Mr Right Next Door

KATIE MONTINARO

Wildflower Publishing

ISBN: 978-0-6450918-1-6 (paperback)

Editor: Laura Boon

Cover art and design: Melody Jeffries

Trigger warnings: anxiety rep, death of a parent (off page) and illness of a parent.

For my Mr Right

Chapter One

JOSIE

According to my mother, women of my age are supposed to wake up to the cries of newborns not the snores of their ruggedly handsome next door neighbour. Some people might not think that is a problem, but today it is. Today I am twenty-nine years old which means I am officially too old to keep waking up in my neighbour's bed. At least, that's what I've been told.

The birds squawking outside the window wake me. They gnaw into my pounding head reminding me of a good night had. I slowly open my eyes and find the room is bright and already warm from the summer sun coming through the sheet that hangs over the window in place of a curtain. I roll over stopping just short of the naked body next to me. I recognise the small diamond tattoo behind the ear I'm looking at. I let out a groan and roll back over trying to sit up. I bunch the soft three thousand thread count cotton sheet around me, the ones I bought on sale six months ago, and steady myself against the spinning room.

A rough hand tenderly runs over my bare back and makes me

shiver. 'We've gotta stop meeting like this.' He laughs. 'Or not.' I don't need to turn around to see the smirk on his face.

I let out a series of noises that sound more like an animal dying than a graceful young lady, but I don't care. I spot the black dress with the spaghetti straps I wore last night on the ground, right next to a matching lacy underwear set. Panic swirls in the pit of my stomach as I realise that if they're on the floor, then I'm wearing nothing at all under this sheet. I pull the sheets higher and try to stand, in the process ripping the sheets from the bed leaving a very naked, very hard, man exposed. In typical Nick style, he doesn't try to cover his modesty; instead he raises his arms above his head and rests in place.

'Oh my God, Nick!' I throw a pillow at him to help him cover up.

'That sounds different this morning. Last night it was more like, 'Oh my *God. Nick!*' he moans and then proceeds to laugh at his own joke.

I throw him a look, which makes him stop. He puts the pillow behind his head, still refusing to cover up. I train my eyes to lock onto his. I'm not allowing them to travel down the thick neckline or the bumps in his shoulders where his muscles ripple. Nope. Not down that curly patch of dark chest hair that lies over the pecs which years of physical work have helped sculpt and define.

'Come on birthday girl, one more round.' His words pull my eyes back to where they're supposed to be – locked and loaded with those baby blues.

'This,' I wave my hands over him, 'is not happening again.' The corners of his lips rise as he hears those familiar words leave my mouth. 'I mean it. No more. I'm going home.'

Clutching the sheet tighter around me, I gather my belongings from the floor.

'Can you at least give me back my sheet?' He lies on his elbow, propping himself up to run his eyes over me. Again.

My mouth dries as I shake my head. 'I paid for these.'

'Because you knew you'd be sleeping on them. Well, not sleeping exactly–'

'Alright! I don't need to be reminded.' I sit on the edge of the bed and try to find my legs under the layers of sheet I have wrapped around me. I slip my feet through the leg holes of my underwear, carefully drawing them up while staying hidden beneath the sheet. I feel Nick roll over onto his back and tap his chest impatiently. I try the same trick with my bra but end up copping a cupful of fabric instead. I abandon the sheet, it floats and lands on Nick, barely covering him. He doesn't bother to fix it. I dress quickly.

'Josie, you don't have to leave. Let me make you some breakfast.'

'It's fine. I have breakfast at home. Besides, I need to take a shower, down a packet of Nurofen and listen to some Adele.'

'I have all of that here – apart from that Adele crap.'

I move around the room finding my shoes and handbag. 'It's not crap. You know, for someone who can be so cultured, at times you're just so...urgh. Besides, I don't expect you to understand.' I get down on my knees and reach under the bed for my missing shoe. 'It's not the same for guys as it is for girls.'

Nick sits up, finally fixing the sheet over him and his bulge. 'What's not the same?'

'Turning twenty-nine.'

'Well, I can confirm that there is life after twenty-nine,' he mocks. I pick another pillow that I bought off the floor and fling it at him. He catches it with precision. 'Don't most people freak out when they turn thirty?'

'I'm not freaking out.'

'*You* are quite clearly freaking out.'

I stop at the foot of the bed. 'I am *not* freaking out.'

'Then why are you in such a hurry to leave?'

'Because! This shouldn't have happened.'

'And yet it *keeps* happening.' He smirks.

I shake my head. 'Not any more. See, this is what I mean.

This,' I move my hands back and forth between us to emphasis my point, 'has to stop. I'm twenty-nine, Nick. Twenty-nine! I'll be thirty next year.'

'I can count.'

'And I'm supposed to have my life together,' I say, ignoring him, 'I'm supposed to be getting married and having kids! Not causally hooking up with my neighbour.'

'I see--'

'It's okay for you. You're a bloke, and blokes aren't expected to settle down until they're in their mid-thirties.'

'Great! Looks like I have some time before I need to panic.' He rubs his hands together in mock enjoyment.

Typical Nick. I start talking about settling down, and he makes a joke. Commitment is not in his vocabulary. That's why this...*arrangement* has worked for so long.

'I'm serious!'

'I can see that.' He crawls towards me reaching for my hand, 'look, Josie, you're freaking out over nothing. Who said you had to have all of that before you're thirty, huh?'

'Everyone! Society! My *mum.* Did you know that a woman loses ninety percent of her eggs by the time she's thirty! Ninety percent!'

'I'm right here. You don't need to shout.'

'It's okay for you because your little swimmers...'

'Don't call them that.'

'... keep working until, like, you die.'

'Did you Google that?'

'It's biology, Nick.'

'Well, biology is science, and science has a way of making everything work beyond its natural limits, so there's no need to worry.'

I drop my hand from his and slide back into my dress from last night. 'I knew you wouldn't get it.'

I turn and leave. I can hear him call after me as I walk the few small steps to the front door and begin to unlock it.

'I'll see you at lunch, yeah? Happy birthday, Josie.'

Walking across the shared driveway to my unit is made worse by the January sun. My feet feel as though they are walking across fire. I do a little hop, jump, jog before landing on my own 'Welcome' mat and walk through to the kitchen.

'Don't say anything,' I say to my roommate Ant, who is cooking a large greasy breakfast. 'That bacon better have my name on it.'

He gives me a wry smile. 'There's so much I could say right now, but I'll spare you. Consider the biting of my tongue my birthday gift to you.'

'And what a gift it is.'

I slump down on a bar stool and rest my head against the cool marble of the bench top. The smell of bacon and the sound of eggs sizzling away in the pan reminds me of just how hungry I am.

'Good morning! That smells good.' A tall, slim man walks past us both and into the bathroom.

I do a double take and look at Ant. He checks to see if the door is shut and comes closer to me.

'Who's that?' I whisper.

'I don't remember his name.' Ant stifles a giggle, and it makes me do the same. He puts a cup of coffee in front of me and its warmth awakens my whole body.

'At least I know the name of the guy I went home with!'

'That's because you always go home with him! *Help me*,' Ant pleads.

The bathroom door swings open, and Ant and I part lightning fast. The stranger with the fresh face and the fresh fade sits next to me and makes love heart eyes at Ant's back. *Oh dear!* 'Hi, I'm Josie.'

'Levi. Bryan, you never told me about your *gorgeous* roommate.'

I try to keep the coffee from spitting out of my nose. Ant turns to us and dishes up breakfast.

'Yes, *Bryan*, why didn't you tell *young* Levi here about your gorgeous roommate?' I tease.

Ant leans against the bench and shovels scrambled egg into his mouth. 'There wasn't a lot of time for talking.'

Levi blushes and looks down at his plate. I tilt my head trying to catch Ant's gaze.

'So Levi, what do you do?' I press on. It really is my best friend duty to get as many details as possible – details my best friend has probably already obtained and promptly forgotten.

'I'm studying education at uni.' The dots connect. 'I'm in my final year. Bryan was giving me some pointers last night.'

'I'm sure he was.' Levi didn't hear me over the love heart confetti he was practically throwing at *Bryan*, but Ant certainly did and gave me a small smirk in return.

'Primary, right?' Ant chimes in, showing off the one detail he has remembered about Levi.

'What do you know about primary school?' I scoff.

'Teaching is teaching.' He shrugs. 'Build a rapport, work to your kids' strengths and make the learning meaningful to them.'

I shake my head with a smile and say no more. Levi looks like his heart is about to explode, and I know that Ant takes his job way more seriously than he's letting on. We both do but getting into the intricate nuances of teaching and education is not really the kind of hungover breakfast conversation either of us are looking for.

'It's such as shame I'm doing primary. Wouldn't it have been *amazing* if I could have done my rounds with you?'

Ant tries not to choke on his eggs, and I try not to let out the laugh I'm holding in. What a treat that would have been! 'That is such as shame, isn't is *Bryan*?' I tease.

'So, Josie, why don't you tell us about your night?' Ant teases right back.

'Nothing to tell.'

'Hmm...the bed hair and last night's outfit begs to differ.'

'Ooo, scandalous!' Levi cups his hands around the mug in front of him, settling into position for gossip.

'Hardly,' I scoff.

'Josie gave herself a birthday present by going home with our neighbour last night.' Ant fills in the gaps for Levi.

'Aw, cute.' Levi's juvenile enthusiasm for my predicament transports me back to my uni days when something like this was far more scandalous than it is right now.

'No, Levi, not cute,' my teacher voice slips out, 'I'm twenty-nine years old. I need to get my life together. I need to settle down.'

'So, marry the guy next door.' Levi waves his hand dismissively.

Ant cocks an eyebrow before smugly sipping his morning brew. I reply with a very mature eye roll and a shake of my head. Marry the guy next door? *Nick?* That's never going to happen. I need someone who is committed, ready to settle down in to marriage, kids, the lot. Not someone who would rather randomly shag his way through the week than even think of the word 'commitment.' No, what I'm looking for is a life partner. I'm looking for Mr Right, not Mr Right Next Door.

Chapter Two

NICK

I'm going to need another cold shower if I don't stop thinking about Josie and last night. But I can't get the image of her in that tight black dress and the way it clung to her curves out of my head. Or of her lacy underwear or the way her hips moved...*damn*. I run my hands through my hair trying to decide on another shower or another run. I spy my shoes by the back-door, and before I know it, I'm forcing my feet through the laced-up runners. Run it is.

The heat hits me with force when I open the door, and I know I'll regret this later, but it's the only way I can stop thinking about her. I hope.

Josie. Josephine Elenore Russo. I've been trying to outrun thoughts of her for the last three years, ever since I moved into my unit. I haven't managed to get very far. And just when I think I'm making some kind of progress, something like last night happens. Again. And I'm back to square one. It's those lips, those perfectly soft, pouted lips. And the hair; the long, thick hair I just want to run my hands through and grab...I run faster.

It's not long into my run before my t-shirt is wet with sweat. I take it off tucking it into the back of my shorts and keep going. I pass a group of girls making their way to the beach and almost knock them over with my smile. Their heads turn as they dissolve into giggles of excitement. I hate myself for doing it, but I like the attention. I need to feel admired by someone other than the one person I'm trying to forget. Josie stirs things in me. Things in me that I shouldn't want. Things I probably don't deserve.

I stop at a set of lights, sucking in air and see a family across the road. I zero in on the mother. She's wearing a see-through cover type thing with her bathers on underneath. A neat little one piece. I scan her from head to toe, her husband completely oblivious to my wandering eyes. Nice face, great handful of tit, hips... she reminds me of Josie.

I groan and hit the pavement harder when the little green man flashes. I can't outrun her. Fucking Josie! I come to a stop just outside a strip of shops and lean against the wall trying to catch my breath. Several minutes pass where I'm free from thinking about anything, mainly because I'm puffing so hard I think I might pass out. I channel all of my minute brain power into controlling my breathing and not dying.

When everything slows down and I feel like I can breathe again, I take in the scene around me. Families, couples – all enjoying the beginning of a new year together. *Happy.* There's the couple kissing over ice cream outside the milk bar, the dad across the street trying to catch a runaway toddler in a nappy, new parents capturing their baby's first trip to the park and a pair of teenagers sucking each other's faces off as they wait for their order outside the fish and chip shop. I want that, I want all of that, and I want that with Josie. A wave of insecurity washes over me like a relentless beast, reminding me that Josie is too good for me.

Or more to the point, that I'm not worthy of her. I try pushing the intrusive thoughts out of my mind like I've been taught to do before it spirals. I can't help it. I focus on the memory of the way she looks at me when I make her laugh and goddamn, I want to make her look at me like that forever. Fuck it! I'm tired of playing around. I'm not really one for making New Year's resolutions but this year is different. This year I'm going after the girl of my dreams.

Chapter Three

JOSIE

Of all the people I expected to be late at my traditional birthday lunch, I didn't expect it to be me. I'm never late, but Ant let me nap a little too long which meant I didn't have time to make myself look the way I had envisaged. A swipe of mascara, a slap of red lipstick and throwing my untamed mane into a bun atop my head, I had to be ready to go. When we arrive at lunch, Nick and Elle, the final member of our crew, look halfway through their first drink. I greet them both with an apologetic kiss on the cheek. Nick's hand lingers on the small of my back, imprinting its mark. I try to ignore it but last night is still fresh in my mind, no matter how hard I try to forget it. It was a mistake, and if I'm going to take this year seriously, I have to forget about Nick and his lingering touches.

'Sorry! Sorry! *Someone* let me keep napping.' I take a seat across from Elle.

'*Someone* needed it. Besides, I had a guest to entertain,' Ant replies.

Out of the corner of my eye, I catch Nick smiling into his

drink. Elle's eyebrow pops over the rim of her sunglasses requesting more information from me.

'You two?' she points between Nick and I, and neither of us say anything. 'Of course. This is what happens when I have to stay home and be mum.'

'Still would have happened if you didn't.' Ant smirks.

'Hey! You should be grilling *Bryan* on his toy boy,' I deflect.

'Who's Bryan?' Nick asks.

'So, I gave a fake name. Who hasn't?' Ant reclines in his seat.

Elle and I raise our hands.

'Bullshit,' Nick calls.

'What about the dentist?' Ant interjects.

'Fake number, not name,' I correct.

'Oh yeah, I've done the fake number thing,' Elle recalls.

'Back when you were fourteen,' Ant teases.

Elle sticks her finger up at him, and we all share a laugh. We tease her and Rich all the time for being high school sweethearts, but secretly I think we're all jealous.

'Anyway, tell us about this toy boy. I live vicariously through you singletons.'

'Nothing to tell. It was fun. It's not happening again. Hence, Bryan.'

'How young was he?' Elle holds in a laugh.

'Old enough to be off P plates.'

'Just,' I jibe.

'So, how was *your* night last night, birthday bitch?' Ant smirks, successfully moving the attention away from himself.

'Oh God, I'm gonna need another drink for this,' Elle snaps her fingers at the waiter. 'Hi, I'll take one of your fruitiest, most alcoholic cocktails please. And a glass of rosé for her and a beer for him.'

'Make it two,' Nick adds as the waiter scurries away with our orders.

He smiles at me and my stomach flips. That stupid crooked smile hiding underneath that bushy beard does things to me that I can't explain. I try to shake my mind clear of Nick. I'm sure I'm still a bit drunk from last night. That's all it is. 'Cocktail?' I question.

'I have spent the past four years being pregnant or breastfeeding. This is my first day of freedom, and I do not intend to waste it.'

'That's what happens when you have two kids on top of each other.' Ant quips.

'Yes, and I love them to bits but I'm glad not to have anyone hanging from my bits for a while.'

'Don't tell poor Rich that,' Nick smirks.

He cups his glass and takes a swig. I try to ignore the way his arm tenses as he does that. The waiter places the glass of wine in front of me, and it couldn't have come any sooner. I hold back from downing the entire glass just to drown out my thoughts.

'The last time I let him do that, I found myself pregnant and running around after an eight-month-old. This,' Elle waves her hands over her bust, 'is a no-go zone.'

'Well, we all know Elle's New Year's resolution. Anyone else want to offer up theirs?' Ant raises his drink. The three of us join him to clink glasses.

'Yeah, come on birthday girl. You're up first,' Elle says.

Butterflies rise in my stomach, and they have nothing to do with how close Nick's knee is to mine under the table, although strangely that is the point I'm hyper focused on. The more I think about Nick, the more I think about this morning, and that feeling rushes through me again – panic. This is the last year of my twenties, the last year I have to prepare for the next stage, or "chapter", of my life as my dad likes to call it. Next year I'll be thirty, and that means responsible adulting. I have this one year to get my life in order. *Breathe, just breathe.*

'I think it's time to get serious about, you know, settling down.'

'Why?' Ant scoffs.

'Because I'm twenty-nine! It's about time.'

'Says who?'

'Ant, don't get her started. She literally ran out of my place this morning freaking out about turning twenty-nine.' Nick shakes his head.

Elle wags her eyebrows at me and mouths, 'tell me later.'

I give a little nod before adding, 'It's a big deal! Elle, back me up.'

'It's true. A woman's fertility drops significantly when she turns thirty.'

'So I've heard,' Nick slouches back in his seat.

'You want to have kids?' Ant looks confused.

'Yes. Not right now but maybe in like two years. I need to find someone first.'

'How very feminist of you.'

'Nope,' I wag my finger at Ant, 'don't go there. I can be a feminist and still want a family.'

'I seem to recall a big speech right around your twenty-first birthday where it was...what was it? 'Men are taught to *be* someone and women are taught to *find* someone.' And then a long-winded speech about how you had to fight the patriarchy.'

'I stand by that.'

'So, what, you just––'

'I'm just ready. I still want my career, equal pay and equal rights, but I also want to get married and have babies.'

'How many babies?' Nick's hands are clasped in front of him, and for once he seems to be taking all this seriously. It throws me.

'A couple. I don't know.'

'And where are we finding said man?' Ant takes another swig of his drink.

'She has a list,' Elle yells and points at me. Her eyes widen in surprise as though her body was momentarily taken over by someone else. *Traitor.*

I groan inwardly. I'd hoped she'd forgotten about the list let alone bring it up. I see the smirk dance across Nick's face. This is the type of thing he loves to hear if only to taunt me with it later.

'Can't wait to hear this.' Nick skulls the last of his first drink.

'We both made lists in like, year eight or something, right Josie? We both had something down about him looking like Zac Efron.'

'Zac Efron has aged well.'

'I'll agree to that,' Ant clinks his glass with mine.

'So, what else is on this list?' Nick appears too invested in my list already, and I regret the day I made it.

'I don't remember,' I lie.

The only thing worse than everyone knowing about the list is everyone knowing I kept it, and that it's currently hiding in my top draw behind my knickers.

'Bullshit. Elle, what was on her list?'

'I don't remember,' Elle lies. Girl code back intact.

I give her a grateful look because we both know the other is lying. We memorised that list like any teenage girl memorised the entire history of their favourite boy band.

'Doesn't matter anyway because I don't have it,' I claim.

Ant and Nick share a look I can't read and don't like. It usually means they're conspiring against me, and it makes me nervous.

'So where are you going to find Mr Right, then?' Ant asks with a smug look on his face.

I know he doesn't believe in things like soul mates and has no desire to settle down and start a family, but I also know that he'll throw his full support into whatever I decide to do. I just need to figure out how to find Mr Right.

'Oh, we could download an app!' Elle sounds excited.

Nick curses under his breath. 'You don't need an app.'

'Could be fun.' Ant chimes in.

'Or you could be met with your untimely demise. Those apps are full of weirdos, Josie.'

'On second thought, Nick's right,' Elle puts her drink down. 'Remember that chick Ant swiped on last year?'

A collective sigh of 'Oh yeah' is released by the group. Ant managed to swipe on one of the clingiest people I have ever met. It took us three months and a restraining order to finally get rid of her. Even now we still look over our shoulders to make sure she isn't lurking in the shadows somewhere. On cue, we all take a sweeping look around us.

'Apps scare me,' I shudder, but I have no idea how to meet people these days. I'm too old to be going clubbing, too young to be sitting around a dingy old pub, and hooking up with someone from work is firmly on my no-go list, so what other options do I have? If only Mr Right would just fall into my lap and make it easy for me, thank you very much.

'Maybe there's someone already in your life...,' Nick says into his next drink.

'If there was, we wouldn't be having this conversation.'

Nick's jaw sets and he shifts in his seat. The only men in my life are Ant and Nick. Ant and I have been best friends for far too long to consider each other in that way. He's like the brother I never had while Nick is completely unavailable. Emotionally. Mentally. In any way excluding physically. He's always down for a good time, just not a committed, long time, let alone marriage and kids.

I don't even know why I am wasting my time thinking about it. Sure, we have fun, and on some level we're compatible otherwise things wouldn't have gone on as long as they have. But we're at completely different stages of life. I'm ready to settle down. He's not. Plain and simple. Doesn't matter anyway. I have my list, my blueprint of what I'm looking for, and a plan will eventually happen as to how I can check those boxes off my list. But right now, I need another drink.

Chapter Four

NICK

By the time we reach the units, Josie is one too many drinks into happy, and she's walking with her arm draped over me. I'm not complaining; in fact it's actually going to make this next part so ridiculously easy that I almost feel sorry for her. Almost.

Ant and I decide in that unspoken manly way to be complete menaces and search their unit for her list. Neither of us bought that she had just thrown it away. She's too much of a hopeless romantic for that despite the fact that she tries to convince everyone otherwise.

Since Elle mentioned the list at lunch, I haven't been able to get it out of my mind. I have to know what is on that damn list. More importantly, I need to know if I'm anywhere close to being in the running for Josie's perfect guy. I know she created the thing when she was a teenager, but when someone like Josie has her mind set on how her future should look, or future husband for that matter, it rarely changes. Josie is the most organised and grab-life-by-the-horns person I know. If she wants it, she'll make it happen. That's why looking at this list is the single most important thing for me to do today.

As Ant opens the door, and we shuffle in, he yells 'now' at me, and I wrap Josie in a bear hug while he runs straight into her room. Having her in my arms again so soon after last night is torture. She wriggles in my arms each time pressing her soft arse into my groin, and I have to think the holiest of thoughts to stop anything from moving down there.

'What are you doing?' Josie whines.

'It's not in the bedside tables,' Ant yells out, ignoring Josie's call.

'Try the knickers draw. Chicks always hide the good stuff there.' I call back to him and immediately try to push images of Josie's knickers from my mind.

'No!' she gasps, 'Ant if you go in there, I swear I will--'

'Gold!' Ant saunters out of the room, waving a folded bit of paper in his hand.

I release Josie and she heads straight for Ant, trying to pry the paper out of his hands. He puts his hand above his head, and it's game over. Both Ant and I tower over Josie whose about five foot nothing, so there's no way she's getting it now.

'Fine,' she slumps on the couch, 'let's just get this over with. I want to preface it with the fact that I was, like, fourteen at the time.'

Ant takes his position in front of the television like he's about to give a speech, and I sit on the arm of the couch. Is it weird that I feel nervous? What if the guy she has written down on that piece of paper is nothing like me? What if she wants some pompous academic type?

'Number 1. Sweet. Number 2. Hot body,'

'Oh God,' Josie wails into her hands.

So far, I'm looking the goods. Ant reads on.

Kind. *Check.*

Nice smile. *Check.*

Funny. Smart. Loyal. *Check. Check. Check.*

Thinks I'm his world. *Fucking check!*

Successful. Umm...

Loves to read. *Shit.*

Zac Efron.

'The clean cut *High School Musical* Efron or the *Down to Earth* Efron?' I ask.

'Now? *Down to Earth*, Efron.'

Efron with a beard and a bit of meat on him. I could be looking in the damn mirror. *Check.*

It's not all bad. I'm most of those things. I still stand a chance. Plus, that was fourteen-year-old Josie. I know twenty-nine-year-old Josie, and I know what adult Josie likes. This can still work in my favour.

'I'm really disappointed by this,' Ant laughs and takes up his position on the recliner. 'I thought it would be far more embarrassing. Kudos to fourteen-year-old-Josie.'

Fourteen-year-old Nick would have had one thing on his list – big tits. Thirty-one-year-old Nick also only has one thing on his list – Josie.

'Okay, well now that's done, I think I'm gonna go lie down.'

'Wait,' I grab her by the arm, 'we haven't given you our present yet.'

Josie sits back down, and Ant presents her with a card. I'd like to take credit for this gift but in all honesty, it was Ant's idea. I *know* Josie, but I'm also a terrible gift giver. It's like I blank out the second I set foot in a shop or pull up a website online. There's just too much choice. It's overwhelming.

'You guys didn't have to get me anything.'

She says that, but I know that if we didn't, she'd be shitty at us for at least two days and then spend the next twelve months bringing it up any time one of us pissed her off. She seems genuinely surprised when she pulls out three tickets to the musical, *Singing in the Rain.*

'There's three tickets there and of course you can take whoever you want––' Ant tries to hide his enthusiasm.

'Oh no, I'll be taking the two of you! We've only been going on about this for like two years.' She turns to me, stroking my cheek then ruffling my beard. It drives me wild when she does that and she knows it. 'Besides, I want to be there to pop this one's musical theatre cherry.'

'Very funny.' I say and try not to think about what I'd like to pop.

'Well, it's an all-expenses night out with us, obviously. Dinner. Three-bedroom apartment in the city for the night,' Josie gasps, her eyes widening like a child at Christmas. and I just want to kiss her. 'Nick organised that. It has amazing views over the city.'

Organising an apartment was easy. I know the city like the back of my hand. I also have a friend with a very wealthy father who bought said apartment as a holiday house of sorts.

Josie turns to me with that smile that lights up my world, and I immediately regret being a gentleman and getting a three-bedroom apartment instead of a two-bedroom apartment. My friend's father has both.

'Guys! Thank you, this is honestly the best.' She leans in to hug me, and all I can smell is her mango body wash and the cocktails on her breath, as she breathes lightly on my neck. I'm sent.

There are three months until the show. I decide immediately that the show will be my deadline to convince Josie that I'm her Mr Right.

Chapter Five

JOSIE

Littleton Beach is a small beachside town along Victoria's south-east coast. When you're a teacher, it feels even smaller. Summer holidays bring the crowds, and the more we go out, the more likely we are to run into some kids from school. Ant and I are making our weekly shopping trip when we're served by one of our students. I don't know who is more embarrassed, the year eleven girl swiping my box of tampons or me. Honestly, this is the worst part about being a teacher; marking, report writing, yard duty, staff meetings – nothing holds a candle to this very moment of being a teacher. Normally when students see you 'out in the wild' they like to pretend you don't exist, and I'm more than happy to play that game but not Ant; he likes to make sure he's been seen.

'Oh come on, it's not that bad. She probably gets a period too,' Ant says as we load the shopping into the trunk.

'How would you feel if she was swiping a packet of condoms?'

'Self-service. Crisis avoided.'

Ant drives, and I play with his Spotify until I find something worth listening to. I know my flicking around to different songs drives him mad, so I keep the flicking to a minimum and settle on a random playlist of nineties pop music. My phone buzzes in my hand, and I let out a sigh.

'Mum?' Ant asks.

He's right so I don't bother responding, there's a special kind of sigh that is reserved for Mrs Lorella Russo. I take a deep breath and answer the call. 'Hi Mum.'

'Josephine, darling, how are you? Listen I don't have a lot of time because I'm dealing with the caterers. Just want to confirm that you *are* bringing someone Saturday night. It will make my place settings uneven if you don't.'

'Wouldn't want to do that,' I mumble.

'Josephine, you know I hate it when you mumble. Is that a yes then?'

I throw my head back against the car seat. I had forgotten all about the dinner on Saturday night at my parent's house to celebrate their anniversary. When Mum first mentioned it to me, I was in the midst of marking year twelve practise exams and getting my final results in before the VCAA deadline. I didn't know I was agreeing to bringing a guest.

In fact, now I think about it, I don't think I did say I would bring a guest. I suspect she thinks that if she makes room then suddenly someone will land in my lap to take home to meet my parents. Out of her three daughters, I'm the disappointment. Sure, I have a great job, respectable even (at times), but I'm not married off. My older sister Franki is married and has been for close to a decade. But even she's teetering on joining me on Mum's List of Disappointments if she doesn't pop out a kid soon. My baby sister Daniella is in a serious long-term relationship which my mother deems as suitable, but I think it's because she is more focused on a diamond on Daniella's finger more than Daniella is. Mum certainly isn't backwards in being forward so I imagine that rock will appear on Daniella's finger any day now.

And me? Well, I'm eternally single and a Very Big Disappointment. The blemish on an almost perfect record of settling her daughters down to respectable men. Turning up single is clearly not an option for Saturday night. Heaven forbid I throw out her seating chart! I know my mother, and if I don't bring someone, she'll bring someone for me. There really is only one option. 'Yes, Mum, I'll bring someone.'

'Splendid. I'll see you both Saturday night. Love to you.'

I let out a frustrated groan after I end the call with my mother.

'Please tell me you are free Saturday night,' I say to Ant.

He shakes his head. 'As much as I'd love to come to another one of Lorella's fabulous dinner parties, I am going to have to decline. But if she's serving any of those mini crab tart things, stuff some in your handbag and bring them home for me.'

He doesn't sound sorry at all. Jerk. I'm thinking about revoking his best friend card. 'Why? Where are you going?'

'Jared's bachelor party.'

I'd forgotten all about that too. Jared from work was getting married and it was the biggest news going around school in term four. Is memory loss something that happens on the cusp of turning thirty? Asking for a friend.

'Urgh! You suck.'

'What about Elle?'

I shake my head. 'It's Rich's week on call, so she's home alone with the kids.'

'Nick?'

I shrug my shoulders. 'Maybe. He's probably got a hot date or something.'

Ant rolls his eyes, just a little, but I catch him. 'What? What was that?'

'What?' Ant tries to act innocent.

'That little eye roll thing.'

'Nothing!' he says an octave too high to be believable. 'Just ask Nick.'

He's the only one in my friend circle that hasn't had the pleasure of attending one of Lorella Russo's infamous dinner parties.

The thought of asking him stirs up a wave of nervous energy. What would it be like to bring Nick home to meet my family? I doubt he's ever done the meet-the-family thing before. It could be fun to see him squirm.

'Fine. I'll ask.'

Chapter Six

NICK

I enjoy living in Littleton Beach. It's big enough that you can walk down the street without running into anyone you know, yet small enough that everyone knows everyone else through a friend of a friend. That six-degrees-of-separation kinda thing. I like it.

It's so different to living in the city where you are truly anonymous, and there is no beach. Having the infamous Littleton beach at the end of my street is definitely a perk of moving here. I take a quick dip in the water most days after work in the summer.

In my first few days of living here, I realised that all through summer the locals travelled with a spare pair of bordies and their surfboard in the back of their ute. I haven't taken to surfing, but I sure love being at the beach. Hot days mean early knock off time on site which means beach time. It's the only thing that's bearable about already being back at work. Living in a coastal beach town is like permanently living in a holiday destination. Something that is easy to get used to.

As the temperature rises, my boss calls time on the day, and it isn't even lunch yet. Maybe I'll have time to catch up with Ant and Josie. I can't imagine having as much time off as they do. I need to keep busy. Just as I'm about to throw my last drill on the tray, the boss calls me into his office. Office is a generous description. It's nothing more than a stuffy old portable with a fan that sounds like it's on its last legs.

'You right?' he asks as the project manager leaves the two of us alone.

I shrug. 'Yeah. Why wouldn't I be?'

'You know, the thing that happened before we went on break. I just––'

'I'm fine.' I say it a little firmer than I intended to.

I don't like to think of the day he's talking about and shut down any further conversation about it. I try to keep my anxiety in check through being physical; the gym, my job, random workouts, but sometimes it's not enough. It's not something I like people knowing about me, so having a full-blown panic attack at the end of last year in front of this guy isn't something I really want to 'talk through'.

'Nick, I just–'

'I said I'm fine.'

He sighs. 'We didn't see you at Christmas.'

'I never made a promise.'

He doesn't know what to say next. We're both trying to navigate this new father-son working relationship thing. I didn't know my father until three years ago when he offered me a job at his construction company. Up to that point, he was no more than a name on a yearly birthday card.

'Nick, I'm trying,' he pleads and runs his hands through his thinning grey hair, 'I just want to know you're alright.'

I nod, not wanting to give him any more. I really am trying to give him a break and get to know him like I promised when I took the job. I just didn't expect it to be so hard. It's hard to look past the man who ditched his wife and kid to create a new family with someone else. There's a lot of unresolved shit there, and today ain't the day to work through it.

'Listen, Gina and I are having a barbecue Saturday night. Why don't you come over? We can sink a few beers and watch the cricket.'

I hold in a humourless laugh. How little he knows me. I hate cricket. I've been to his house once in the time I've lived here in Littleton Beach. On every inch of his display-like home are family photos hanging in frames, constantly reminding me that I am an intruder on this happy family, *his* family. Never mind that I was his family first. Once was enough. I've pulled out every excuse since not to go back there. I figure we can work on the father-son-getting-to-know-you-thing at work.

'I'll see.'

This is the right answer because he smiles and doesn't keep pressing me about the thing that happened before break.

'Great. I'll get Gina to get some extra snags. Go on, get outta here. It's too bloody hot.'

I don't wait for a second invitation and leave as quickly as humanly possible. Now I just need to find a reason not to show up on Saturday.

Chapter Seven

JOSIE

People who think teachers only work nine to three are delusional. Most days I'm there before eight and leave after five. And still come home and do extra work. This is why my school holidays are generally booked up with appointments I never get around to attending during the term.

Typically, they're all crammed into the final weeks of summer break. Today's appointment is the optometrist. I'm not especially loyal to any one place but catching sight of the person who is about to spend the next hour in a darkened room with me while I try to read letters off a board has me changing my mind. He looks more like he belongs on the cover of some fashion magazine. His brown hair is slicked back to perfection but not greasy; this is a man who knows his limits. His suit looks tailor-made, and his shoes are shiny. His eyes, *oh my God*, his eyes...they're an emerald pool that I'm drowning in, framed of course by round tortoise-shell glasses that highlight the small flecks of amber around the irises of his eyes.

He reaches out his hand for me to take. 'Josephine? I'm Milo.'

'I-it...it's Josie,' I stutter.

His hand feels smooth and warm, and I might be holding it a little too long. I use the time to quickly scan *that* finger and notice no ring and no tan line.

'You ready?' he smiles, and I nod, following him to one of the backrooms.

He points for me to sit in the large chair that dominates the room. He takes a seat on a swivel chair and sits so close that our knees are almost touching. The air feels electric. He smells like freshly shaved man and I'm ridiculously close to losing all self-control. So, turns out I'm turned on by a good-looking guy in glasses. Who knew?

'Do you work at Littleton Beach Secondary?' He tilts his head to the side, a little playful, a little bashful.

Another pitfall of teaching in a relatively small town is I've either educated every person I meet or someone they know. Littleton Beach Secondary College is the only public school in the area, so most families choose to send their kids there instead of having them catch a forty-five-minute bus ride to the closest private school.

I nod in reply to his question. *Please don't be the father of one of my students.* I couldn't take it if the guy I've been crushing on for five seconds and imagining a white picket fence kinda life style with is the father of one of my students. He would be completely off limits.

'I thought I recognised you. You gave a speech at the awards night last year.'

My heart crumbles, but I plaster on a smile as if being recognised for my speech-giving abilities is a compliment.

'I did. Along with educating the minds of our future leaders, I am privileged to be a coordinator which means I get to stand in front of parents at award ceremonies and mispronounce their names,' I say sarcastically, and Milo lets out a deep belly laugh. 'You have a good memory. Did I mispronounce your child's name?'

He shakes his head. 'I don't have children,' he says as my body floods with relief, 'but my Godson attends your school. I came to support him. He received an award for music.'

I can't stop the smile and blush that spreads across my face. I can date a student's Godfather, right? I mean, they're not even related. It's just a fancy way of a friend telling another friend that they trust them enough to look after their kid if they die. I bet the kid isn't even one of my students. I don't ask the name. It's insignificant.

'You have a good memory.' I repeat, tucking an invisible strand of hair behind my ear. I'm thankful that the room is dark, and he can't see what a dork I am.

'I never forget a pretty face.' Milo's cheeks flush as though he said something that only his brain was supposed to hear. He clears his throat and continues, leaving no time for my brain to unpack what just happened. 'So, what brings you to see me today, Josie?'

I flash him my best smile. 'I think my eyesight is getting worse.'

He matches my smile and rolls to his computer, tapping a few buttons. 'Says here you have a prescription. You don't appear to be wearing your glasses though...contacts?' I shake my head and he gives me a wry smile. 'Josie, have you been naughty and not been wearing your glasses?'

The way he says naughty makes me tingle – everywhere. I can only nod and keep my legs crossed.

'Alright. Let's get to it.'

Getting your eyes tested is an extremely intimate process. Milo has to get in my personal space to change the lenses on those hideously heavy glasses that look like something a caricature of a mad scientist would wear. He then asks me which one is better, number one or number two? I tell him number two, and he gently reaches out and changes the lens. His fingers brush the sides of my ears as he adjusts the glasses, and it makes me weak. Our knees knock a couple of times, and each time he apologises with the goddamn sexiest smile I've ever seen.

I deliberately place my hands on my knees, so the next time our hands will gently brush past one another. I feel like I'm a fifteen-year-old again with a high school crush, you know those ones where you're instantly attracted to someone without knowing the faintest thing about them, and yet you cannot imagine how you'll be able to live without them knowing you exist? Yeah, it's intense.

'How's that?' he asks, no louder than a whisper, his eyes looking straight into mine.

'Much clearer.'

He takes the heavy round glasses with all the different lenses off my face and checks the health of my eyes. I want to say something funny, flirty, but nothing comes to mind. Is it inappropriate to flirt with your optometrist? He keeps smiling at me and his gaze lingers on mine. I think he *wants* me to flirt with him. Am I crazy?

He asks me to put my chin on the strap and look through the machine as he checks my eye health. 'You have very pretty eyes,' he says from behind the machine.

'I bet you say that to all the girls.'

He lets out a chuckle. 'I think I'd be fired if I did.'

My heart skips several beats as The List pops into my head. He's smart, funny and kinda looks like he could be related to Zac Efron. Maybe. A distant relative perhaps. I try to steady my breathing. It's been a while since a guy has openly flirted with me besides Nick, who doesn't count, that I've almost forgotten what to do.

'Sorry, I don't mean to make you uncomfortable. That was inappro–'

'It's fine,' I rush to interrupt, 'It's kinda nice to have someone flirt with me?' The infliction in my tone makes it sounds like I'm asking him if he's flirting with me because my self-conscious self needs that reassurance.

'I find it difficult to believe that I'm the only one flirting with you.'

I roll my lips together while butterflies swarm in my stomach. 'It's been a while.'

'Well,' he breaks the tension, pulling the machine away from me, 'I think you're in need of a glasses upgrade. Your prescription has degraded a little. I can take you out the front to show you a few different pairs....'

He looks like he's deciding if he should say what he's thinking. I silently beg him to.

'Then...ah, perhaps we could take them for a test run Saturday night at the movies?'

The red in my cheeks deepens, and I chew the bottom of my lip. Is this really happening? Is this gorgeous man asking me out? I can practically feel the text messages to Elle writing themselves.

'Will the glasses be ready in time?'

He runs his hand along the shaved sides of his head and slouches back in his seat, satisfied he's secured the date. As if anyone could ever say no to him. 'I can give you some contacts until they do. That way you could try those and see if the prescription is right. And if they're not, then at least you'll have someone who can drive you home.' He smiles, showing off his dimples. Dimples! That's it, I'm gone. Done.

I can't help but smile back at him. 'That sounds like a plan.'

'I could come and get you at six. We could do dinner and then a late movie.'

Just as I'm about to accept my stomach drops. Saturday night. Although this seems like the perfect opportunity to get out of going to dinner at my parent's house, it won't be worth the hell my mother will put me through for the next six months for missing her event. Even if he is an optometrist.

'Shoot. I have a family thing Saturday night. Maybe Sunday night instead?'

Not missing a beat, Milo accepts the proposal, and I suddenly feel like a nervous ball of energy is bouncing around in my chest.

He walks me out to the front of the store with his hand placed on the small of my back. He guides me over to the rack of designer glasses and helps me pick out the perfect pair. The lady who runs the store is eagerly trying to force her opinion on me, but I don't hear her. I only hear Milo and take the pair he likes the most. Another customer comes in and steals him away for an examination.

'I'm sorry, I have to go. Those look great on you. Nice to meet you, Josie. I'll, um, I'll see you soon.' He flashes that dimpled smile at me, and I turn to jelly.

The woman begins to tell me about all the lens options they have, but I don't look at her. Instead, my gaze follows Milo as he escorts the customer into his room. As he reaches the door, he turns back to look at me one last time, smiling, and I wonder if I've just been conned into buying the most expensive pair of glasses on the shelf.

Chapter Eight

JOSIE

'Do you think it's too soon to ask Milo to be my date for Saturday night?' I muse as I sit on the couch eating ice cream from the tub. Ant came back from the petrol station with two tubs of Ben and Jerry's ice cream because we don't share ice cream. Or chocolate. Flatmate rule number one.

'Yes, you stalker freak.'

I let out a groan. 'But he is so hot.'

'I think I need to get my eyes tested. Where did you get yours done again?'

'Oh, it's in the shopping centre, right between Piss and Off.' I stick my finger up at him, and he laughs.

'Didn't you ask Nick already?'

I shake my head. 'Not yet,' I say with a mouth full of ice cream.

I haven't been avoiding him so much as I've been avoiding the thought of attending another family dinner. Dinner with my family is always an over-the-top occasion. My parents come from Italian migrant families where both sets of grandparents had to work hard to provide the basics for their children. My dad talks of a birthday party he had when he was eight because it was the only one he was allowed to have. The neighbour's kids came over and they were allowed to share a packet of the good biscuits and a bottle of lemonade.

Mum's upbringing wasn't much different. She often talks about her 'good dress', a navy button down that she once tore a small hole in when climbing a fence. It was enough to send my Nonna into a blind rage and ban Mum from playing outside with the other kids. From then on, her role was to be in the kitchen and raise the babies, lessons that started from such a young age that my mother can't remember being encouraged to be or do anything else. A lesson she has since passed onto my sisters and me. A lesson society encourages whilst trying to say it isn't. You don't need to look too far into my past to see where my anxieties come from about turning thirty, unwed and childless.

'You're leaving it a bit late to ask him, aren't you? It's tomorrow night.'

'I'm hoping I fall into a coma between now and then.'

Ant lets out one of his big belly laughs to which no one is immune, and I laugh along with him. We fall into our usual rhythm of dissecting the movie we're watching and talking endlessly about random nonsense until the film finishes, and I have a slight bellyache from all the ice cream I absentmindedly consumed.

'Right, I'm off to bed.'

'But it's only ten! Piker,' I protest.

'I have a big night tomorrow night. I need my beauty sleep.' Ant fans himself.

I scoff. 'Sure.'

'Go next door and ask Nick about tomorrow night.'

'He probably already has plans.'

'Why are you putting this off?'

'Why are you so hell bent on me asking Nick to come to dinner?'

Ant waves his hands dismissively. 'Fine, let Lorella's wrath rain down on you like dragon fire for the next six months because you fucked up her seating plan.'

I roll my eyes. 'Fine. I'm going.'

I knock on Nick's door giving him far more respect for privacy than he ever gives us. He uses our front door like it's his own and often just wanders in unannounced. I've tried endlessly to get him to knock before entering but it seems to be a skill he can't quite master.

He takes his time getting to the door, and I'm suddenly very aware of the actual time and what, or who, he might be doing at this hour on a Friday night. I turn to leave at the same moment he opens the door, sweaty, shirtless and hair tussled.

'Hey Josie, you good?' he puts both arms up and leans against the door frame, conveniently blocking my view of his unit.

I wring my hands together and clear my suddenly dry throat. 'Sorry, I didn't mean to interrupt....' I point inside at nothing but implying everything.

He looks behind him and back to me with a mischievous grin. 'You wanna come in?'

I furrow my brows, confused. 'Aren't you *busy?*'

He catches my meaning and laughs. 'There's no one here. I was just doing a bit of a workout.'

'At ten o'clock at night?'

'I had energy to get rid of,' he shrugs, 'unless you can think of a better way for me to burn it off?'

I roll my eyes and push past him as I enter his unit. It feels like an extension of our place, mainly because I forced Nick to deco- rate. I took him shopping, loaded up the trolley, and he paid. If it were left to him, he'd have nothing but a recliner and a few plates to eat off. At least now it feels like a home.

'I told you Nick, that's not happening again.'

'You say that all the time,' he laments.

We walk to the kitchen and I can see an array of dumbbells and a skipping rope lying on the floor. Nick reaches around to the kitchen sink and pours two glasses of water. He quickly downs his and makes another.

'So, what brings you here this late if it's not that?'

I cringe inwardly at the suggestion. I place value on our friendship and am a little disappointed that he doesn't feel the same way. Things between Nick and I have been casual for a long time, probably too long for something that hasn't developed into *something* else by now. I guess it just works that way. Besides, he's not really the settle down type of guy.

'I need to ask a favour.' He raises his eyebrow as an invitation to continue. 'I have this family dinner thing on tomorrow night, and I was wondering if you'd come with me?'

Something flashes in his eyes momentarily. Fear? Panic? Then he replaces it with the look he normally gives to blueprints he's trying to make sense of. He clears his throat. 'Like a date?'

My stomach drops like one of his discarded dumbbells is attached to it, and I inwardly kick myself for making things awkward. Nick and I hang out all the time as friends, but there's usually someone else around like Ant. The only other time we hang out alone is, well, to not really hang out. We've never done anything just the two of us that requires both of us wearing clothes. I think I may have overstepped the line. He clearly looks uncomfortable.

'No, not a date. As a friend,' I say hastening to clear up any misunderstandings.

'So...you want me to go to your family dinner as your...*friend*?'

'Look, I know you don't normally do this stuff--'

'What stuff?' He leans against the kitchen bench, and I try not to be distracted by his near nakedness and the way his shorts hang dangerously low off his thick hips.

'The whole going to meet a girl's family thing--'

'What makes you say that?'

He seems offended. 'Come on, Nick! I've had a front row seat to the parade of women you've brought home over the last three years. Not one of them has hung around more than a night.'

'Except for you.' He tilts his glass at me before downing its contents.

'That's different.'

'Hmm, how so?' There's a glint in his baby blues that's pure trouble. He scans me with those mischievous eyes, and I try to keep it together.

'We're friends, Nick.'

'*Friends.*' He says the word like it's dirty.

'And I promise I will make it very clear to my family that that's all we are.'

'So, no fake dating then?'

I let out a little laugh. 'You've seen one too many teen flicks.'

He plasters a smile on his face, but it seems false. 'Just friends then.'

'Just friends.'

Nick takes another large gulp of water, keeping his eyes fixed on me. I feel hot under his gaze, and the hairs on my arms stand to attention as if on auto pilot. I remind my bits to calm down and tell them, firmly, that we're no longer reacting to Nick like this. We have a real date on Sunday.

'Don't look at me like that!'

'Like what?' He feigns innocence.

'Like trouble.'

'I'm just curious as to why I'm getting the call up.'

'Ant is going to a bachelor party, and it's Rich's week on at work, so Elle's home alone with the kids.'

'So I'm a last resort?' He stands tall, almost looking down at me.

'It's simply your turn. As my *friend*, you're merely completing your friendly duties.'

'Kinda like a hero then?'

'More like a sacrificial lamb.'

'You really know how to entice a guy, Josie,' he deadpans.

'Just making sure you're fully aware of what you're consenting to.'

He folds his arms across his chest, and I can see he's holding back a thought. What I wouldn't give to have unfiltered, V.I.P access to his thoughts. Nick can retreat into his own mind and when he does, I feel like someone suddenly hit the brakes when we're traveling one hundred kilometres an hour. It's jarring to say the least.

'Still processing?' I ask hesitantly. The thought of him declining my offer makes sweat gather at the back of my neck.

He shakes his head. 'Oh no. I'm fully committed to attending. Just wondering what's got you so scared that you're asking *me* to go. You know, as your *friend* and all. Why not just go on your own?'

'It will throw off the seating plan.'

'It'll what?' He jerks his head forward as if I am speaking a different language that he needs to decipher.

'You'll see.'

Chapter Nine

NICK

As I drive to the Russo family home, I have the distinct feeling I've taken on something far greater than a quiet family dinner. My first tipoff was when Josie showed up at my place in an off-the-shoulder, figure-hugging dress. I've never wanted to be a piece of fabric more than the piece clinging so tightly to those hips. She made me change from a t-shirt and shorts into an ironed shirt and dress pants. I'm just hoping my Rexona for men holds up against the summer night and nerves. I've cranked the air conditioning up in Josie's car, which she insisted we take over my ute, to the point of freezing the poor girl. Her skin has broken out in small bumps, and her nips poke through the dress. Bonus.

The second tipoff was the way she gave me a list of rules on how to behave around her parents. From all of the manic rambling, I got the general gist of must-be-on-my-best-behaviour-tonight. She's spent the car ride furiously rubbing her hands together, either to keep warm or to calm her nerves. I take her hand in mind, draw it up to my mouth and plant a short kiss on

40

it. It takes all the strength I have to pull my lips away from her soft skin. 'Tonight will be fine, Josie. Don't worry about it.'

'Yeah well, we'll see if you still want to be my friend after Lorella Russo has chewed you up and spat you back out.'

I could easily make an inappropriate joke right about now but something in the way Josie is moving makes me think it wouldn't be a good idea. She's different to the Josie I know. She's more ridged in her movements. Those glorious hips of hers don't sway like they're meant to, and she stands at an impossibly straight angle. She looks as wooden as the planks I use on site.

When we enter the front door, I see why. From the front, the house looks like any other family home on the street; double storey, neat gardens and an unused 'welcome' mat at the front door. Stepping inside is like stepping into the pages of some home magazine: marble floors, a large chandelier in the entry and art that looks confusing so it must be expensive. Something in me must change because Josie grabs my hand and tells me not to worry.

'I didn't know your folks were loaded,' I whisper so it won't bounce off the walls and find human ears to land on.

'We're not. It's all just for show.' She says flatly.

She doesn't let go of my hand, so I give it a little squeeze in support. She looks up at me with those big brown eyes and gives me a sad smile. I just want to take her in my arms and get her out of here. No wonder she doesn't speak about her family much if seeing them makes her this miserable.

'Josephine, darling.' An older woman dressed in white accented with chunky jewellery comes towards us with open arms. Josie reluctantly drops my hand and stiffly pats the woman on the back.

'And who is this young man?' she looks me up and down, seemingly impressed with my outfit but not my face. It's probably the beard. You either love them or hate them, and I'm guessing this woman is the latter.

'This is my friend, Nick. He's our neighbour.'

Unsure of the social etiquette here, I put my hand out for her to take, and she does so with distain. Apparently, something Josie said has turned her right off me. I'm off to a horrible start.

'Well, we're all at the table. Waiting. You're late,' she sings as a warning.

Josie apologises, and I feel like an idiot. It's my fault we were late because I had to change, and I didn't have an ironed shirt ready to wear. Josie had to take my shirt back to her place to quickly iron out, and I tried to distract her with my charm. I take one for the team and apologise to her mum, owning up to my mistake. She looks over her shoulder at me with a look that could melt ice.

We step into what can only be described as a movie set. It's so over the top with candles, shiny cutlery and people dressed in their finest that I suddenly wish I had worn a tie and studied the script better. The rounds of introductions are made, and I immediately forget everyone's name except for Josh. He sports a tattoo on his hand and I find myself wondering if that was Lorella Russo approved. He also looks as miserable as I feel. I take in Josie's family and can see the resemblance between her and her sisters. They're all beautiful; long dark hair, the same big brown eyes and perfectly painted pouty lips, but Josie really is the queen of them all.

I remember to be on my best behaviour, which means listening to some blonde gym junkie tell the table how clever he is for running his own business and how he's about to launch a new line of something. I tune out. I don't give a shit what Mr Muscles is about to launch unless it's dessert, and we can get the fuck out of here. Josie hasn't said a thing all evening and has had her hand firmly planted on my thigh under the table for most of the night. I've made a mental puzzle out of the intricate patterns on the table cloth to keep my mind from focusing on her hand and wishing it was planted a little bit higher up my leg.

Mr Muscles, who belongs to Josie's younger sister, Daniella, finally shuts up, and there's an audible sigh of relief from everyone, free to now talk about anything else. Unfortunately, that seems to be me.

'Nick! Why don't you tell us a bit about yourself?' her father asks. All eyes land firmly on me.

Mr Muscles has a smirk on his face and a dare in his eye, challenging me to beat him and his story about his gym. I'm game for the challenge but there really isn't one. I get the sense that everyone already thinks he's a bit of a wanker, so I've already won.

'Ah, not really much to tell I'm afraid.'

'Nick is a builder. He works for his father's company,' Josie jumps in and beams with pride as she tells her family about me.

It makes my heart swell. Among other things.

'Will you be taking over the company from your father one day?' her mother asks, taking a sip of her wine while looking every bit the Disney villain. She scares me.

'Not if I can help it.' I smile.

Mr Muscles scoffs and confidently places his arm around the back of his girlfriend's chair. She looks about as comfortable with it as someone who has a stick shoved up their arse.

'Have we met you before? You seem very familiar to me?' her father asks.

He seems less uptight than his wife, and a lot older too, but I've already decided I like him. Maybe it was the way he topped up his glass behind his wife's back and sneaked an extra helping of potato that sealed the deal. He looks like he's afraid of his wife too.

'I don't think so–'

Josie freezes and squeezes my leg. She turns to me with wide eyes in what I'm about to learn is a warning.

'Not formally but we have seen you before. A *lot* of you,' her mother snarls. 'I believe you and Anton were providing a show for all of your neighbours when we came to visit.'

It takes me a minute to figure out who Anton is before I can even start to unpack the rest of what she said.

Josie rubs the back of her neck and turns to me with flushed cheeks. 'It was the day after your footy grand final two years ago,' she says discreetly into my shoulder.

I'm distracted by her flowery perfume. An image from that night of us tangled in her bedsheets flashes into my mind. I'm one hundred percent certain no one saw us do that.

As if reading my mind, Josie shakes her head and continues, 'The nudie run.'

She says it so quietly that I have to ask her to repeat herself. The table looks at me, expectantly, and I feel like my stomach just dropped out of my arse. Great first impression to make. I look over to Mr Muscles and his shit eating grin, and I think, yeah, you won buddy.

After three courses, dessert, cheese platter and coffees, which I respectfully decline, I think the night is coming to an end. I couldn't be further from the truth. We're ordered into the lounge room by Franki, the oldest of the Russo sisters. She takes Josie by the hand, whispering furiously as they leave the rest of us in their wake. I take my time leaving the table, hoping to avoid any further conversations. I allow everyone else to leave ahead of me, except one of the other partners, who has the same idea.

'Josh,' he holds out his tattooed hand.

I give it a firm shake. 'Nick.'

'I'd like to tell you that these things get easier...,' we pause in the dining room checking no one can hear us before Josh continues, 'but I'd hate to give you false hope.' He says it as a joke, but it sounds loaded.

'Yeah, I don't think I'm making a very good impression.'

He scoffs. 'The only way you can make a good impression on Lorella Russo is if she sees your bank account.'

'She seems to like you.'

Josh lets out a humourless laugh. 'I'm half Italian and my folks have money. Plus, I tamed her wild child.' He uses air quotes around the term 'wild child' and suddenly I want to know more. I give him a look that tells him so. 'Don't get too excited, Lorella's version of wild is quite tame to what most people would think. Franki, my wife, was a bit of free spirit, a drifter. She's the kind of person who leads with her heart. I think Lorella was happy when we met. You know, stable, focused – that's what she wants for her girls.'

Suddenly Josie's freak out on her birthday makes so much more sense. I watched Franki at dinner tonight, and I didn't see one glimmer of a free-spirited drifter who leads with her heart. Has this guy changed her? Has Lorella? I'd never want that for Josie. I never want her to change.

'Yeah right,' is all I can think to say.

'Don't worry, though. Josie will be next to fall in line. They all do.'

Fall in line? Who the hell is this guy?

'You might have your work cut out with Lorella, but I can tell you've already won Josie over.'

My ears prick up at the compliment. I want to know more, so I go fishing. 'We're just friends.'

'Doesn't look that way from where I'm sitting.'

It's exactly the stroke my ego was looking for. *Thank you, douchebag.* 'Josie calls the shots,' I shrug.

Josh shakes his head at me. 'Lorella does. She might not be impressed with you now, but if you can get Josie to settle down and pop out a few kids, you'll be golden. Then maybe think about taking over that family company, and you're set for life.'

Josh pats me on the back and leaves the room like he's just laid down some infinite wisdom. He can piss right off with all his scheming. I've never lived my life to impress anyone, and I'm certainly not going to start now, even if the person I need to impress is Josie's mother. Love me or leave me, that's my motto. The only person whose opinion I even remotely care about is Josie's. I follow Josh into the lounge room where I am confronted by what looks like a PowerPoint presentation on the TV screen. Josie is standing up the front with an apologetic look on her face looking like she'd rather be anywhere but here. She clutches a piece of paper as her sister begins to speak.

'Take a seat everyone. Mum and Dad, you're up the front. Right, great,' Franki clears her throat as I take up a seat next to my new best buddy, Josh. It's either sit next to him or Mr Muscles. Slim pickings. The sister continues, 'As you know, we're gathered here today to celebrate the union between our parents, Lorella and Enzo, who are celebrating their fortieth wedding anniversary.'

The sister pauses, and everyone applauds. Forty years is pretty impressive, I'll give them that, even if Papa Russo has to sneak extra potato salad behind his wife's back.

'So, we'd like to share this presentation looking back at their love story.'

Daniella dutifully glides over to the wall to turn down the lights, but not before my eyes connect with Josie, sharing a look in which we each beg the other to save them.

Chapter Ten

JOSIE

I throw the keys in the bowl on the stand next to the door and allow Nick to follow me inside. Tonight's dinner was a tremendous mess, and he took it all in his stride. There was a certain sense of comfort that his presence bought me tonight, but I can't tell him that. With Nick, he takes compliments one or two ways; he'll either use it to try and bed me or take it and run away avoiding all social contact.

I need neither response from him right now. We head straight for the lounge room. I flick my heels off, not caring where they land and stretch my legs out on the couch. Nick lifts my feet up, taking them in his lap as he flops on the couch next to me. He knows exactly what I need. His cold hands touch the soles of my feet and begin to work out the tension I'm holding.

'You have magic fingers,' I moan and lay my head back.

'Wouldn't be the first time you've said that.'

I laugh and let him have the joke. I'm too tired to try and stop him. 'Thank you for tonight. My family can be pretty...well, you saw them.'

I shift my head to the side so I can see him. He gives me that grin that looks like he's smiling from the inside out. I like that one best on him. 'What?' I say, somehow grinning too.

He shakes his head and slowly moves his hands from my feet up my calves. My body tingles at the familiar roughness of the callouses on his hands. I give in just for a moment before I pull myself together and sit up, sliding away from him.

'Just friends, remember,' I say, forcing a smile.

He throws his head against the leather back of the couch and lets out a sigh. His shirt strains again his muscles, and I remind myself not to drool.

I can't be with Nick, not if I'm taking this whole settling down thing seriously. No matter how much I may have wanted something to happen in the past, nothing ever has. I've wasted months wishing for something that he can't give me. So I've given up. Well, at least tried to. I can't deny the butterflies that swirl in my stomach when I see him, especially when I see him like this; relaxed, calm, almost vulnerable. But he's not. Nick doesn't do vulnerability. That's why nothing serious will happened with Nick; he's not that sort of guy. I can't afford to get my heart broken by someone who never really wanted it in the first place. We're better off just being friends.

Nick opens his mouth to say something but is suddenly interrupted by a high-pitched giggle coming from the door. Nick and I turn in sync to see a petite blonde woman curled under Ant, feigning a protest at his affections. They stumble into the wall and fall into fits of laughter together. Nick and I share an amused look. I can't help myself.

'Hi ho sailor,' I say which makes Ant and his companion look in our direction.

'Sorry, didn't think anyone was home.' Ant straightens up and holds the girl's hand.

'Well, don't let that stop you. As you were solider,' Nick announces, and Ant gives him a salute before rushing the woman into his bedroom.

'Oh God. I hope they settle down quickly. I'm too tired for this tonight.'

Nick shrugs. 'You can always stay at mine.'

I shoot him a suspicious look to which he throws his hands up defensively and adds, 'As friends, of course.'

There's a hint of disappointment in his voice that matches the one in the pit of my stomach. 'Thank you, *friend*. But I'll be fine. I'll listen to a podcast for twenty minutes, and it'll all be over.'

There is a loud crash followed by more laughing from behind Ant's bedroom door.

'Twenty minutes, is that all?' Nick winks at me and my lower regions flutter.

I have got to get my brain talking to everyone else in here otherwise this *friends* thing is going to be a lot harder, maybe too hard to fight.

'They both seem pretty drunk.'

'Even then I'm not that quick.'

My cheeks flush as several memories simultaneously flash in my mind. I try to push them out, but they don't budge. I stand up, and Nick mirrors my actions, straightening out his pants.

'Okay, well I'm off to bed. *Alone*,' I emphasise, and he simply shrugs. 'Thanks again for tonight.'

Nick winks at me and kisses me on the cheek, lingering a second longer than friendly. My eyes fall to his lips hidden beneath his beard as he slowly pulls away, and I find myself wondering how much harm one little kiss could cause. One soft, little kiss. He must think the same as he rubs his lips together. Something nags at the back of my mind reminding me that this would be a very big mistake. I pull back, and he clears his throat stepping away. We share an awkward smile as he leaves and sees himself out.

I grab at the back of my neck, pushing down as I bring my hands forward. Just friends. It's all it ever can be.

Chapter Eleven

NICK

I should have just kissed her. I've done it hundreds of times before, so why did this time feel different? I pace around my kitchen hoping the answer is in a cupboard somewhere as I forcefully open and close them. Shit. I run my hands through my hair and rip off my shirt. Frustration builds up inside me and I need to do something – *anything* – to escape my own skin. The waves appear in my stomach. I know what they're signalling, and I'm not going to let them beat me.

I stride over to the dumbbells sitting on the stand and take one in each hand, griping them so tight my knuckles turn white as I begin my routine starting with bicep curls. I move at a steady pace, squeezing the muscles each time I lift. I focus on my breathing to quieten the noise in my head. I do a set of fifteen then pick up the skipping rope and do a quick one-minute jump. It gets my heart racing and is enough of a distraction that I feel the waves disappear.

This is how I've been managing for the last three years, before that it was with an unhealthy attachment to all the wrong things. Spoiler alert: I wasn't managing; I was in self-destruct mode. The waves in my stomach are the first signs of my anxiety returning, and if I can get physical, I can push through it.

Mum always said I was a bit of a nervy kid. I guess having your father abandon you at a young age will do that to you, but I never had panic attacks until she passed away, and I was left with no one. It's what prompted my father to reach out and what made me move to Littleton Beach three years ago. A change of scenery and a change in friends was the first step in getting myself out of the hole I had dug.

I haven't shared that part of my story with anyone except Ant. He found me one morning about two years ago suffering through a pretty severe attack, so bad he rushed me to the hospital because we both thought I was having a heart attack. When it turned out to be a panic attack, I begged him not to say anything to anyone, especially Josie, because I felt embarrassed. I've been pretty good at keeping it under control but the thing about anxiety is, it just pops up whenever the fuck it wants. There's no reason tonight should have caused it to rear its ugly head, and yet here I am, entering into my second round of curls and one-minute fast jumps. Sweating it out has been the one consistent thing that has worked for me, and man, I am sweating like a pig.

The knock at the door surprises me, and I throw my dumbbells down to answer it.

'Hey,' Josie's big brown eyes are like a damn arrow through my heart, 'why are you all sweaty again?'

She's standing in my doorway in a very silky, very short black night dress, clutching her pillow. I feel a sense of déjà vu as I'm pretty sure I've dreamed of this very moment.

I shrug my shoulders trying to pass off that working out this late at night is a completely normal thing to do. 'Just a little workout.'

'Is this like a thing you do now? Stay up late and, like, workout? Are you and Ant not really going to the gym when you say you are?' The accusation in her eyes is cute.

'You know, Josie, for someone who just wants to be friends you sure are making a lot of late-night visits to my house.' I can't help but mess with her a bit.

I catch her eyes flicker over my chest, so I flex my pecs. I like making her blush.

'Can I sleep here tonight? Ant and the blonde are so freaking loud, and I'm too bloody tired to try to wait them out.'

I stand aside and let her in. I'm going to be the perfect gentleman too and offer her the spare bedroom, although it's the last place I want her to sleep. She eyes the sports equipment and looks back at me.

'Were you like, preparing for something?' I have no idea what she's talking about and it must show because she adds, 'Like were you expecting someone? 'Cause if you've invited someone over, I can leave.'

I look to the equipment and then back to her trying to piece together how this all fits with what she said. I must really be an open book right now because she elaborates for my benefit.

'I've seen videos of Chris Evans doing push ups before filming scenes, so his muscles are like bulging and big.'

I laugh at the absurdity of the situation. She thinks I'm working out to impress someone else? 'Hang on, you think in the fifteen minutes since I left your place that I've gone and called someone to come over for the night?'

She unapologetically shrugs her shoulders. Is that what she thinks of me? That I have an endless list of chicks I can randomly call to hook up with? That I would even want to? I've just been out with her all night, with her family no less, we almost kiss, and she thinks I'm back here dialling up a booty call. I haven't been with anyone *but* her in more than a year.

I think about telling her just that, but I don't. What will it achieve? She's made it perfectly clear that she just wants to be friends. I want more. I know I do but coming straight out of the gates with that little truth bomb will likely frighten her away. I've gotta take it slow with Josie. I've gotta get her to see me in a much better light than she apparently does right now. I've gotta make her fall in love with me.

'There's no one coming around. I really was just working out. Tryna clear my mind.'

'I'm sorry if my family messed with you tonight.' She bats her eyelashes at me and I see a sadness in her eyes that I hate. I almost cave in and tell her everything. Hell, I don't want her to think this is her fault. I open my mouth to say something, but she beats me to it.

'If it makes you feel any better, they behaved the same with Chad when Daniella first started dating him. I think the fact that he's a successful business owner has won my mother over. She was willing to overlook his heritage.'

'What do you mean?'

She rolls her eyes and takes a seat at my bench as though this simple question has a complicated answer. 'My parents, especially my mother, have a thing about my sisters and I only marrying Italians.'

'Ah, she's a racist.'

'Not exactly. She's a snob. She wants us to marry good Italian men with good jobs. Chad is some English Australian mix, but he has a successful business so money trumps heritage – despite the fact that he's an insufferable jerk.'

'I thought it was just me who thought that!' I exclaim a little too excitedly.

Josie shakes her head and swallows a laugh. 'No. We all hate him. He's so controlling and such a show pony,' she pulls a disgusted face, 'but Daniella seems to be head over heels for him. Josh comes from a good Italian family so he's safe from my mother's criticism, and he does something in the corporate world. Essentially, they're both professionally important enough to meet my mother's marriage material checklist.'

'And then you bring me there, an Aussie bloke, a tradesman

with a beard and no aspirations to take over the family business––'

'Yes, I'm a huge disappointment to my mother at the best of times.' She flashes me an apologetic smile. I just want to yell and scream at her mother for not seeing the incredible daughter she has in front of her.

'Josie, you're not a disappointment.' I move towards her.

'I'm a twenty-nine-year-old single woman with no marriage prospects who lives with her best friend from high school. Also, being a co-ordinator is not good enough. I should have aspirations to be Principal.'

I hate hearing Josie talk down about herself; she's so much more than any of those things.

'Who the hell would you ever want to be a principal? I don't even know why you want to be a teacher!' My joke makes the corners of her mouth lift, and I can't help but smile back at her. 'Is this what that freak out on your birthday was about?'

'I do want to settle down and have a family, but I just haven't met the right guy yet, and biologically, I'm running out of time.'

I'm not one to subscribe to lists and should-dos, so I try hard to connect with what she's saying, but it just doesn't make sense to me. 'I think you're putting too much pressure on yourself, Josie. Everything will work out. You're too amazing not to have all of that happen for you.'

My sincerity goes over her head as she dramatically plants her head on her hands and then gestures wildly to the gods. 'But when? When! When is Mr Right coming into my life to sweep me off my feet, marry me and put his babies in my belly?'

I should just tell her how I feel. Forget taking it slow. Where has slow ever gotten anybody anyway? I know she only thinks of me as her friend, but I know we're great together. We wouldn't have carried on this long if we weren't.

I open my mouth to talk but she beats me to it again and dashes all my hope.

'Who knows, maybe Milo will be the one. He ticked every item on my list, at least at a surface level, so maybe he'll be it.'

'Who the fuck is Milo?'

She waves her hands dismissively at me. 'Didn't I tell you?' No, you bloody did not. 'Milo is my optometrist. We're going out tomorrow night.'

Well, fuck me. Now what do I do?

Chapter Twelve

JOSIE

It's not even half an hour into my date with Milo, and it's already the best date I've ever been on. He's smart and funny and can hold an intelligent conversation without swearing or making some ridiculous joke. This must be what it feels like to be a grown up. Milo orders a red wine that costs more than the meal itself, and I feel a little bit swept up. Maybe he is the one; is it too early to be thinking about that?

'I was so nervous about asking you out. I didn't want to come off as creepy, but...I just knew it was now or never.' He pushes his plate further towards the middle of the table to indicate he's finished.

I wipe the corners of my mouth with the napkin and use it to try and pat away a blush that has coloured my cheeks.

'I had no idea! But I'm really glad you asked. There was no way I was going to do the asking.' I stifle a laugh.

His eyes sparkle in the candle light as a large grin takes over his face. He looks every bit the leading man in this light and that shirt; I'm finding it difficult not to fall all in.

'I was surprised you were single. Girls like you, well....'

'Girls like me what?' I ask, feeling like a high schooler flirting with her crush.

'Come on, Josie. You must know how beautiful you are. You must have guys fighting each other to get a date with you.'

I want to laugh hysterically; guys fighting over me? Is he joking? No guy has ever fought over me. I guess that was the problem with my ex; he never fought for me or us. I haven't exactly been inundated with offers since we broke up almost five years ago. Unless you count Nick, which I don't. That's just a bit of fun, for both of us. He doesn't see me as anything serious anyway. So no, no guys have been fighting over me.

Although I'm flattered by his compliment, I try to deflect the attention; something ingrained in me tells me I'm not worthy of this man's compliments or affections. 'Me? What about you?! How is a handsome, successful man like yourself single?'

He swirls the wine in his glass. 'Handsome, huh?'

Milo's attempts at flirting are a little awkward, like the cockiness doesn't really belong to him, like he borrowed it from someone else. Not like with Nick, flirting with Nick comes easy. So does the confidence. Nick flirts with such ease that even when he's being cocky it's kinda sexy–wait, why am I thinking about Nick right now? Probably because Milo brought him up. Or I did. Someone did, right? I shake all thoughts of Nick out of my brain and concentrate on the man in front of me.

'Okay, rapid fire answer time,' I announce to a stunned-looking Milo.

'And what exactly is that?'

A little perplexed that he hasn't a clue about rapid fire questions and answers, I explain. 'We get five questions each. Think getting to know you stuff, but you have to answer with the first thing that comes into your mind. And you have to answer, no sitting on the fence. No filter. No explanation. You game?'

He sips at his wine. 'I must admit, I am very good at games.'

I grin. A competitive side underneath all that well-presented, well-spoken man? Everything inside me electrifies. There's a hint of playfulness in the grin that spreads across his face, and my lady bits flutter.

'Ladies first,' he gestures, and I begin.

'Cats or dogs.'

'Dogs.' *Tick*. Excellent start.

'Best flavour ice cream?'

'Vanilla.'

'Vanilla?' I ask surprised.

'Is that one of your questions?'

I hit an imaginary stop button. 'Pause the game. Vanilla?'

He chuckles. 'I thought there was no explaining?'

'I change the rules as I go,' I shrug.

His laugh deepens, and he plays along like the good sport I know he is.

'It's simple. Vanilla goes with everything. Any topping flavour is enhanced by adding it to vanilla ice-cream.'

'That's because it's boring and has no real flavour.'

'And,' he raises his finger to accentuate his point, 'when ordering two scoops of any flavoured ice-cream, it should always be paired with vanilla, so the flavours don't clash and––'

'No way!' I interrupt, unable to control my sudden indignation about vanilla ice-cream, 'You've clearly never lived on the edge wondering if your choice of bubble gum will go with peppermint choc chip.'

'And does it?' Impertinence dances across his tongue.

'Of course not! Nothing goes with bubble gum.'

'Vanilla would.'

'Bubble gum flavour is the worst and ruins everything. Even vanilla. But you keep trying it with everything else until you find the perfect combination. It's like ice-cream roulette.' My passionate ice-cream outburst sends us into fits of laughter. 'Okay, okay. Time on. Summer or winter?'

'Neither. Spring.'

'That wasn't an option!'

'I change the rules as I go,' he shrugs, playing on the words I said moments ago.

'Well then, to follow the rules or break them?' This time I take a sip of wine.

He cocks his head as a small blush colours his cheeks. 'Depends on the rule, or the consequence for breaking it.'

The temperature of the room skyrockets, and I gulp more of my drink. I fan my face like a sensitive fifties housewife who just saw the neighbour's gardener with his shirt off. *How very improper, Sir.* Milo smiles into his glass of wine and sips.

'Last question,' he reminds me.

My mind is completely blank. I try and sift through the darkness for something flirty to say back, but all I can think about is breaking all the rules with Milo. There's something dangerously sexy about a well-presented man who harbours a naughty mind.

'I might hold onto my last question,' I say, trying to come across as mysterious, but really, I'm just trying to give my mind a moment to recover.

'Fair enough. My turn then?'

'Fire away.'

'Flowers or chocolates?'

I throw my hands up in mock outrage. 'Impossible to choose between. Both.'

'You have to pick one. No sitting on the fence, remember? Your rules.'

'I thought we established that I was a rule breaker?' A wry smile dances across my face.

Milo wags his finger at me, and I find his authority a turn on. *Who am I?*

'We established that I was the rule breaker, and you were the rule changer.'

'Well, I'm breaking my own rule and choosing both.'

Milo pushes his glasses to the bridge of his nose before folding his arms across his chest. I notice the way his shirt tightens in all the right places, not enough that his shirt looks like it is about to be ripped to shreds by his muscles, but enough to remind you that he has them hidden away.

'Fine. Flowers. Unless it's the little chocolates you get from speciality shops that combine weird flavours like salted lemon.'

'I'm sensing a theme here...,' he leaves the end of his sentence hanging as if it's an invitation to complete it for him.

'Only with sweets. The sugar cancels out anything funky. I'm as picky as all heck with regular foods.'

'Well, based on that I think I already know the answer to my next question, but I'll ask it anyway - home cooked meal or fine dining?'

'Home cooked meal. At least I know what I'm ingesting.'

'Have you ever been to a fine dining restaurant?'

'Is that one of your questions?' I tease, and the corners of my mouth lift.

He thinks it over for a moment before nodding.

'No, I haven't been to anywhere I'd consider fine dining. No-one in my circle of friends is really a fine diner.'

Milo rubs a hand over his clean shaved chin before taking the wine glass to his lips. The movement is more mesmerising than it has the right to be and highlights how quickly I am falling for this man. *Lord help me.*

'If you've never been, then how do you know you don't like it? And that's not one of my questions by the way, I'm merely musing out loud.' We share a laugh before he continues, 'Books or movies?'

'Wait,' I hold up my hand, 'we both need to answer this at the same time.'

'You're right,' he plays along. 'This could be dealbreaker territory.'

I nod. 'On the count of three. One, two, three–'

'Books,' we say in unison and raise our glasses to clink together.

'That could have been awkward.' Milo blows out a breath.

'We'd have to end the date here. I'd have to find a new optometrist!'

'I'd have to take my Godson out of your school!'

'Don't get me wrong, I love movies–'

'But the books are always better.' He smiles and finishes my sentence. 'There's only one more thing to ask then....'

'Ask me anything. I think we got the big one out the way, so...'

A knowing smile flashes across his face. He recovers by looking at his glass before working up the courage to look me in the eyes and ask, 'Short term? Or long term?'

'Long term,' I answer without hesitation.

His gaze holds mine as if that was the perfect answer.

Dinner flies by, and as red wine flows through our veins, we become more comfortable around each other. I keep finding reason to gently touch his arms or his shoulder, and each light touch sends a surge of electricity through my body.

'How many times exactly has this trick worked before?' I smile over the rim of my glass.

'What trick?' His eyes shine in the candlelight.

Honestly this is like something out of a movie. A cute little restaurant by the beach, a handsome leading man and enough chemistry to create a Big Bang. I'm living my very best Kate Hudson life right now.

'Tell a client she has pretty eyes, flirt and ask her out. How have they all worked out in the past?'

He swallows a grin. 'I'll tell you in the morning.'

I let out an overdramatic gasp. It might be the wine talking, but it also might just be me; I feel like a teenage girl with a crush. Isn't this what falling in love is supposed to feel like? Okay, maybe not love right away but definitely lust.

'Only if you play your cards right,' I wink.

'Is that so?' He tries to cock an eyebrow but can't and instead cocks both at the same time. It makes me giddy, and I giggle.

By the time we're in the cinema I'm comfortable enough to sink into Milo's chest and have his arms firmly around me. As the lights turn down, Milo shifts in his seat, angling his body towards mine. He ducks his head, so his lips linger by my ear and his warm breath tickles at the spot just below my earlobe.

'Would it be a terrible idea if I kissed you right now?'

Everything about him is intoxicating: his cologne, his breath, his voice. It's not the most romantic place for a first kiss with a new man, but I throw all romantic notions out the window along with my self-control.

'I don't think it would be a terrible idea.' I bite down on a smile.

Milo reaches forward and cups my cheek. His mouth make the short trek from just below my ear to my lips, leaving a trail of excitement along my jawline as his lips edge closer to mine. When they finally meet, everything around us melts away.

We steal kisses throughout the film like horny teenagers, and by the time the credits roll, I've already decided to take him back to my place.

'I never got to ask my last question,' I say, running my hand over his chest as we pause by the car in the carpark.

'Do you want to ask it now?' He brings his lips impossibly close to mine.

I nod.

'What is your last question, Josie?' he asks barely louder than a whisper.

I lick my lips. 'Your place or mine?'

I watch his Adam's apple bob up and down. He runs his hands over my bare arms. 'Wherever you feel most comfortable.'

I suggest my place and feel a sense of excitement and adrenalin run through me as he accepts my offer. My body tingles in all the right ways as I bring home a guy on the first date. It feels a little bit naughty and it's doing strange things to my body – things I like. It's not normally my style. Normally I'm cautious and wait the acceptable amount of time (whatever that is anymore) before bringing someone home, but something about this feels right. Looking into his eyes feels like looking into my future, and I somehow know that tonight won't be the last time we see each other.

Ant is sitting up watching TV alone, and I feel a sense of relief that Nick isn't here. I don't know why I care so much about it, probably because I know he will give me hell for bringing Milo back to my place. Ant cocks one eyebrow at me as we walk into the lounge, fingers intertwined.

'Ant, this is Milo,' I say.

Ant doesn't move from the couch but beams a bemused smile. They share an awkward wave at each other.

'Well, we're just going to...in there,' I don't know why words fail me as Ant stifles a laugh at my awkwardness.

I push Milo towards my bedroom and look over my shoulder at Ant who gives me a thumbs up and mouths the word 'hot' at me.

I lean against the closed door as Milo reaches for me around my waist. He pulls me in and kisses me deeply. I run my hands through his hair and push into him.

He lifts away slightly and says, 'Should I be worried that your flatmate is a guy?'

I shake my head. 'We've been friends forever. He's more like a brother.'

Milo is satisfied with my answer, thank goodness, because I don't have the concentration to go into Ant's complex dating life to quell the insecurities of the male ego. The fact that he straight up accepts my answers turns me on even more. He lifts me up and walks me over to the bed, gently placing me down on my back. He pushes my knees apart with his and gently lowers on top of me.

'You sure about this,' he whispers in my ear as he kisses down into the crook of my neck, a definite weak spot.

I let out a satisfied groan. I've never been surer about anything in my life.

Chapter Thirteen

NICK

I really should have made better use of the weekend to do grown up things like food shopping because being without food on a Monday morning is the biggest inconvenience and the worst start to my day. I'm not the best person to be around when I'm hungry. But none of this is really my fault. I didn't get much sleep over the weekend, so I felt hung over without the joy of actually having any alcohol.

This is all very clearly Josie's fault. I thought I could handle her sleeping in the room next to mine on Saturday night, but as it turns out, I spent the whole night talking myself out of walking into that room and making love to her over and over again. And then on Sunday night, all I could do was think about the date she was on, hoping desperately that it sucked major balls. With Josie occupying most of my brain space, food shopping wasn't even a consideration.

I make my way over to Ant and Josie's place and let myself in. Ant's up and eating cereal at the breakfast counter before their first day back of term one. He nods at me, and I nod back at him as a greeting.

'Forget to do your grocery shopping again?' he says around a mouthful of food.

'Something like that.'

I take out a bowl and pour myself the same cereal as Ant. I lean against the counter and shovel the crunchy, tasteless mess into my mouth. 'What the hell is this?'

'Some gluten free crap Josie bought. Taste like cardboard, right?'

'Taste like nothing good.' This doesn't stop me from finishing the bowl just as Josie and some tall stranger exit her room.

My eyes narrow in on Mr Clean-Shaven and everything within me tenses. I immediately don't like him. 'Who's that?' I say, nodding to the man holding Josie's hand.

'Milo,' Ant replies.

'He's food?'

'Technically, it's a drink.'

'Technically, it's only a drink if you add milk to it, so technically, he's a form of granular food.'

'Technically, you're both being rude,' Josie frowns.

I don't even pretend to care that we're talking about Mr Foodie like he isn't there and hearing everything we're saying. If he's too precious, he can fuck right off. I give him the once over, deciding that I'm easily a foot taller and broader. Score two for me.

'It's okay,' Foodie's lips touch Josie's and stay there too long for my liking. 'I've got to get home and ready for work.'

Ant gives him a nod, and I stand with my arms folded across my chest. He looks like he could fulfil every item on her list; damnit he even looks like he could be related to Efron. And if she let him stay the night after just one date, the date couldn't have been as bad as I was hoping it would be. This isn't good news for me and my plan to make Josie fall in love with me.

'Do you two think you could have been any less mature?' she fumes after Mr List Perfect leaves.

Ant and I don't say anything, and she switches into full teacher mode. 'The way you both conducted yourself just then with Milo was completely unacceptable. How uncomfortable do you think you made him? He's such a lovely guy and didn't deserve to be treated like that.'

'Sorry, Miss. Does this mean you're going to give me a detention?'

She pushes past me completely unimpressed with my attempt at humour.

'You know, Josie, most people are pretty chill after sex. Did the Backstreet Boy not really know what to do?'

She gives me her best teacher glare which does nothing to stop the jealous beast inside me. I admit I'm acting like a bit of a dick, but I can't help myself.

'He knew *exactly* what to do,' she slams the cutlery draw shut, 'twice.'

I wince at her words. It was better when I just assumed they had sex rather than actually know they did. The confirmation makes me feel sick. She storms off to the bathroom and slams the door shut.

'Man,' Ant shakes his head at his cereal, 'you messed that up.'

I rub at my beard. 'Yeah, I know. Shit!'

'It's been cute watching the two of you play at this little game for the last three years, but seriously, it's getting a bit old.'

'What do you mean?' I play dumb. I know exactly what Ant means. We've had this exact conversation approximately four hundred and eighty-six times in just the last year alone.

'This whole you-like-her-and-she-likes-you-but-we-don't-tell-each-other thing is tired. Just man up and tell her how you feel.'

'It's a bit more complicated than that,' I protest, gesturing to the door the Bieber wannabe just walked out of.

'Oh please, she didn't sound like she was having that great a time. Not even once.'

It shouldn't, but the reassurance from Ant brings a smile to my face, and I feel like I'm a high schooler who just discovered his dick is bigger than all the other boys.

'Look, I know for a fact that neither one of you have been with anyone else but each other for at least the last year. The amount of time you spend with each other – you're practically dating already. Just get on with it.'

'You're mighty impatient this morning. What's up your arse?'

Ant walks around the bench and drops his bowl into the sink. He's big and broad like me, probably bigger thanks to his Greek genes. He's a looker, so I can only hope that the Pinterest Pin-Up was somewhat intimidated by the fact that he is Josie's roommate.

'Nothing,' Ant shrugs.

'Blondie didn't do it for you the other night?'

Ant leans against the bench next to me. 'I don't know, man. I've been talking to Levi a bit.'

'The guy from New Year's who thinks your name is Bryan?'

Ant rubs the back of his neck and lets out a laugh. 'Yeah, I cleared all that up with him.'

'Good for you, man. Does Josie know?'

Ant shakes his head. 'Nah. And I kinda wanna keep it that way, yeah? You know how she gets. She'll have us married off before the end of the week.'

I nod, a gentleman's agreement. 'Didn't really peg you as the Daddy in a Sugar Daddy situation.'

Ant elbows me. 'Fuck off.'

'Seriously, a toy boy? I always pictured you as the boy. All the other dudes you've gone for have been older.'

Ant shrugs. 'Maybe that was the problem.' He runs his hands through this thick, curly black hair. 'I don't know. Just thinkin' out loud I guess.'

I start to offer more support, but Josie enters the room like a hurricane, clearly still pissed at my earlier performance. Man, I'd hate to be her first period class today. I use her entrance as my cue to leave.

'Hey,' I nod at Ant, 'gym tonight?'

He nods. We both know it's code for 'talk about this later'.

'Bye, Josie,' I offer, but she just grunts at me.

I've got to figure out a way to keep my cool about this guy and get back in Josie's good books. It'll be hard to make her fall in love with me if she's mad at me. Besides, this thing with the Directioner won't last, at least that's what I tell myself to get through the day.

Chapter Fourteen

JOSIE

Today I feel like every teenager has decided to return to school and be a little turd. I spend most of my morning following up incorrect uniform offences and the afternoon chasing down waggers, all while trying to teach my three English classes. All in all, it's a pretty lousy first day back compared to the completely not lousy night before.

Milo was the perfect gentleman all night and into the morning. I didn't get much sleep and it's probably adding to my irritability as I pull Connor James out of his fifth period math class. Poor Connor. I can already feel a whole day's worth of frustration about to unload on him for his poor choice in skipping fourth period.

'Yes, Miss?' Connor swaggers out of the classroom and into the corridor with me, hands in pockets, trying to pass off as cool to his mates looking through the classroom windows.

'We haven't even been back a day, and you're already skipping class.'

Connor makes the mistake of feigning innocence, claiming

has no idea what I'm talking about. It's only fuel to the fire. *Today is not the day, Connor.*

'Don't,' I hold up my hand to his face as he is about to speak, 'it has been a really long day so let's just cut the bull – I know you were wagging because Mr Daly-Hennen caught you.' Connor wisely closes his mouth and lets me continue my tirade. 'We spoke at the end of last year, remember? We had your mum here, and we spoke about how you were going to change this year, because year eleven is important. Remember that little conversation?'

He nods and shifts on the spot. Something in his stance reminds me of the way Nick was this morning which angers me further. 'And I don't really care to know what you were thinking. In fact, I'm taking a big wild guess here, Connor, and am going to say that you weren't really thinking. And then I'm told, on top of wagging, you gave Mr Daly-Hennen lip when he questioned you.'

I paused for dramatic effect, and Connor takes this opportunity to speak. Wrong move, Connor. 'Yeah, but Miss, he was being a–'

'I don't care what he was being,' I interrupt, raising my voice even louder, 'you were wrong. You were clearly in the wrong to treat him like that. Mr Daly-Hennen is a lovely man, and you had no right to speak to him like that, Ni–, I mean, Connor.'

I catch myself by surprise as I almost say Nick's name. That idiot has had enough of my brain space for the day. And Mr Daly-Hennen isn't a nice man, in fact he probably deserved the lip that Connor dished out to him, but it is very clear to me that this is no longer about Connor.

'Right, so,' I recover, 'you'll have two lunch detentions this week for wagging and the Mr Daly-Hennen stuff. Okay?'

Connor rolls his eyes, and I give him a stern warning look. He shuffles back off to class, and the jeering of his mates follows me as I storm off to my office.

I can't believe I let Nick and his childish outburst bother me all day. I should be basking in the glow of all the right things that happened last night, but all I can focus on is my anger towards Nick from this morning.

The final school bell doesn't come quick enough and as soon as the day is over, I take my frustration to the one place and person I know who will take it all way.

'Great, she's just woken up from her nap,' Elle says as she hands me her fifteen-month-old baby girl, Harlow.

I snuggle into her and immediately all my troubles melt away. There has never been a child as snuggly as Harlow. I drink in her sleepiness and the way she smells like jasmine and wrap her in my arms so tight that she may just fall back asleep. My ovaries practically shout at me, *'Let's make babies!'*

'So, what's got Aunty Josie in such fuss this afternoon?' Elle uses her baby voice as she approaches us with a bottle.

Harlow snatches it out of her mother's hands and feeds. I change my tone too, to match Elle's and suddenly it feels like we're on the set of a very grown-up version of *Sesame Street*.

'Well, Aunty Josie is mad at Uncle Nick for being a big meanie today.'

Elle lets out a familiar groan. 'What did he do this time?'

With a sudden burst of energy at the sounds of the *Bluey* theme song, Harlow leaps from my lap to join her brother, Jaggar, in the lounge room. I pout after her.

'Don't worry, she'll come back. Now, tell me what is going on?' Elle edges closer, eager to gossip.

'So, I went on a date last night with this really cute guy.'

'What? Okay, we're coming back to all that goss, but get the Nick stuff out of the way first.' Elle's eyes light up.

'Okay, well, this morning Nick was really rude to him. Like, him and Ant were talking about him like he wasn't even there when he was literally right there.'

Elle shakes her head and wags her finger. 'Whoa. Back up.

This *morning*? So, you took him home on the first *date*? Go, Josie!'

'I know!' We fall into giggles like we're fourteen again.

'Must have been one hell of a date!'

I sigh. The date, yes. 'It was. He was just so...I don't know how to describe it. Perfect? Like, he ticks everything on my list.'

Elle sits back with a satisfied look on her face. 'I can see why Nick was a jerk then.' I look at her confused. 'Oh come on, Josie. You and Nick have practically been dating for like the last two years, and then you come home with Mr Dreamboat. It's no wonder he was a dick. He's totally jealous.'

I scoff. No way is Nick jealous. Nick doesn't want anything serious with anybody. If anything, his ego is probably bruised because I've found someone else to spend time with which means a permanent end to whatever it was that we have been doing for the past two years.

'I know you don't like hearing it–'

'It's not that I don't like hearing it, Elle, it's just not true.'

'Oh, believe me, it is. He likes you. You should see the way he looks at you. It's so bloody obvious.'

I shake my head. 'It's just casual. It doesn't mean anything.'

'Mmm-hmmm. So, you're telling me that if Nick was to declare his undying love for you, you could easily brush him off?'

I shift in my seat and wish that Harlow would return so I could hide behind her. I've pictured it, the whole thing with Nick, white picket fence and all. In my mind I've heard him tell me all the things I've ever wanted to hear. But it's nothing more than a fantasy. Nick hasn't given any indication that he wants anything serious in all the time I've known him.

'It's a stupid question because it's never going to happen.'

Elle rolls her eyes. 'One day the two of you will wake up and realise you've been in love with each other all along.'

'Nick and I have fun together. That's it. Besides, you should have seen the way my mother looked at him at dinner the other night. Boy! She was not impressed.'

'Of course she wasn't. You bring Nick, a beard-wielding, rugged, sex-on-legs lumberjack to dinner...'

'What!' I can't help but laugh.

'...of course Lorella is going to hate him. He doesn't look like a good Italian boy who just stepped off the pages of European *Vogue* and don't even get her started on the fact he's a mere tradie! *'Not good enough for you, Josephine.'* She mimics my mother perfectly and it only starts a new round of laughter from me.

'Forget. That. And why the hell was he at your parent's house anyway? Josie! You have so much to tell me!'

I catch Elle up on everything from the weekend, including every intimate detail of my night with Milo.

'You should see him,' I practically swoon, 'if you put 'guy in suit and glasses' into Pinterest, he would pop up. And he reads! He's smart, an optometrist, can you believe it?'

I continue to list Milo's qualities and details from last night. She practically breaks out into a hot sweat as I recount our night, perhaps indulging in the finer details a little too much. I can't resist. I built him up to be something or someone who could deliver a happy ending after a magical night. The truth is it was okay. Just okay.

I don't know whether it was just nerves on both our parts, but the sex didn't produce the fireworks I was expecting. And it certainly wasn't twice like I led the boys to believe this morning. It was barely even once. But embarrassment stirs within me, and I don't want to let anyone know, especially not after the scene I caused in the kitchen this morning, or the way I just spoke about him to Elle. No-one needs to know that the date was great, but the sex was definitely not.

That stuff builds anyway, right? First time with someone new gets the better of everyone. It's only been Nick for so long that I'm too attuned to his body and his cues. I just need to relax a bit and learn Milo's body and cues. Surely that's it. I need to give Milo the benefit of the doubt because everything else about him ticks the boxes on my list.

Chapter Fifteen

NICK

Monday is just following where Saturday and Sunday left off – grinding on my last nerve. Maybe it's the sleepless weekend, maybe it's the Magic Mike in Josie's bed this morning, maybe it's the fact that the apprentice is too damn slow, but I feel like I'm the pot on the stove about to boil over. My day doesn't get any easier when I'm cornered by my father as I'm about to leave to meet Ant at the gym.

'Nick, a word?' he nods his head to the side by way of telling me to meet him over there, away from other people.

It's never good when the boss wants a private word, even worse when the boss is your father, and you blew off family dinner. 'Whatever it is, can it wait 'til tomorrow? I'm having a shocker of a day.'

He removes his hard hat and looks at it in his hands. 'Nick, I wanted you to come over for dinner this weekend because there's something we need to discuss.'

'Then right now probably isn't the place or time to–'

'Would you just,' he pauses to calm himself, avoiding a scene, 'look, we need to discuss a few things, so I'd like it if you came over tonight. I realise that having dinner with your brothers and your stepmother–'

'Your wife and kids,' I correct him.

'Nick,' he pleads, 'I realise that it still may be difficult for you to be a part of our family, and I shouldn't pressure you into it. Look, come over tonight after you've had your dinner, and we'll talk.'

He looks worn out and tired, and as much as part of me wants to accept the offer and is curious about what he has to say, the larger, stubborn part of me always wants to make him work for my attention.

'I've got plans tonight.'

'Do you think you could possibly reschedule them?' he snaps. 'I don't know what more I've got to do to get you to forgive me. I can't change what I did, but I'm sure as hell tryin' real hard now to make it up to you.'

He stares me down, and I can't move. I'm hyperaware of the boys walking past us to clock off. My cheeks redden as a consequence of pushing him further than I intended. Not wanting to create a further scene, I reluctantly accept. 'I'll see what I can do,' I say as I walk past him to my ute.

Pulling into the gym parking lot doesn't relieve the stress I've built up from the long day. Normally on the drive over I feel the stress drift away but not today. At least here nothing could get any worse, unless I drop a weight on my foot or something. I catch Ant in the parking lot. He jogs up to me.

'Ant-Man.'

'Nicolai.'

Our stupid little greeting brings a smile to my face. Maybe there is hope for this day yet.

Ant and I fall into our usual routine of talking nonsense and spotting each other on the bars. When I moved to Littleton

Beach, he was the first friend I made, possibly my first true friend ever. Although my old life is only an hour away, it seemed too far for my so-called friends to visit, and as the months dragged by, they started dropping like flies.

I guess I didn't make it easy for them though. I hit a dark place after my mum died. It was sudden, and we weren't prepared although nothing can really prepare you for the loss of a parent. Growing up, it was just the two of us, and then it wasn't.

She worked hard to make sure I didn't miss out on anything, but I was a stubborn teen back then and didn't really see the opportunities she gave me. She never chastised me for it though, believing that I'd find my own way at some point. I'm not sure I have yet to be perfectly honest. However, Mum showered me with enough love and support for whatever my dumbass did that it certainly made up for having only one parent.

Right up until the end, she was trying to help me figure out my life, my direction. Trish at the hairdressers was looking for someone to do odd jobs around her house? Nick'll do it. Joan's husband was looking to take on an apprentice landscape gardener? Nick'll give that a go. The local post office were in desperate need of someone to deliver packages? Nick's your man. She never failed to talk me up, but I sure as hell failed her every time. I never stuck at anything for too long. Until now.

Never saw myself as much of a builder although I've always been good with my hands. I put myself through trade school though, as a mature aged student, on a whim after stumbling upon a careers open day. Do I like what I do? Sure. Keeps my mind busy and my body active. Do I like working with the old man? More than I thought, although you'd never know it from the way I treat him. I'm trying, but there's some part of me that always wants him to have to work hard for my attention and affection, as if it's some sort of delayed payback for everything we went through after he left.

It's a cycle. I act like a dick. I feel bad because I acted like a dick, so I act more like a dick. Back in my old life, in the city, that behaviour was inflamed by women and partying until my body seized up with regret and anxiety. So I'd do it all again until all the big feelings went away. But they never did.

That's why moving here was important. After hitting rock bottom when Mum passed away, I knew nothing would change unless I moved away from the places and people who were enabling my destructive behaviours. Mum would never have wanted that for me. So, after Dad contacted me with his condolences, I had a choice to make. I decided in that instance that I needed something to change immediately, and he gave me an out.

I was curious to know more about the man I share my genetics with, so I took the opportunity. It was never meant to be a long-term plan. I didn't plan to put down any roots here – no friends, no romance – just stay long enough to break a few bad habits and figure out my next move. It wasn't until this big, curly-haired Greek God dragged me to the gym and insisted I join his footy team that I started to feel like my real self and wanted to stay. I didn't see Ant coming, and I owe my life to him in many different ways.

'Hey, how was Josie today?' I ask, in between breaths. I swear Ant snuck an extra couple of kgs on the bar.

'Dunno. I only caught her on my way here. Think she said something about going out with Milo again tonight.'

I let out a groan that's more about Milo and almost definitely not about the weight crushing my arms.

'She's seeing him again? They only went out last night.' I sit up and wipe my face with the towel. 'You think she's serious about him?'

Ant shrugs, and I hate it. He's normally so confident in anything he says so I know the shrug is more about letting me down gently.

'I thought this morning you said it wouldn't last long?'

'It's probably still true. You just have to ride it out until then.'

'And watch them play loved up couples? No thanks. I mean, what's so good about that guy anyway?'

'Um, he's successful and insanely hot.'

'You're not helping, Ant.'

'I'm sorry, but it's the truth. If Josie is hell bent on this list thing and this guy ticks all those stupid boxes then you know she won't give up without a fight.'

I do know. That's what worries me. What if she fights so hard she ends up marrying the guy all because he fits some stupid list? Where will that leave us? There's more to a relationship than what looks good on paper. Her determination is one of the things I love about her. When she wants something, she goes and gets it. But what if she's got the wrong 'it' this time? I've just got to find a way to make her see that she's not supposed to end up with him, she's supposed to be with me.

'Hi, guys. Hi, Nick.' Tori, the girl on the front desk walks past us. She flicks her long, blonde hair over her shoulder and turns to give one last smile.

Ant chuckles and slaps me on the shoulder. 'Every time, man, every time.'

'Yeah, I know.' My eyes drop to my towel.

'Is there something else bothering you, man? Normally you can't resist checking Tori out.'

Ant and I switch positions; I spot him as he effortlessly pumps the iron. I try not to feel a little embarrassed by how easily he is showing me up. I feel those familiar waves start to creep across my stomach and instinctively put my hand over them as if to calm them down. I know the trigger this time; it's about going to see my dad tonight.

After three years we still don't know each other very well, and the fact that I can't predict what he wants to talk about scares the shit out of me because I can't prepare for it. Growing up, I always had a plan for any situation. Even now, when I walk into a room, I plan my escape should anything happen. I'm not sure exactly what I'm preparing for, but at least I have a plan.

Take the gym for example. Apart from the front entrance, I know that there is an emergency door about five metres to my left and out the back, and past the pool there is a fire escape door that is alarmed. Next to that door sits an axe in a glass case which would easily break one of the seven windows in the corridor that lead up to that fire escape door. I also know that 238870 is the code into the staffroom, which is off the corridor to the right and has a back door that leads out to the rear carpark. I'll give you one guess as to how I got in there.

My point is, I've always got a plan. I can predict how the people around me will behave and respond to almost any situation that matters in my life; all except one, my father. The thought of having to go to his house and meet with him tonight makes me feel queasy.

'Nah, man. Just had a shit day.'

I know I should tell Ant. I know that Ant will actually talk some sense into me, but I can't bring myself to do it.

Ant and I make the rounds and finish off with a slow walk on the treadmills. His watch rings, and to my horror, he answers it. I have a real thing against people using loudspeaker or video calls in public. Not everyone wants to hear your life story. I'm about to hop off the treadmill and disown him when I hear Josie's voice come from his wrist.

'Hey, it's me, I can't talk long–'

'Why are you whispering?' Ant says much louder than a whisper, and the irony gets me.

'Because I'm in the bathroom, and you're probably at the gym!'

At least Josie gets it. I think?

'Correct. Nick and I are doing a cool down on the treadmill. Say hi.'

Ant thrusts his wrist in my face, and I push him away. 'I am not speaking into your wrist in public.'

Josie hesitates a moment before she says hello to me. Despite my horror that everyone in the gym can hear our conversation, I reply with the same strained greeting. I eyeball Ant who has zero understanding of the social boundaries in this whole scenario.

'Okay, well…I um, I'm just ringing to say I'm at Milo's. That I'm staying at Milo's tonight, so ah, yeah, don't wait up.'

My stomach drops, and those stupid waves increase.

'Okay, well, call me if he turns out to be an axe murderer and tries to kill you in your sleep.'

'Ant! That's not funny.'

'Well, Nick's laughing. Actually, he looks horrified, and I can't tell if it's because I'm talking on loudspeaker in public or if he's concerned for your safety.'

'Both now, you jerk,' I say.

'Okay, well you *both* have nothing to worry about. I'll see you tomorrow.'

She makes a kissing sound and hangs up. I punch Ant in the arm.

'What was that for?'

'You know.'

Nothing about this is sitting well with me. I don't doubt that she's safe. I know from personal experience (which was more accidental than anything else) that she can throw a wicked knee to privates if needed. I'm more worried about her falling for the guy. We go to the lockers and collect our things. Anger pulses through my veins like a drug, and I can't help but be a little heavy handed with the doors.

'Nick, relax man. I'm sure she'll be okay.'

It's not just that though. The waves in the pit of my stomach increase and bile rises from my stomach. I close my eyes and practise breathing until they both subside a bit. Little sleep plus my dad plus Milo is not a good combination for me.

'Nick,' Ant places his hand on my shoulder, 'don't go all straight white male on me. If something's up, tell me. Is it Josie?'

I stand up and give him my best fake smile and head out of the change room doors. 'It's nothin' man. Josie can do whatever she likes. Doesn't mean I have to like it though.'

'Doesn't mean you need to take it out on the locker either.'

'You got a better option?'

Tori spots me the second we round the corner, her big doe eyes zone in on me and a flirtatious smile dances across her face. 'Have a good session, boys?'

My feet take me to her, and something falls over me like a protective shield. I'm all wry smiles and charisma. 'It was good, but I just don't feel very tired yet. Still feel like I've got a bit of energy to burn.'

Tori's cheeks flush, and she bats her eyelids at me. 'Well, maybe you need to add some new exercises to your routine.'

'Any come to mind?' I run my eyes over her body.

'Um,' she grabs at her ponytail and twirls the ends through her fingers, 'a few.'

'Hmm, I have a few in mind too. I wonder if they're the same?'

She chews the corner of her lip, and I know I've got her. I'm such a jerk.

'What time do you get off tonight? Maybe you could come round and show me what you're thinking?' I reach around the desk for the pen and paper in front of her and scribble my address down.

She folds the bit of paper and slides it under the collar of her shirt into her black bra strap. 'I finish at eight.'

'I guess I'll see you after eight then.' I tap the counter and slide away.

Ant shakes his head, and we fall into step making our way out. I don't turn around, but I can see Tori's reflection in the glass, and she hasn't taken her eyes off me.

Chapter Sixteen

JOSIE

I can't really concentrate on what Milo is saying because I'm too busy scanning his apartment for signs of him being an axe murderer. *Bloody, Ant!* So far, the most disturbing thing I've found is a shelf full of collectable *Marvel* paraphernalia. Hardly incriminating. I'd be more concerned if *Scream*-themed collectables were sitting on his shelf, but it's superhero stuff. Maybe he sees himself as a protector of the innocent? I mean, he's an optometrist for God's sake. Optometrists don't go around murdering innocent women, right? RIGHT?

'Josie.' My name in his mouth snaps me out of my wild imagination. 'Where'd you go there?'

'Sorry, was just thinking about something Ant said.' I wave my hands dismissively and flash him my best smile.

He returns the gesture and continues chopping the vegetables for the salad he is throwing together. There's something very sexy about a man who can take charge in the kitchen. I just have to stop my mind from wondering about his expert knife skills. He does seem awfully comfortable with a knife in hand. I take a seat at the bench and try to forget anything murderous with a glass of wine.

'So, what's the deal with you and Ant?'

The question catches me off guard, but it shouldn't because it's always one of the first questions a guy asks when they learn I live with another male. It's predictable if not a little disappointing. I'd like to just once not have to defend my friendship with Ant. Just once.

'Ant and I have been best friends since high school. Completely platonic.'

'You two have never gone there?'

Most people find this completely incomprehensible but no, we've never 'gone there'. There was one time in high school where we were matched together in a game of Spin the Bottle. We were about to kiss and the dread that filled both our souls was suffocating. We were saved by Janie Crossman skinny dipping in the pool. After that, we agreed never to play Spin the Bottle with each other again and that we would forever and always be just friends.

I know though, that Milo's follow up question will be something where he'll want me to define Ant's sexuality as if that is some seal of ego approval that Ant is not a threat. I refuse to do that. It's no-one's business but Ant's.

'Ant is like the brother I never had. We've only ever been friends, and only ever *wanted* to be friends. Is that going to be a problem for you?' I add. My tone is a little clipped, short.

Milo shakes his head. 'I'm sorry, I didn't mean to offend you....'

I'm not offended but I'm also not surprised by his line of questioning. Most guys are threatened by a female-male friendship, except for Nick. It's never been an issue for him. I try to put myself in Milo's shoes and think about how I would feel if he had a female roommate who was attractive. I would probably feel insecure and want a full run down of their history too. Guilt sinks into my chest.

'It's fine,' I lie. In truth it makes me feel a little flat. 'I get it.'

'Sorry, I guess I shouldn't assume...I mean, I am still trying to figure out your living situation and how you came to be with Ant and the other guy.'

It dawns on me that he thinks Nick lives there too. I mean, what other conclusion could you make at seeing two men eating breakfast together in my unit.

'Oh, Nick doesn't live there. He's our neighbour. He pops in every now and then for breakfast when he forgets to do his food shopping.' Or runs out of food. Or if the mood strikes him to pop over. He doesn't really need a reason. I keep that part to myself. 'I had been struggling to live with my parents since, well forever really, but when I finished my teaching degree and got a full-time job, it was just unbearable. So, Ant and I decided to buy a place together. I was already practically living with him and his then partner in their rental anyway. They broke up, and Ant needed to move out. It just made sense.'

I can see Milo sift through the information I just dumped on him. His shoulders soften and relax. I run my finger around the rim of the wine glass.

'Are you okay, Josie? Did I say something wrong?'

Yes. And no. It's not so much what he's saying as the fact that we're having this conversation. The whole vibe feels off. The magic of our first date, only just last night, has gone. I shouldn't have slept with him. It always ruins things. *Too soon, Josie, too soon.* It's the only conclusion I can reach in order to make sense of why things feel different.

We stay in silence for a moment – him scurrying around the kitchen unloading what looks like precooked and packaged pasta onto plates, and me sitting there watching, spending too much time in my own head. He brings over the food and lights a couple of candles. Despite the ambience, I'm just not feeling it.

Although I've faced those questions before about Ant, I feel kind of disappointed in Milo for asking them. He seemed to be different to the guys I've dated before, more mature, worldly and intelligent, so I didn't expect them from him. I know I'm playing into the double standards charade that happens when you date someone, but I can't help it.

I blame my attitude on this being one very long day. I shouldn't have committed to seeing him after the first day back at school. It's always a draining day. Maybe that's it. Maybe it's not really Milo at all but a culmination of everything that has happened today from dealing with Nick and Ant this morning to school to seeing Elle and now fronting up at Milo's house. Too much social interaction in one day. I'm sure that's it. I'm sure that's why I'm feeling the way I am. It's me. Not him.

Milo leans over, and our lips touch lightly as I reject his request to part my lips and grant his tongue entry into my mouth. We share a strained smile as we part, neither one of us comfortable enough to call out the elephant in the room. I look at the meal in front of me. Perhaps eating will make everything better?

Although nothing has been said between us about our sleeping arrangements, we both know that I've committed myself to staying the night. I set the expectations when I took him back to mine on the first date. Except now I've changed my mind. Worried about what he might think, I try to rack my brain for an excuse to leave. When we've finished dinner and moved to the couch, Milo drapes one arm over the back of the couch and the other rests on my leg. His thumb draws circles on my bare thigh, and it makes my skin tingle in a good way. A sign for me that perhaps all is not lost, that perhaps I'm just too much in my own head tonight. He leans over and places a kiss just below my earlobe, and I announce I need to use the bathroom.

Inside his very white, very clean bathroom, I fish my phone out of my pocket and message Elle.

JOSIE

I need your help.

When she doesn't message me back immediately, I text Ant.

JOSIE

I need your help.

Ant replies instantly and relief washes over me.

ANT

Does it require a shovel and body bag?

JOSIE

What? No!

ANT

Disappointing. What's up?

JOSIE

Can you ring me saying there's some sort of emergency and that I need to come home immediately?

ANT

Why?

JOSIE

Because I need an excuse to get out of here. I'll explain later.

ANT

HAS HE HURT YOU? OMG is he really an axe murderer?

JOSIE

NOTHING like that. I just feel uncomfortable.

ANT

Then just say you have to leave.

JOSIE

Ant, please. Can you just ring me?

ANT

Sure. When?

JOSIE

Give me five minutes.

ANT

xox

JOSIE

Thank you xox

I flush the toilet even though I didn't use it and wash my hands. I join Milo on the couch and his affections pick up right where they left off. It's the longest five minutes of my life before Ant rings. I answer the phone and stand up, away from Milo so he cannot hear.

'Ant? What's wrong?'

'Quick. There's an emergency,' he deadpans down the phone to me.

I keep up the theatrics on my end. 'Oh no! What's happened?'

'A-an emergency,' Ant stutters before whispering, 'you didn't tell me to come up with a story!'

I gasp for Milo's benefit. 'Of course. I'll be there right away.'

'You owe me.' Ant whispers down the line.

'Okay, hang tight. I'm only about twenty minutes away.'

I end the call and grab my bag, avoiding eye contact with Milo as I apologise for having to leave.

'Is everything alright?' Milo is genuinely concerned, and a pang of guilt stabs me in the heart. I have well and truly screwed this night up.

'No, Ant's hurt himself, and he can't reach Nick. I think I'll have to take him to the hospital.'

'Oh, do you want some help?'

'No!' I say a little too quickly, 'No, thank you. Ant gets a bit funny around hospitals.' I edge towards the front door, 'he doesn't like them and turns into a bit of a baby, so he'd be far too embarrassed if you came along. Thank you though.'

I let myself out and Milo follows me to my car. 'Ring me later and let me know how it's goes. I'm happy to come over and help if you need–'

'Thank you,' I cut him off and open the driver's side door,

'and thank you for a lovely dinner. Really. I'll, um, I'll call you tomorrow?'

Milo nods, leans in and plants a soft kiss on my lips. For a moment, a very brief moment, I forget about Ant and his emergency.

'Drive safe,' he says as we pull apart. I hop in my car and drive home as the feeling of his lips on mine lingers.

As I pull into the driveway, I notice a blonde woman leaving Nick's place. Typical. I roll my eyes and try not to take in too much about her perfect little body or notice how anger swirls in my chest at the sight of her. My jaw clenches, and I slam my car door shut. When I walk through the door, I see Ant on the couch, eating ice-cream out of the tub. I grab my own out of the freezer, a spoon on my way through and flop down beside him.

'Wanna talk about it?' he says with a mouthful of ice cream.

I shake my head. 'Not really. I saw a blonde leave Nick's.'

'Mm, that's Tori from the gym,' he picks up his phone to check the time, 'She's leaving pretty early.'

I let out a groan. 'Does he just pickup chicks wherever he goes?'

Frustration taints my tone as I stab at the ice cream, which inconveniently refuses to allow the spoon to penetrate it's surface easily. Rude.

'Says the woman who is dating her optometrist.'

I give him a little shove and take a large scoop of ice-cream. My phone buzzes and it's a message from Elle.

ELLE

Sorry, I was trying to get Jaggar to sleep! Argh! What's wrong?

JOSIE

Hey, that's ok. All good now. Was just needing an excuse to leave Milo's house.

ELLE

Oh honey, sounds awful. Josie, remember you
never need an excuse to leave. Just walk out!
Love you xox

JOSIE

Love you xox

Chapter Seventeen

NICK

We probably had very different expectations of how tonight was going to go. I can see it in her eyes as I begin to hand Tori her clothes. She doesn't fight or argue. She just sheepishly gets dressed.

I know I'm being an arsehole, and I can feel my inner demons telling me as much, but I made a rule long ago about letting girls stay the night, except for Josie. She breaks all my rules. The thought of her right now makes me feel ashamed of what Tori and I just did, but it shouldn't. She's made it very clear where we stand and what she thinks of me. I guess I wanted to test a theory I had about being able to be with other people guilt-free, and unfortunately Tori was just the perky-tits guinea pig placed in my way. I'm a horrible person.

I open the front door for her and find my father standing there, fist raised about to knock on the very door I just flung open. Greeting him in my briefs has me feeling a little exposed.

'So, this is thing you couldn't reschedule?' My father's voice is laced with disappointment and frustration.

Tori's eyes are wide, and she looks at me in panic. I run my hands down her arms and give her a reassuring smile. 'Sorry. I'll call you tomorrow, yeah?'

She lets out a sigh and nods. She gives my father an awkward wave as she hurries past him and into her car. I block the entrance to my unit and give my father my best pissed off look.

'Surprised you know where I live. You know, since you've never visited before.'

'My invitation must have been lost in the mail, hmm?'

There's a tense stand-off, and we stare each other down for a brief moment before the silence makes me uncomfortable, and I cave first. 'Look, sorry you came out here but I'm pretty tired so I'm just gonna–'

'Yes, I can see you've had a very busy night.' He pushes past me and enters my house.

'You can't just barge in.'

'Nick, there doesn't seem to be any other way now, does there?'

He lays his jacket over the back of the couch and takes a seat at the kitchen bench, all the while I'm standing in my jocks by the open front door, which I finally slam shut making a point.

'Look, I'm really–'

'I'm dying, Nick.'

His statement floors me. Time stands still but my surrounds whirl around me. I'm taken back to the moment the doctors told me that my mother had died, that her injuries from the car crash were too severe, and she couldn't be saved. The empty hospital hallway where the world moved on around me, but my world stopped. Time stood still. I'm taken back to walking into our silent, dark home wondering if I would ever feel anything ever again.

'Nick,' he says again, quieter his time.

'I heard you,' I say, barely louder than a whisper.

My throat is dry. I run to the kitchen and drink straight from the faucet. He says my name, but I turn the tap to its full capacity and let the water I can't catch in my mouth trickle down my chin and over my bare chest. I duck my head under the running tap and shake it like a dog as I pull away.

'Nick,' he pauses and waits for me to shut the water off, 'this isn't how I wanted to tell you. It's just...you've been so bloody hard to pin down, and I–'

'I'm sorry.' I fix my gaze on a spot on the plain cream tiles and allow the water to drip from my hair and body onto the floor.

My father lets out a sad sigh, rubbing his hands down the legs of his jeans. 'Nick, I know this must bring up a lot of...memories about your mother,' hearing her name feels like a punch to the gut, 'and I wish I could make this easier on you. I know I haven't been the best–'

'How long?' I force myself to speak. I don't need to hear the speech about how he's been a shitty father and how he's trying to make it up to me. I don't need him to repent his absentee fatherly sins. I haven't needed anything from him in thirty-one years. I don't need anything from him now.

'Six months if I'm lucky. Pancreatic cancer.'

I drop my head back and let it roll between my shoulders. My mind is running fast, and I only catch a word here and there. I'm reminded of my last moments with my mother, and those first few moments without her. The pain was unbearable. I couldn't breathe. I'm finding it hard to suck in a breath now.

'Nick, I'm leaving the company to you.'

I snap my head forward. 'I don't want the company.'

'Then sell it off and take the profit. I honestly don't care at this point.'

'Why don't you leave it to your other sons?' The ones you preferred to build a life with. The ones who never had to eat two-minute noodles for a week straight or live in hand me downs from the neighbour up the road.

'Because I want to leave it to you. I may not have done a lot right in my life, but at least I can do something good with what's left of it.'

I shake my head to try and stop the chaos inside. 'I can't do this right now.'

'I know it's a lot to take in.'

I let out a humourless laugh. 'You think?'

'Nick, listen, take tomorrow off and come and meet me at my place, and I can explain everything. I can even get my lawyer to come over to show you everything you need to know about the business side of things and what you'll be signing on for.'

I grab at the kitchen bench to try and steady myself. The waves are peaking in my stomach. I have that familiar feeling of wanting to outrun my skin, to escape my own body, my own mind. My father collects his jacket and sees himself out just in time to miss me vomit into the kitchen sink.

Chapter Eighteen

JOSIE

I'd like to blame Ant's snoring for keeping me awake but truth be told, I just can't seem to switch my brain off. Things were weird tonight with Milo but were they *weird* weird, or did something else make it weird?

I haven't been able to stop thinking about Nick all day, mainly how mad I am at him for being here this morning. I didn't want him to meet Milo, not yet. Not during this first awkward stage of dating someone new. And certainly not coming out of my bedroom after the first date. As hard as I fight against societal expectations that dictate a woman should not bring someone home on the first date, I can't help but let old voices haunt me.

I'm ashamed that I didn't want Nick to see Milo this morning because I didn't want him to think less of me for bringing him home on the first date. And I definitely didn't need him giving Milo the hard time he did. I pushed to see Milo tonight out of spite and anger towards Nick.

Milo called during the day after I had that run in with Connor and I was already wound up when I agreed to seeing him again. Not that I have a reason not to but twice in twenty-four hours is a bit...soon? I'm frustrated that I'm second guessing everything, second guessing *myself*. All I know is that I was too much in my own head about everything and worrying about things that didn't even exist. When I found out that Ant was talking to me on the phone at the gym and that Nick could hear the conversation, some part of me was glad. Just to spite him, I decided to stay. *Let Nick stew on that.* Then, another part of me immediately regretted it and wanted an out. I wanted to see Milo, sure, but I wasn't so sure I wanted to go any further than that. Yet, I set the expectations last night. My thoughts circle and go over the same thing over and over again.

I sit in the lounge room dressed down in my favourite crop and leggings, scrolling mindlessly through social media for something to entertain me when there is a knock at the door. I contemplate waking Ant up because only trouble would knock past midnight. I grab at the broom on my way to answer the door and remind myself to talk to Ant about getting a viewfinder put in the door. Another knock sounds, this time a little louder than before. I hesitantly answer the door and let out a sigh of relief as I see Nick standing there dressed in a dark hoodie pulled over his head.

'Now who's making the last night calls?' I tease and immediately get the sense he's not in the mood to play. His eyes look wide with fright, and he's shifting on the spot.

'Ant up?'

I shake my head. 'No, he's asleep. What's wrong?'

'Just, you know, feel like going for a walk and wanted to see if he wanted to come with me.'

'It's past midnight! What's going on?'

I haven't seen Nick like this before. It's worrying. He starts to pace, swearing under his breath. The outside light above his head dances around him casting his face in shadows.

'Nick, are you in trouble?' I am surprised by how high pitched my voice is.

He lets out a manic laugh. 'Nah, nothing like that. I just...I'm just gonna go. I'll go by myself. It's fine. Sorry to have woken you.'

'Nick,' I grab at his arm, feeling the shake running through his body, 'I'll come with you.'

He protests, but I insist while I grab the closest pair of runners I can find. I'm out the door in seconds worried that if I take a moment longer, he'll be gone, and I can't let him be alone in this state. Something has him spooked.

'Do you want to talk about it?' I offer as we power walk our way down the driveway and into the night.

He shakes his head. Our steps fall in sync, and I try not to reveal just how out of shape I am. Nick has his hands in the front pocket of his dark jumper. I reach out and thread an arm through his, and he looks at me with a half-smile on his face and slows the pace. He scrubs a hand over the hood and brings it down. I have the urge to run my hand through his hair, to flatten the scruff from the hood but I refrain.

We continue to walk in silence until we reach the beach at the end of our very long street. We cross the quiet road and sink into the sand as we make our way to the shore. I pull him back to stop so I can take my shoes off and let the coolness of the sand fall over my feet like the gentlest of silks. He does the same. The salt from the sea hangs thick in the still night air. The moon is on show glistening across the water. The cloudy sky sparkles with millions of shiny, small dots.

'It's breathtaking.' I say, swept up in the moment.

Nick stops and looks out to the horizon. I curl both my arms around his and pull him in closer. He lifts his arm up and around me, inviting me to shelter in his embrace. I wrap my myself around his waist, and he smiles down at me.

'I don't think I've ever been to the beach at night,' I muse.

'Best time to come.'

I place my head on his chest and can hear his heart beating. It seems faster than it should be. I gently lay my hand on his chest and he places his over the top of mine.

'Nick, are you okay?'

He looks away back to the horizon, the moon illuminating his face, bathing him in blue. The beach is abandoned, and we have the place to ourselves. Without sign of life, it feels like we're the last two people on earth. Suddenly my mind feels free of all the chaos and is replaced with thoughts of Nick.

I push away slightly knowing this can't happen when his warm hands slide over my exposed lower back, pulling me in. I stare into his eyes, and it's like falling into history. I know he will kiss me, and I know that I want him to.

Chapter Nineteen

NICK

Our lips touch for the briefest moment before I push harder against Josie and make her mouth move in time with mine. She runs her hands around my neck, and it sends a shiver down my spine. I want her now, here. I want her all the time. I want her forever. She plays with the ends of my hair on my neck and pulls me closer to her. I snake my hands under her top and up her back where my fingers dance around the clasp of her bra. I could easily unclasp it with one flick of my fingers, but I don't. She pulls away from me trying to catch her breath. Her hands reach for her swollen lips, and she's shaking her head.

'Nick, I can't. I'm seeing Milo.'

Fucking Milo. I bring my hands up to rest on top of my head and pace. For one brief moment it finally seemed like my world wasn't going to end, and now it feels like everything is crashing down around me, back to reality. 'Milo? Really Josie? Come on!'

'Hey, hang on a second. He's a really great guy.' She pauses in time to hear my groan of disbelief. 'He is! And he's ready to settle down and have kids and everything.'

'He's everything you want, huh? Everything on your stupid list? Do you love him?' I'm shouting at her now. Lucky there's no one else here to witness my epic tantrum.

'It's a bit too early to make that assumption!' There's a break in her voice. Hesitation? Uncertainty? Whatever it is I'm going to use it and make her see she's making a big mistake.

'Really? Well, if he's everything on your damn list then why did you kiss me like that, Josie, huh? Because that's not how you kiss someone if you're in love with someone else.'

I don't wait for an answer. I stride over to her, cup her head in my hands and press my lips against hers. She doesn't pull away immediately, and I have my answer. We stay that way for what feels like minutes, but I know it's only seconds before she does pull away and takes two steps back from me.

'Stop, Nick! Stop! You can't keep messing with me like this!'

'Like what?'

'Like this! Nick, I'm with Milo now because, yes, he's everything on my list and because I want to grow up! I want to stop screwing the guy next door who is afraid of commitment.'

'Who said I was afraid of commitment? When have you ever asked me?'

She lets out a frustrated grunt, but I continue, 'Josie, when have you ever said you wanted something more than just a casual thing with me? I haven't been with anyone but you in the last year.' She scoffs, but I ignore her and continue, 'I haven't wanted anyone else and in case I haven't made things perfectly fucking clear tonight, I want you, Josie.'

I stop short of telling her I love her. Because I do. I have for a long time. However, it would be meaningless to her right now. She can see my temper has flared, that I'm a mess, and if I say it now, I'll come across as some dishonest arsehole throwing a toddler tantrum. No, I need to pick the right moment to lay those heavy words on her.

'Is that what you told the blonde leaving your apartment tonight?'

Shit. She saw that? *Shit. Shit. Shit. Shit.*

The one time, the ONE time, I see someone else in more than twelve months and she has to see that.

'It's not what it looks like.' I pull out the oldest line in the book, knowing damn straight it's exactly what it looks like, but it meant nothing at all.

'So, you're telling me you didn't fuck her tonight?'

My eyes dip, and I shift on the spot. I don't like the way that sounded. Curt. Crisp. Accusatory. Guilt engulfs my lungs making it difficult to breathe. The bluntness of the curse word coming from her mouth feels unnatural but also kinda hot. In all the time I've known Josie, cussing has been a very limited part of her vocabulary. That's her parent's influence and her goddamn need to people please. Hearing her say the word tells me more than anything else.

'Yes, okay, but it's not like that. It meant nothing it was just–'

'Exactly, Nick. You are not ready to settle down. You're not ready to get serious about *anything*.'

I drag my hands over my face. 'Josie, you're not hearing me. I'm telling you I'm ready. I want these things. I want to be with you, but you're so blinded by your stupid list that you're missing the point.'

She throws her hand up. 'I can't do this right now, Nick.'

'Do what? Have an honest conversation about how you feel? I bet it's scary, huh? Because if you have to be honest with me then you have to be honest with yourself, and if you do that then you'll realise you're not that into Milo.'

'Don't lecture me about being honest, Nick. Why did you come over tonight, huh? To see Ant at midnight? What for?' She crosses her arms over her chest.

The beast inside me swirls, and I do everything I can to keep it from coming out. If I tell her about my anxiety and the panic attacks then I'm admitting weakness. She doesn't want a man she has to look after. She wants a man to look after her, as she should.

I can't let her know about this, so yeah, I'm lecturing her about being honest when it's the one thing I can't be right now.

'Don't change the subject.' I snap.

'Don't avoid the question.'

We stare at each other, both daring the other to answer first, both being stubborn enough to refuse to be the first to break. The whole reason I came looking for Ant in the first place is because he is a master at helping me get my thoughts in order before I speak, otherwise I end up like this, a mess of words and thoughts and coming across frustrated.

Ant is the only person I've confided in about my panic attacks, and he said he'd be there whenever I need him. This isn't the first time I've knocked on his door at midnight, and we've walked and talked. This is just the first time Josie has caught me. I take a step closer to her and she doesn't budge. I take it as a sign that she's willing to hear me out.

'How can I possibly prove to you that I'm ready for every-thing you want if you never give me the chance?' I say quietly.

Her stance softens a little. Her shoulders slump but her arms remain folded across her chest. 'I'm with Milo.'

'You've had two dates! That's hardly anything serious, Jose. Wait! Hang on, aren't you supposed to be there now? Weren't you staying over?'

She shifts on the spot. 'Something came up.'

She looks down to her right foot and then back up again, her tell that she's lying. It boosts my confidence and a smirk escapes. 'Trouble in paradise already?'

She rolls her eyes at me. 'Everything is fine.'

'Can't be too fine if you didn't want to stay over. Especially as he was so good in bed last night. Twice, wasn't it?' I bait her, and she bites by giving me her best pissed off look.

'Jealous, are we?'

'Josie, you've always come back to my bed,' I point out which only infuriates her more.

'Is this what this is about? You're jealous because you can't have your favourite play toy anymore?'

'Who said you were my favourite?' My grin broadens, and she huffs, turning to stalk off. I grab her by the hand. 'Sorry, sorry.'

'See, you can't even have a conversation without making it sexual.'

'You're the one who referred to yourself as my favourite play toy!' I have her there, and she knows it.

She turns to face me and lets out a sigh. 'I like Milo. I want to see where it goes, okay, Nick?'

I hold up my hands defensively. 'Fine. But why not date me too? Give me a chance.'

I surprise us both with my words. Where did that come from? I don't want her to date both of us. I want her to date me and only me. After the shock of my words wears off, Josie scoffs, and I'm not going to lie, it stings.

'Date you? Nick–'

'Why not? You know the goods work, and they work better than *fine*, even you can agree to that.' I stare at her, and she gives me a look that shows she concedes and reluctantly agrees. I continue, 'So, let me date you. Properly. Roses, romance, the whole lot. Let me show you what life would be like if you chose me.'

The words hang in the air between us. She searches my face for something. Sincerity? She doesn't need to look very far because I'm deadly serious. I'll pull out all the stops to make her realise that I'm her Mr Right.

'And Milo?' she asks.

I'm really beginning to hate the name.

'Date us both.' I shrug my shoulders.

'Both? At the same time?' Her eyes widen in shock, and I know this is something that she would never have thought to do.

'Why not? Guys do it all the time. Date us both and then see who–'

'Fulfils my list,' she cuts in.

I can see the wheels turning in her mind. 'And then decide who it is that you want to wake up next to every morning for the rest of your life.'

'Same thing.'

I move closer and take her hand. I'm surprised when she lets me. I bring it up to my lips and gently kiss her hand. 'I have one request.'

'Of course you do.' She pulls her hand back and places it on her hip.

I raise my eyebrows at her, knowing exactly what she's thinking. She's expecting me to make some remark about taking sex off the table for both of us. And true, while I prefer her to never sleep with Mr Dreamy again, I'm not about to tell her what to do with her own body.

'Forget the list,' I say, and she looks at me confused. 'Throw it away. It's clouding your judgement.'

'I'll have you know that list has stood the test of time. It's just as relevant today as it was when I was fourteen.'

'Jose, most of your list could be attributed to a dog. Sweet, loyal, kind. Do you want me to get you a puppy?'

'There were other things on there too,' she counters defensively.

'If you could create a new list, what would be on it?'

'The same things. Those things still count.'

'Those things are also qualities you look for in a friend. Bloody hell, Ant ticks the boxes. Elle does too.'

'Neither one of them look like Zac Efron.'

'I've been here through your Channing Tatum, Chris Evans and Pedro Pascal phases all in the last three years. The latest one is that guy from *Yellowstone*.' I particularly like that last one, a big bearded tough guy. Gee, I wonder who he reminds her of?

'I'm changing the locks on the unit tomorrow.'

'Point is, you've changed. Your list has too.'

She looks up at me with her big brown eyes, a hint of annoyance in them. She knows I'm dead right. 'Fine. I'll throw the list away.'

'So, does that mean we have a deal?' I put my hand out for her to take.

She looks from it to me. 'I need to think about it.'

I can work with that. It's better than a no. 'Okay then.'

I retract my outstretched hand, and we start to make our way back up the beach. In everything that has unfolded, I'd forgotten the reason I came down here in the first place. I'm grateful for the distraction. I push thoughts of my father out of my mind, deciding it's a problem for later in the morning. Right now, I've got a chance to make Josie really see me, and I'm going to make sure I don't mess this up. It may just be about the only good thing I have going for me.

Chapter Twenty

JOSIE

I'm distracted and highly caffeinated at school the next day. I survive on auto pilot until I can leave at the end of the day and see Elle for an emergency coffee date. I'm early, but I always am because I don't have to get two little humans ready and out the door with all the tools they need in order to let their mum enjoy an hour of adult conversation.

We picked our favourite little cafe just opposite the beach which even on a stormy day like today, still has a picturesque outlook. I take a spot in the corner where there is some room on the floor for Harlow and Jaggar to play and wait for Elle to arrive.

I haven't had much sleep, I kept replaying my conversation with Nick last night over and over again whilst actively avoiding text messages and missed calls from Milo. Nick on the other hand, has given me much appreciated space. Or is he avoiding me like I'm avoiding Milo? Does he regret what he said last night?

He was already wound up about something, which we never got to the bottom of, so maybe he was just spewing nonsense without thinking. I drag my hands over my face. I've gone around in circles with the same inner dialogue since last night. I look around. Still no sign of Elle, so I pull my phone out of my bag and begin mindlessly scrolling through social media.

'Josie?' My head swivels at my name to see my older sister Franki standing next to the table, smoothie in hand.

'Hey,' I give a small wave and put my phone face down on the table, 'what are you doing here?'

It's not odd that she's here. We live in a small town, so it makes sense to run into someone I know every now and then, but I rarely run into one of my sisters, especially Franki as she's always so busy at work. Although today she doesn't look like she's come from her executive office job. She looks like she's just come from the beach. Franki doesn't wait for me to offer her a seat. Instead she sits across from me, sucking on the straw to her smoothie.

'You look stressed,' she states.

'I am not stressed,' I lie, acting defensive. 'Why aren't you at work?'

She shrugs her shoulders. 'Took the afternoon off. You meeting Nick?'

I feel my face instantly flush at the sound of his name. Great. 'No, what makes you say that?'

She slouches back in her seat with an amused look on her face. 'You bought him to dinner the other night. You're waiting in a cafe for someone. Logical conclusion. And you're as red as a tomato.'

I bring my hands to my face and try to pat the blush away, which doesn't work. 'I'm meeting Elle actually.'

And just as I say her name, she comes through the door in a fluster, dragging her kids behind her. We stand and the three of us greet with short hugs and cheek kisses. My sister moves over a seat and Elle sits down in between the two of us. She pulls out some toys and lays them on the floor for Harlow whilst pulling out the iPad for Jaggar.

'If someone dare says anything about using a device to pacify my son, I'm going to knock them out,' she states in a huff.

'Rough day?' Franki asks.

'Night and day. Harlow is teething, and Jaggar is being a turd. I love them, but I'm ready for someone else to clock on for half an hour so I can rest. Where is my backup parent?'

'He's at work,' I point out, and Elle gives me a little smile. 'Why didn't you tell me? We could have met at your house or cancelled....'

Elle wags her finger at me. 'No, if I have to stay within those four walls another minute, I will in fact go crazy. We all needed to get out, plus you said it was a moral dilemma emergency.'

Franki makes an excited sound. 'Oh, I love those.'

'Well, you weren't invited.' I give my sister a mocking look, knowing full well she has zero intention of leaving.

'Two heads are better than one, and besides, Franki is by far the best of your sisters so...'

'Thank you, Elle. At least someone recognises that.'

The two of them share a giggle, so I concede and let Franki stay. Elle's right though, of my sisters, Franki is the only one I'd trust to go to for advice on anything. My younger sister Daniella is far too self-absorbed. Maybe it is serendipitous that she's here.

'Before we start, I need to order food and drink otherwise we've got about five more minutes before all hell breaks loose with these two,' Elle laments.

I offer to pay considering I was the one who dragged her out and after placing our order, I'm forced to spill the beans. I decide there is no easy way to explain what happened, so with two ticking time bombs afoot, I come right out and say it. 'Nick asked me out.'

'What?' Franki and Elle both exclaim.

'I actually don't see why this is a dilemma. He was practically the protective boyfriend at dinner the other night, so it makes sense,' Franki says.

'What about the optometrist?' Elle asks.

'What optometrist?'

'Josie went out on a date with an optometrist that ended very well, if you catch my drift.'

They continue to talk about me like I'm not sitting right in front of them.

'Oh!' Franki gasps, 'Josephine, you little minx.'

'Okay, okay, that's enough,' I put my teacher voice on. 'Look, I need some serious advice, and if you two can't–'

'Sorry, sis. I promise I will behave and give you my best sisterly advice.'

'What she said,' Elle adds. 'Now, take it back a step and explain it all.'

I start by filling my sister in on Milo before telling them both about last night. I leave out the part where Nick was feeling anxious about something because it doesn't seem right to share that detail, but I tell them everything else, word for word as I have been replaying it in my head.

When I finish, they sit in silence. Franki stares at me like I'm a puzzle she can't quite figure out while Elle stares off into the distance thinking about her response. Our drinks and food arrive signalling a restart to the conversation.

'Just so I'm clear,' Franki clears her throat and leans forward, bringing Elle's eyes back to the table, 'Nick, a.k.a the sexy lumberjack, wants to essentially lay his log in your garden permanently but you aren't sure because some nerd who looks at people's eyeballs all day wants to...there are no good euphemisms for this one. How long have you known the optometrist?'

'A few days,' I say sheepishly.

'And she's been doing the dirty with Nick for two years,' Elle grins.

My sister's eye widen in further excitement. 'As if there is any competition. Josie, come on. You already know the answer to this.'

'It's not that simple,' I protest. 'Nick is not the settle down type. He's been perfectly happy with our arrangement, and he only wants to date me because he doesn't want me to date anyone else.'

'Because he loves you,' Elle adds.

I shake my head. 'Because he's jealous and doesn't want to seem like a loser.'

'How does this make him a loser?' Franki asks.

'I move on and he has to find a new play toy, which by the way, he has already done. I saw one leaving his house last night.'

'After he asked you out?' Elle looks at me confused.

'Before,' I shake my head. 'It doesn't matter. What matters is that it just proves he's not ready to settle down.'

'But hang on, sis, didn't you also just sleep with some random guy on the first date?'

I open my mouth to say something, but nothing comes out, so Franki continues. 'From where I'm sitting, it looks like neither one of you are ready to settle down. Why not just continue to have fun? You're both young.'

'Oh boy, here we go,' Elle mutters.

'Says the woman who has been happily married for the past eight years,' I give my sister a look and she shifts in her seat. 'Look, I'm thirty next year. I should be settling down and having kids.'

'*Should be,* isn't the same as wanting to,' Franki points out.

'I do *want* to. It's *should* and *want.* I mean look at you two, you're both married, and Elle, you have kids.'

'And I wouldn't change it for the world, but you have to really want it with the right person,' Elle soothes.

I notice Franki's silence on the topic. *Interesting.*

'Look, Josie, the way I see it, there are two very different things going on here. Firstly, you don't have to do anything by any certain age. It's the twenty first century, for God's sake, we're throwing all that archaic bullshit out the window.'

'Here, here,' Franki raises her smoothie.

'And secondly, you and Nick have been in love with each other since you first hooked up. I don't even see why you're debating this.'

'Because how do I truly know he is the guy I am supposed to spend the rest of my life with? I can't wait around forever waiting for him to be ready to settle down.'

'But he said he is,' Elle taps the tabletop like she just made the final closing argument.

Franki holds up her finger. 'Just to play devil's advocate here, if we're throwing away all that archaic bullshit, and if you're really not sure, why not date them both?'

Elle rolls her eyes. 'Because it seems like a waste of time when we already know what the outcome will be.'

'I can't date two guys at once!'

'Why not?' Franki asks in all seriousness. 'Guys do it to women all the time. As long as you're open about it, and it seems Nick already is, then what harm is there? That way, you can see who it is that really makes your heart sing. It's just dating.'

I sit back in my seat, cupping my drink. *Just dating.* I don't even know how I would describe the difference between dating and a relationship because all of my relationships have happened after one date. Isn't a relationship just one long string of dates anyway? And how does that differ from anything Nick and I have been doing for the past two years? Have we secretly been in a relationship this whole time? My head spins.

'I think it's pointless, but what your sister says makes sense, Jose. Guys date multiple women all the time. As long as everyone knows it's not exclusive and knows that you're just trying to figure out your heart, then what's the harm. You're all adults. But,' Elle pauses for dramatic effect which make my stomach twist up in knots, 'I will add this: what happens to your friendship with Nick if you choose Milo?'

I let this sink in. My friendship with Nick has been easy, flirty and physical. If I take away the flirty and physical, do we even have much of a foundation for friendship anyway? Would it make things awkward between Ant, Nick and myself?

'I thought you said she would end up with Nick anyway?' my sister accuses.

'And she will, but she also needs to think about the wider implications if she makes a stupid decision.'

'Clearly, you're Team Nick,' I mutter.

'Yes. I cannot be clearer,' Elle smiles. 'I love Nick, and I think the two of you are perfect for each other.'

'I, personally, have only met Nick once, and I cannot believe you would even consider passing up a man like that. However, I support your right to choose.'

I shake my head. The unconscious bias I am looking for is not to be found amongst these two. It's all well and good for them to be Team Nick, but they don't know him like I do, not really. As a friend, Nick is loyal to a T. He will help you argue that the sky is green if you ask him to, but in terms of being in a committed relationship, he's skittish. And stubborn. He may think he wants to settle down now that the threat of me leaving him behind for someone else is real, but if he was so ready to settle and so sure of his feelings for me before, why didn't he say anything earlier?

'Josie,' my sister's voice brings me out of my thoughts, 'date them both. Satisfy your own curiosity because you do not want to make a mistake and settle down with the wrong person.' Her eyes bore into mine, flooded with sincerity, 'And if it doesn't work out, then enjoy having two men fight it out for you, having the most impressive sex of your life.'

This draws a snort of laughter from Elle. 'Impressive?'

'Trust me, if a guy thinks he is in competition with another guy, he brings his A-game to the bedroom. Every. Single. Time. Enjoy, sis.'

Chapter Twenty-One

NICK

Having the front unit in our block means I own the prime people watching space. Which is exactly what I have done all day. I've sat on my couch, stuffed my face full of chips and watched people walk past. I called in sick today. After dad's bombshell last night, I've gone into active avoidance mode like the respectable adult I am. He's not the only one I'm avoiding. I'm also avoiding Josie. I'll admit, my ego was bruised when she didn't jump into my arms on the spot and declare she was done with that imposter and would devote her life to me immediately. Instead she's left me hopeful which is much worse. Hopeful is bad because it gives you permission to daydream, to think of what could be. Hopeful gets you all excited about the future when in reality, it can be taken away in a second. Crashing down from hopeful is a long and painful fall. A flat out 'no' is fine; you know exactly where you stand. A 'yes' is great too because it's a promise that both parties are going to try to make it work and at least you know she likes you.

'Let me think about it' is torture. You have no idea of how she feels about you, you have no idea if she is leaning more one way or the other, and you have no idea what you're supposed to do. Do you give her space to think about it, or do you take things up a notch and try and persuade her into a yes? But then if you do that, how will you know if she was going to say yes anyway or if you have forced her into something she didn't really want to do? I don't want that.

These damn thoughts have circled on repeat in my head since we arrived home (separately) last night. And so, not knowing what to do, I pick avoidance. And stalker. I'll admit I got hardly any sleep last night and have dozed on and off throughout the day, but you can bet your last five bucks that I was staring through the crack in my blinds at Josie's place this morning hoping to catch Ant by himself to ask him what I should do.

Bloody, Ant. All of this could have been avoided had he been the one to answer the door last night. Then I wouldn't have run my mouth off and invited trouble.

Just as I'm about to get up and raid either the fridge again or the pantry, likely both, I see Ant's car pull into the shared driveway and immediately race to the window. I watch Ant exit the car alone and know this is the perfect opportunity to grab him for a chat. Without a care for how I look, I race out the door, jumping the small hedge and surprise Ant as he unlocks his front door.

'Good God man, you scared the shit out of me.' Ant clutches at his chest dramatically.

'You alone?'

'I am, but I wish I wasn't, you lunatic.' He looks me up and down. Dressed in old worn grey sweats with dark circles under my eyes and nothing else, I'm probably not looking my best. 'You been to work today?'

I shake my head. 'It's a long story.'

Ant opens the doors and his arms, gesturing for me to follow him inside.

'What time is Josie getting in?' I ask, looking around the unit for signs of one of the people I'm avoiding today.

'She was meeting up with Elle after work, so she probably won't be home 'til later.' Ant drops his belongings on the kitchen bench and reaches into the fridge for two soft drinks.

'She tell you anything?'

Ant shakes his head.

'Did she seem happy this morning? Or more like....'

'You two hook up last night?'

I wish. I shake my head. 'Nah, nothing like that.'

'Then what's got your knickers in a knot?' Ant smiles over the rim of his glass.

I run my hands through my thick head of hair and let out a sigh. 'I told Josie that I had feelings for her.'

Ant does a double take. 'When did this happen?'

'Last night.'

'Last night?' Ant almost shouts in disbelief. 'When last night? I didn't see you.'

'I came over after...' thoughts of my dad pop into my mind and bile rises in my stomach. I push them aside. 'I came over looking for you, to see if you wanted to go for a run, but Josie answered.'

'What time?'

'Midnight-ish.'

'Midnight? Geez, Nick. You alright?'

No. 'Fine.'

He stares at me like he's waiting for me to continue, like he knows I'm not alright and have more to say. He's one of the few people who can read me like a damn open book.

'We'll get to why you needed a run at midnight in a sec, but let's circle back to telling Josie how you feel. What did she say?'

I scratch at my beard. 'Nothing.'

Ant's mouth hangs open like a cartoon character. 'Elaborate.'

I throw my hands up. 'I told her how I felt, and she said she didn't believe that I wanted to settle down. Basically said that I'm pursuing her because of that eye doctor.'

'And are you?'

I give him a look. 'Seriously, man?'

He holds his hands up defensively. 'I needed to ask. It just seems like a strange time to suddenly tell her how you feel. I mean, *we* can all see it. But she'll think it's suspicious timing.'

'Yeah well, timing has never been my strong suit.'

'So what happened next? You just left it at that?'

I crack my neck from side to side. 'Not exactly....'

'Oh geez.'

'I kinda encouraged her to date us both and see who she likes better.'

Soft drink spurts out of Ant's mouth and nose as he laughs and chokes at the same time. 'You what?'

'You heard me.'

'I know, I know. I just wanted to hear you say it again.'

I flip my middle finger at him as he continues to calm himself down. Tears are now rolling down his cheeks, and I don't know whether it's from the laughter or the burning sensation of having spouted soft drink from his nose. I hope it's from the soft drink, the bastard.

'That's gold.'

'Shut up.'

'So what's the plan, Romeo?'

I rub my hands along my sweats. 'Obviously, I have to beat him, have the better dates.'

'Obviously,' Ant says dryly, 'because you love her, right?'

Because my world would damn near crumble without her. Because I wouldn't be able to breathe without her. Because I can't imagine a future without her in it. Yes, because I love her. 'Are you questioning my intentions? Seriously, Ant!'

'Look, I am one thousand percent behind you if you can look me in the eyes right now and tell me you love her. Not just have a crush or infatuation or because she's someone you enjoy boning–'

'Boning? Come on, man.'

'If you can tell me that you are unconditionally in love with her, and that you are dead serious about settling down, white picket fence, kids and all, then I will back you, and I will help you.'

'Didn't peg you as the romantic type,' I say dryly.

Ant throws his hands up. 'See. You can't.'

Anger spikes in my gut. 'Why? Because I made a joke?'

'Are you gonna take this seriously? I'm filling in as the big brother she doesn't have, and I want to hear from you that this is serious, and not some schoolyard trick because the new guy has come in and is getting all the attention.'

'Alright, you want to know how I feel?' I raise my voice without meaning to, but I can't seem to control it anymore. 'She is the first thought I have in the morning and the last thought I have at night. When I even *think* about the possibly of her sharing her life with someone else, it makes me sick to my damn stomach. When she's hurt, I'm hurt. When she's happy, I'm fucking delirious. She is like the damn air that I breathe. So yeah, I am in love with Josie.'

Ant stills and lets my words hang between us. My heart is racing, saying all those words out loud for the first time to someone is bloody scary. Ant's eyes shift slightly, and I still. 'I swear, if you tell me that she is standing behind me right now, I'm gonna....'

'She's not,' Ant says seriously, 'I've never heard you speak like that before. About anyone.'

'Yeah, well, Josie isn't just anyone.'

'Man, I'm about to jump over this bench and kiss you. That was romantic as hell.'

I laugh out a sigh of relief. 'Thanks, man.'

'Why the hell didn't you just say that to her?'

I shrug even though I know the answer to it. I'm afraid she won't feel the same. I may not have said exactly those words last night, but I told her I wanted a future with her, and she didn't say a thing back. She gave me nothing, not any sort of indication that she feels a shred of what I'm feeling, and until I'm sure, I'm not saying anything further to her or anyone else.

'You can't tell her.'

Ant rolls his eyes.

'Seriously, Ant. I mean it. She's so hell bent on this idea that she has to settle down before her next birthday that she's not thinking straight.'

'Then it seems perfectly reasonable to tell her.'

I shake my head. 'No, I want her to come to her own conclusion about how she feels. I don't want her to think she loves me just because it will help her meet her deadline.'

'Fair. So, then, what's the plan?'

'I have no fucking clue.'

Chapter Twenty-Two

JOSIE

I can no longer ignore Milo's text messages. I'd think he's being a little excessive, but I did leave his place in a rush citing an emergency. As I walk through the door, I have every intention of messaging him back straight away, until I see Nick. Shirtless. Sitting at my kitchen bench, shirtless. Because of course. If I was a woman looking for a sign, this could be it; he keeps getting thrust in my path. Half-naked. Yet, he also lives next door and has been in our back pockets ever since he moved in, so I'm claiming normal Nick behaviour, not a sign from the universe. I hate the way my eyes automatically scan over his defined chest and abs, but I hate the way my body responds even more. Tingles every-damn-where! He notices, of course, and a smile beams out from beneath that scruffy beard of his.

'Josie.' He nods.

'Where is your shirt?' I proceed to make my way around the opposite side of the bench and pour myself a glass of water despite not needing it. 'I'm starting to think you don't own any.'

'Doesn't look like it bothers you.'

My cheeks flush, and I bite the inside of my lip. When I notice a piece of paper on the bench, Nick is quick to retrieve it and fold it away in his pockets.

'What's on the paper?' I push my glasses up the bridge of my nose.

Nick shrugs. 'New gym routine.'

Ant stifles a laugh besides me, and I give Nick a look that tells him I do not believe a word he says.

'You come to a decision yet?' Nick straightens up with both hands in his pants pockets.

'I guess he told you?' I turn and say to Ant.

'I heard a rumour.'

I turn back to Nick. My whole body is screaming out to touch him, but I restrain myself. I should be awarded a medal.

'I haven't spoken to Milo yet.'

'So? If he doesn't agree it's only because he knows he doesn't stand a chance.' Nick's confidence continues to stir my whole-body tingles.

'You're so confident.'

'Of course I am,' his eyes dart to Ant and then back to me, perhaps showing a small sign of insecurity. 'Everyone knows how this is going to end. You're the only one living in denial, Josie.'

I turn to Ant for back up. He folds his arms across his chest and leans back into the bench. 'Don't look at me. I'm here for the entertainment.'

'Big help, Ant.'

'Hey, don't blame me for the situations you find yourself in. For once, this does not have my fingerprints all over it, which is sad, to be honest.'

'I don't even know how I found myself to be in this situation in the first place, *to be honest*.'

'Oh, boo hoo, Josie. Two hot guys fighting it out for you. That's what dreams are made of.'

'He has a point,' Nick chimes in with a devilish grin.

'Fine! Fine, I'll do it.'

Nick rolls his eyes. 'Don't want to twist your arm or anything.'

'No, everyone is right. You and I have...well...,' I point between Nick and I unsure of how exactly to define what we have been, 'and Milo is....' I mean, words, any time you'd like to appear would be great. Cheers.

'Right. So?' Nick prompts.

'So, how does this work exactly? I just date you until I figure it out? What if I fall for both of you? Or neither of you?'

'Well, that's not gonna happen,' Nick chimes just as Ant says, 'Three dates.'

'Three dates?' Nick and I say in unison, his tone surprised, mine horrified.

'You expect me to know after three dates?'

Ant simply shrugs. 'I figure you already know Nick. This is just a chance to see if you're compatible as a proper couple. If it can be more than boning and moaning.'

'Oh God,' I say running my hands over my face as Nick lets out a chuckle.

'And you've already sampled Milo's goods, so same-same. You want to find out if you actually *like* him, if you're compatible.'

'Anyone can behave for three dates, even him.' I point to Nick.

'True.'

'Hey!' Nick protests.

'Sorry, man, but she has a point. Okay, what about this? Let the boys plan the first two dates, and then I'll team up with Elle, and we'll plan both third dates which will be designed to test your compatibility as a couple.'

'I'm in.' Nick issues a dare with his eyes.

I stare him down, thinking it over. I feel I'm taking this a little more seriously than anyone else in my life right now. I don't need my dating life turning into *Couples Survivor*. I need to be serious about this. I need to be on the road to settling down. How can I possibly know after three dates which man I want to be with forever?

'Think of it as a wicked story to tell the grandkids,' Ant spins one last sales pitch at me.

I let out a small chuckle. I look between the two of them and I think back to my earlier conversation with Franki and Elle. I can't deny the sense of excitement in the air, the anticipation that is all encompassing.

'Alright. Deal.'

Nick's satisfied grin is infections, and I find myself smiling back at him.

'I can't believe I just let you game show my love life.' I say to Ant.

'This is going to be fun!' He claps his hands together like an excited child who just won the big fluffy toy at the fair.

'Wait, what if Milo doesn't agree?'

'Then I guess it's game over. I win.' Nick winks

I'm nervous about speaking to Milo. It was a lot easier when all I was going to do was send him a message, telling him Ant was fine and that I was sorry for running out last night. Now, I actually have to call him. I don't think a text message saying, 'Hey, sorry for running out, all is good. By the way, I'm dating you and another guy, and you have three dates to prove yourself to me,' is really going to cut it.

I shake my hands out like I'm drying them to see if that makes me feel any better. It doesn't. There is a queasy feeling in the pit of my stomach that I know won't disappear until I make the call. I take this to mean that I do have feelings for the guy. I guess I won't know for sure until I call him. Time to get this over with.

'Hey,' I croon as he answers the phone. 'It's Josie,' I add unnecessarily. Everyone has caller ID these days.

'I know,' I can hear the smile in his voice, 'you're a hard woman to get a hold of. Is everything okay with your friend?'

'Oh, yeah, Ant's fine. Nothing a couple of stitches couldn't fix.' I grimace and quickly move on hoping he doesn't ask any more questions. 'I wanted to apologise for rushing off....'

'No, don't be silly. You did what you had to do.'

'Right.'

An awkward silence falls between us. I'm not too sure how I bring up the whole double dating thing. *Hey Milo, by the way, I want to see other people while seeing you. Hey Milo, I've been conned into double dating. Hey Milo, I'm moving to Siberia.*

'I'm glad you called,' he says down the line. His voice is chocolate-smooth, and I almost melt at the sound of it. 'I wanted to apologise. Last night felt....'

'Weird,' I add, and he sighs down the phone.

'I'm glad you thought so too. I thought maybe it was just me, that I had said something to offend you or....'

'No, no, not at all. It's just...I mean maybe we took things too far too quickly? Not that it wasn't fun. I mean, it was great.' I speak fast and my words sound like they're running into each other.

'No, no, I get it. Yes, perhaps maybe a little too quickly.'

Now it's my turn to let out an audible sigh. 'I didn't know how to bring it up.'

'Look, I like you Josie, and I would like to continue to see you...'

I'm beginning to notice how Milo never finishes a sentence, and it's annoying me. Could I build a life with someone who cannot finish a sentence when things get awkward? I wait until the silence forces him to speak, but it's too much, and I speak instead, much to my own annoyance.

'Me too. It's just....' I try doing a Milo to see if he'll step in and complete my sentence, but he appears comfortable with awkward silences. I inwardly groan. Now I've noticed this little quirk, I can't help but feel frustrated by it. 'Can we slow it down? Do you mind if we get to know each other over a few dates?'

'Absolutely. I'd really like that.'

I dramatically wipe non-existent sweat away from my brow for nobody's entertainment other than my own. 'And, I mean, don't feel like you have to, you know, just date me. I mean, I don't want to take away from anyone else you're dating or getting to know.' I cringe at myself in the mirror. *Smooth, Josie, smooth.*

He chuckles. 'I'm not seeing anyone else.'

My stomach drops. 'Oh.'

'Buuut, I take it you are?' He says it in a friendly manner, like an adult trying to coax an obvious answer out of a child.

'Well, I mean,' I let out a puffed laugh, 'there is someone. One someone else who I'm sort of making my mind up over. But it's totally, you know...I mean, this is what dating is about right? As long as everyone is on the same page, and I mean...we're all getting to know each other. And–'

'Josie,' he chuckles again, 'it's fine. I'm a big boy. I can handle the fact that you want to get to know both of us.'

'Really? You're okay with this?' To be honest, this isn't exactly the response I was expecting.

'Well, it's just *one* other guy, right?'

'Yes, just one, and I won't be adding anyone else in the mix. I promise. And if you want to date someone else, that's fine too.' I hate the idea though. Yes, I know I'm a walking, talking hypocrite.

'Josie, I'm just interested in *you.*'

A pang of guilt snaps in my chest. Urgh. What am I doing?

'Look, Josie, I've got to go but just promise me one thing.' I'm nodding even though he can't see me. It's the least I can do. 'Just let me be the first one to take you on a date. Friday night.'

'Deal.'

Chapter Twenty-Three

NICK

I'm a morning person. Actually, I'm a my-brain-won't-shut-off-so-I-get-little-sleep person which inevitably means I'm a morning person because I normally see so much of it. What I've never been is a take-an-early-morning-dip-in-the-ocean person, until now. I read something online that said it was supposed to help reduce stress, promote deep sleep and spiritually cleanses my aura, whatever the fuck that means.

I don't think the 'reduces stress' part works upon first entering the water because my body goes into a state of stress and refusal the second the icy cold water touched my toes. It may be summer but that means nothing to the water temperature unless you're living further north. Even then I'm not convinced it means anything. After the swim though, I understand the buzz. I do feel refreshed, I do feel more settled, and I notice my mind racing less. There are a few other people doing the same thing, and a few others taking an early morning walk along the beach, all of whom appear to be much older than me. It makes me think of my dad, and an instant wave of nausea rolls through the pit of my stomach.

I'm towel drying myself close to the water's edge when a silver fox of a man approaches me from the water with a sunny smile. 'Beaut morning for it.'

I return his smile and nod agreeably. 'Sure is. You do this every morning?'

He stands proudly with his hands on his hips, apparently not feeling the urgency to dry off. 'For fifteen years. Rain, hail or shine, you'll find me here.'

I'm in awe of his dedication. I reckon the second it even threatened rain, I'd stay in bed.

'A few of us meet up every morning then get a coffee afterwards. Have a chat. Men's group. It's been the best thing I ever did.'

I nod, not sure quite what to say. Is it rude to probe further? Ask why it's the best thing he ever did? Or is he giving me an in to ask? Shit, I never know quite what to say around new people. Especially ones that could be old enough to be my dad. Or granddad.

'I'm John, by the way.' He sticks out his hand, and I shake it.

'Nick.'

'So, Nick, what brings you down here?'

I chuckle nervously. 'What makes you think something bought me here?'

'Ah, the ocean calls to us all when we need it.' He gives me a knowing glance and despite the fact that it's fresh and we're standing around in our bathers, I feel oddly at ease around him. The ocean cleansed his aura good.

'I guess you're right.' I shrug.

'Seventy-five years on this earth, I hope I've picked up a thing or two about reading people.'

Seventy-five? Shit, this man looks better than most forty-year-olds I know. Hell, maybe I will keep up this swimming thing. But if he started fifteen years ago, that makes him sixty when...

'Trying to figure it out?' he asks.

'Sorry?'

'Why I started this?' He points out to the ocean and looks at it lovingly.

'I mean....'

'I lost my wife, fifteen years ago. Stage four. It was sudden once they finally diagnosed her.'

'I'm sorry for your loss.' I look down at my feet and move the sand over them.

'Something tells me you know a thing or two about loss.' I look back up at him, and all I see is kindness in his dark eyes. 'Look, I know to a young bloke like you, we may just be a bunch of old codgers, but you're more than welcome to join us for coffee if you'd like to.'

I've never done well around older men mainly because I lacked a father figure growing up. My male teachers were the ones I always clashed with the most at school, taking out my abandonment issues on them. I know that for a lot of young boys in the same position, there is a pull to latch on to any adult male figure, but for me it was the opposite. I rebelled against them like two north poles on a magnet. There's something about John, though, that doesn't seem as confronting. I guess that's how I find myself in a coffee shop with five other elderly gentlemen discussing my issues. A surprisingly plot twist to *The Life of Nick*.

'You just need to remember that you know her better than this other bloke and trust in your gut,' Clancy, seventy-eight, says to me.

'What sort of a name is Milo anyway?' George, seventy-nine, chimes in.

'Just remember your manners. Hold the door open for her, pull her chair out–'

'And never let her pay. I don't care about all this feminist nonsense. The man should always pay on a date.'

'It's not the done thing these days, George,' John chuckles.

Georges waves his hand dismissively. 'Nonsense.'

'Son, if you want to marry this young lady and spend fifty years together like me and my Mabel, then you need to remember this one phrase.' Clancy leans forward and I mirror him just as he is about to drop a ball of wisdom in my lap. 'Yes, dear.'

The other men around the table chuckle and agree.

'Happy wife, happy life,' George confirms.

'Well, we're a bit off the mark there. We haven't even had our first proper date yet, and there's this other guy–'

'Oh, forget the other guy. You show your lady from the very beginning how you're going to treat her, and you keep it up. That's your one job; you be her safe space, her comfort, her friend, her ally. That's it.' John lifts his coffee up and tips it towards me to make his point.

'What about providing for her?' I ask, confused.

'She doesn't need you for money. You said she's a teacher, right? That means she's a smart cookie. Educated. She can provide for herself. You need to give her something that she can't necessarily provide for herself, a partner. In the truest of true sense. Someone she can trust to pick up the pieces when the world falls apart, and it will. Someone to share a life with, even the little moments.' A sad smile spreads across his face.

'I tell you, Nick, when your person leaves this earth for whatever comes next, you realise it was never about the big things. It was always about the small things. Telling her you love her every day. Compliment her for something small. Listen to her, hold her, cry with her. Go with her to something that you have zero interest in just because you want to spend time with her. At the end of it all, it's not how much money you make or what flashy thing you can buy her, it's about how you make her feel.'

The table falls silent, and I glance at the men around me to see them quietly nodding. The heaviness of experience, heartbreak and loss feels like it's wrapping its arms around me in comfort. I sit with it for a moment before the waitress comes over and takes away our cups.

'I guess you have work to get to this morning, Nicky boy.' George chuckles as we all stand to leave.

I guess so even though I'm still undecided about whether or not I'll go.

'Ah, the perks of being old – retirement.' Clancy slaps me on the shoulder. 'Good to meet you, young man.'

I thank him and tell Clancy and the rest that it was good to meet them too, and it truly was. I didn't think this is how my morning would turn out. As we exit the coffee shop, John puts his hand on my shoulder to indicate for me to wait back for the others to leave.

'Nick, there are few things in life that we can outrun. It all catches up with us eventually. If, and I suspect there is, something else troubling you, you know where to find us.'

'Thanks, John. This morning has certainly been...' Eye opening? Educational? Comforting? I don't quite know how to put it. '...interesting.'

John lets out a deep chuckle. 'We'll see you round, Nick.'

I head back to my unit, walking in the opposite direction to the men. I turn back and watch them go, walking along, sharing a laugh, and I can't help but feel my world has shifted ever so slightly in the right direction.

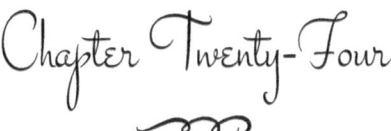

Chapter Twenty-Four

NICK

The effects of the morning don't last long when I arrive home to find a familiar ute in my driveway. My father is leaning against his car, sipping from a takeaway coffee cup. His eyes stay trained on me as I make my way up the concrete driveway, towel over my shoulder, hair still damp with salt water.

'What are you doing here?' I say by way of greeting.

His grey eyes look into mine, and he pauses for a brief moment before responding. 'Making sure you get to work today.' He looks at his watch. 'Better late than never.'

'I've got sick leave. I'm entitled to take it.'

'You don't look sick to me.'

I let out a frustrated laugh. 'Wouldn't expect you to understand.'

He steps forward, brow furrowed, serious expression on his worn face. 'I understand better than you think, Nick. You and me,' he points between us, 'we're not too different. I've been an avoider all my life...'

'I know.'

He ignores the jibe and continues, 'but the funny thing about cancer is you can't avoid it. So, you can choose to talk to me now or on my deathbed because, boy, they're our only two options, and they're both fast approaching.'

I avoid his gaze. I run my hands over my beard, stroking it as I absorb what he just said. It's the same sentiment I heard only minutes ago from John.

Nick, there are few things in life that we can outrun. It all catches up with us eventually.

'I'm already late for work,' I mutter.

'I don't think your boss will mind.' The joke falls flat; there's no humour in his voice.

Backed into a corner, I feel that all too familiar feeling of wanting to outrun my own skin crawl up the back of my neck and reach around my shoulders to my chest. The nausea sets in. I suck in a deep breath and let out a sigh.

'Tonight. We'll talk tonight.' As I say the words, I'm already thinking of how I can get out of it.

'My place or yours?'

'Here. Eight.'

He gives a curt nod. 'Done.'

We stand facing each other awkwardly. Before he leaves, he gives me an address of a job we're working and tells me that he expects me there within the hour. I'm left standing in my driveway feeling numb.

I know why he sent me to this job. We're putting the frames up on the bottom floor of what will be one of those mega mansions with beach views. Frame day is a busy, intensive work day which means little time to think about anything else and with the sun beating down on us, the only other thought I have is being back at the beach.

The property is along Littleton Beach Road or Millionaire Row as us locals call it. All the houses here are two to three stories high. The house next to the one we're working on has a garage below ground like the Bat Cave. All the neighbours around here try to outdo each other. Another house on the street boasts a home cinema, bowling alley and full-size basketball court – indoor and out! This one we're working on is considered to be on the conservative side because it's only seven bedrooms and nine bathrooms big. It doesn't have a private bowling alley, but it does have an in-ground pool that would make most five-star resorts blush and a hidden library that goes over both levels of the house.

It's not something I've ever dreamed of for myself. Growing up without much, I never strive to have it all. A modest roof over my head is all I want. It's more about the people I share it with. And that thought brings me back to Josie. Having seen her family home, I wonder what she wants. I've never known her to be a materialistic kind of girl, but maybe she's trying to build up to the comforts she grew up with. My aspirations are far less grand, and my stomach churns as I wonder if I'll ever be enough for her.

When I picture my future, I picture the whole shebang – wife and two kids, dog, white picket fence. I visualise little kids sports on the weekends and DIY projects. What I don't picture is this: a mega mansion where the house feels nothing like a home, and you employ people to do jobs that you are more than capable of doing. I know that sounds judgemental, but, fuck, who needs a bowling alley in their house?

Despite being busy, the day drags, and by the time I make it home, I just about pass out on the couch from exhaustion. As I sink into the soft leather seats of my three-seater, I hear a knock at the door followed by someone opening it and hollering my name. The day suddenly seems brighter just hearing her voice.

'I need help.' Josie walks into my lounge room in a black dress that she's clutching from the front. 'I need you to help zip me up. I know it's probably inappropriate under the circumstances, but I'm out of options.'

I fold my arms over my chest and sink further into the couch, letting a smirk dance across my face. 'Going out somewhere, Josie?' I tease.

She gives me an unimpressed look. 'I'm going on my first date with Milo tonight, and Ant has inconveniently disappeared off the face of the earth, so I have no one to help zip me up. By the way, do you know where he is?'

I have a strong suspicion he's with a bright-eyed, pre-service teacher, but he's sworn me to secrecy, so I simply shrug and play innocent.

'Whatever. I'll grill him later. Nick, I can't do this zip up on my own. Please help?'

'Maybe you should pick something else to wear then.'

'Nick! Please. This is, like, the only nice thing I have to wear. He told me to dress up.'

My ears prick up, and I cock an inquisitive eyebrow her way. 'Oh yeah? Where is he taking you?'

'I have no idea. He just said to dress up in something fancy. This is the fanciest thing I own so I need help zipping it up.'

Shit. He's taking her somewhere fancy? I'd given some thought to our date and after my conversation with John, George and Clancy this morning, I was going to take her to the drive in. She's never been and has been on about it since we first met. Maybe I need to change my tack. If he's doing a fancy whatever, maybe I need to do the same.

'Nick!' Her pleas drag me out of my thoughts. 'Please.'

As much as I enjoy seeing her half-dressed in my loungeroom, I cave in, stand and help her zip up the back of her dress. I immediately regret it. The dress is figure hugging and it takes all my strength not to run my rough hands down her hips. Damn. I definitely need to rethink the drive in.

'Thank you.' She spins around to face me, pushing her long dark hair over her shoulders.

'Don't mention it.'

She pauses and looks me up and down. 'You good?'

'Yeah,' I lie. 'Why?'

She tilts her head. 'You look...I don't know, tired.'

I feel worse, but I try not to let it show. 'Was just about to jump in the shower. I'm sure that'll refresh me. You could join me if you like.'

This earns me a blush and a small smile. 'You're incorrigible.'

'What? Wouldn't be the first time we've showered together.'

'Is that what I have to look forward to when we go out on our date?'

'If you play your cards right,' I shrug, 'I'm not against it.'

'I didn't mean it like that. I meant like, just a date of... you know what? Doesn't matter. I am about to go on an actual date with Milo, so I need to finish getting ready.'

She already looks beautiful. If I tell her, she'll dismiss me saying she hasn't even done her make up or hair yet, but it doesn't matter to me. She looks beautiful all the time. A longing grows in my chest only to be outdone by the strong hold of jealousy. When I set this up, I didn't think I'd be seeing her before her dates with him. I mean, realistically it was always going to be a possibility, living next door to her and all, but I didn't think I'd be the one helping her get ready for a date with the other guy. Feels like a punch to the guts.

'Well, I hope it's a terrible date.' I place my hands in my pockets and rock on my heels.

'Gee, thanks,' she says dryly as she walks towards the door.

'Pleasure. Oh and Josie, if you need help getting out of that thing later, you know where I am.' I wink and she lets out another small laugh before leaving and shutting the door behind her.

Chapter Twenty-Five

JOSIE

Did I intentionally go over to Nick's house to gauge his reaction to my outfit? I can neither confirm nor deny. I did need help zipping up my dress, but I may have stretched the truth saying this was the only fancy thing I own.

I own another dress in red that would also fit the bill of what Milo had sent me in a text message earlier today, but my gut instinct was right, judging by the way Nick was practically drooling over me. And damn if it didn't do things to me that I was not expecting. Since Nick declared his intentions and since it seems like everyone in my life has declared Nick my perfect mate, I've started to allow myself to imagine. It's dangerous territory because for so long I've pigeon-holed Nick as a commitment-phobe.

When I first met Nick, I was instantly attracted to him: beard, broad, the epitome of a manly man. A dangerous smile and eyes you can easily get lost in. There was something alluring about him, and I found myself just wanting to be around him. He made me laugh and brought out a fun, flirtatious side of me that I hadn't really seen before. With him, I could be a version of myself that I always felt had been hidden away under the expectations of my family. Be the good girl, the sensible girl, set an example for your younger sister – be *that* girl.

With Nick, I didn't have to be anyone other than myself. He gave me the freedom to figure out who I actually was without the pressure of expecting more. It felt like everyone else around me always expected me to act a certain way, say the right thing and be the good girl while Nick expected nothing from me. He never scolded me for saying the wrong thing or for voicing what I wanted.

The trail of beauties leaving his apartment in the beginning showed me that he would never take a relationship seriously, and no matter how quickly I was developing feelings for him, I knew they wouldn't be reciprocated. I talked myself into having fun. I talked myself into believing that he was never going to be that guy, and now I've been talking myself out of falling for Nick for so long that it has become an automatic response, a kind of self-preservation. I'm a little scared to jump back in with my feelings. I try to push Nick out of my mind. I need to focus on Milo, not Nick. I need to give Milo a chance to see if he is where my happily ever after begins. Because even though Nick has declared he's ready, experience has me concerned.

I re-read the text from Milo again to get myself in the mood for our date.

MILO

Dress to impress. I'll pick you up around five
for a night of fine dining and fun.

Fun I can handle. Even the late scramble to get ready after a busy day at work is doable, but I'm nervous about the fine dining part. I'm a notoriously picky eater, unless its sweets, and fine dining usually means small dishes of things you wouldn't dream of serving your dog let alone a human. If it's raw, difficult to pronounce, set menu or part of an animal that isn't breast, rump, wing or drumstick then I'm out. I'm the furthest thing from a foodie, and the idea of fine dining edges up close to a nightmare for me. Let's just hope his idea of fine dining is an overly priced Italian restaurant. No-one can stuff up pasta.

I'm ready at five p.m. I'm pacing the entry way as I look down at my watch to see he's already ten minutes late. There's been no call, no message, no communication as to why he's running late. Did he forget we had a date? Maybe I got the day wrong? Has he forgotten where I live? Maybe he's been in a car accident? As thoughts race around my head, I pace faster, back and forth. My phone buzzes in my hand. A message from Elle in our group chat; which has been named and renamed numerous inappropriate things until we collectively settled on one that made the most sense and would cause the least amount of embarrassment should anyone stumble upon it.

Finding Mr Right

ELLE

Where is he taking you? The suspense has been too much.

JOSIE

It's a quarter past five.

ELLE

And? What are you wearing? What is he wearing?

JOSIE

I'm wearing that little black strapless dress we bought on sale last year. Him. No idea. He's not here yet.

FRANKI

Strike one.

JOSIE

Should I call him?

ELLE

NO!

FRANKI

HELL NO! He's late, he should be calling you.

JOSIE

Am I being stood up?

ANT

Nick would never be late.

JOSIE

He lives ACROSS THE DRIVEWAY! He has no excuse.

ANT

Just saying...

ELLE

You're not being stood up. I'm sure there is a reasonable explanation.

FRANKI

Which he should have already messaged to you by now.

JOSIE

What if he was in a car accident and can't message me?

FRANKI

Do you know how unlikely that is?

ANT

Agree with Franki.

ELLE

Maybe he got held up at work?

ANT

Disagree with Elle.

JOSIE

Not helping Ant. BTW where are you? I was in serious need of your assistance earlier. I had to ask Nick to help zip up my dress!

ELLE

WHAT?!

FRANKI

NO! OMG SIS!!

ANT

laughing face emoji THAT was your only option? Couldn't have found another dress that you could zip up yourself?

JOSIE

No. This dress is perfect.

ANT

Could have worn the red one.

JOSIE

Where are you?

ANT

Nice deflect.

JOSIE

Same to you.

FRANKI

I'm grabbing my popcorn. This is better than anything on any of the streaming services.

ELLE

Has he shown up yet?

JOSIE

no

ELLE

He's officially twenty-three minutes late.

FRANKI

Call it.

ANT

Yep. Done. Game over. Do you want to tell
Nick or shall I?

JOSIE

Oh wait! He's just pulled up. IN A BENTLEY!

ELLE

All is forgiven.

FRANKI

eye roll emoji he sounds like a wanker.
Abort.

ANT

What kind of Bentley?

ELLE

Does it matter?

JOSIE

Gotta go. Bye xox

I open the door to find Milo in a very well fitted grey suit with a light blue checked shirt looking like a poster boy for Armani.

'I am so sorry I'm late, Josie. I had to fit in an extra client, and my phone died somewhere between walking them into my rooms and the end of the appointment. I don't have a charger.'

'Your fancy car doesn't have a charger?'

A wry smile spreads across his face. 'No. I truly am sorry, Josie. Not making a very good first impression, am I?'

I can feel a blush running up my neck. I have Franki's voice in my head telling me to call out his BS excuse, and Elle's voice telling me to accept the apology and move on. Ant's voice is in there too, laughing.

'Still, I was raised to be a gentleman and I am sorry. Please allow me to make it up to you. I promise the rest of the night will be one you won't forget.'

The plea in his green eyes has me melting, so I agree. 'Well then, let's get this date under way,' I say and walk out the door, closing and locking it behind me.

Instinctively, my eyes dart across the driveway to see Nick leaning against the outside wall just by his front door. He's showered and changed since I saw him last as evidenced by the damp mop of dark hair sitting water tossed on his head and the black tee that hangs beautifully off his frame. His hands are in his jeans' pockets which drags them down ever so slightly, showing off the trail that leads below the belt buckle. His expression is unreadable. I give him a short wave, and he nods in return.

'Nice ride,' he calls out, crossing his arms over his chest.

'Thanks, man,' Milo smiles whilst guiding me to the passenger side.

'Shit, if I had of known how much I'd make staring into people's eyeballs, I might have studied harder.' A smirk spreads across Nick's face, and I shoot him a warning look.

'What can I say?' Milo tries to be humble.

'Oh, I think the car says it all, really.'

'Have a good night, Nick,' I rush to add before he can say anything else.

'Be safe out there, you kids.'

Milo shuts the door and strides to his side of the car, taking his time, I guess in an effort to show Nick that he isn't intimidated.

'Wasn't he the guy in your kitchen the other morning?' Milo says, putting on his seatbelt.

'Yes. Sorry about him. He's a little...'

'Jealous?'

'I was going to go with childish, but sure, jealous probably works too.'

Milo lets out a small chuckle. 'Well, I would be too if I saw some other guy taking you out. You look beautiful by the way.'

I look down, but my cheeks don't flush as expected. 'Thank you.'

'He's not the other guy you're seeing, is he?'

There's something in the way he asks the question, almost jokingly, as if Nick couldn't possibly be his competition. Or maybe that's just how I read it. I don't know. I look out the window. Nick is like a statue, still in place watching our every move, expression back to being unreadable.

'No,' I lie and turn my attention back to Milo, 'he's just a friend.'

This seems to satisfy him as he relaxes back in his seat. I'm not really one for fancy cars; for me, a car is merely a thing to get you around. They're fairly indistinguishable, and ones like this, well, if I hadn't recognised the Bentley symbol, you could have told me it was any type of car, and I would have believed you. However, the one thing that does stand out about this car is how plush the leather seats feel. You sink into them. Milo looks at me before he starts the engine, and I think it's a cue for me to compliment his car, so I mention the seats.

'You can heat them or cool them. Want to see?'

I'm intrigued so I nod, and he presses a button. Moments later I have a cool, wet sensation coming from my seat. I know I didn't just wet myself. And the car certainly doesn't get me that excited.

'Takes a bit of getting used to,' he notes before driving out the driveway.

'Yeah, it feels wet.' My face scrunches up at the feeling. 'I think I'm good. I don't think I need my seat cool.'

Milo presses the button again and the wet sensation disappears although I still feel uncomfortable in my seat. Aside from that...it's a car. What more can I say? It drives. I don't understand the fascination with them. The roads these days are pretty good, so most cars drive smoothly. Is it really worth the down payment on a house? I'm not convinced.

Turns out that Milo is taking me into the city. As most of the peak hour traffic is heading our way for the weekend, away from the city, we have a relatively quick run in. He pulls up to one of the swankiest hotels in Melbourne, and the flutter of nerves settle in my stomach. It's a sleek modern building that lacks any real warmth or feeling of invitation from the outside. The valet opens Milo's door, and another does the same on my side, offering me a hand to hold as I step out.

I take it and suddenly feel like I should have paparazzi taking my picture. Milo waits for me on the steps. I take him in again, and there is no denying his handsome features, the strong jawline freshly shaved for the evening, and the way his green eyes make all sorts of promises. I try to shake off the reservations I have and take his hand as he walks me into the hotel. There's a large, marble water fountain smack bang in the middle of the lobby, and a grand stair case just behind it that veers off in two different directions.

'We're going up here.' He squeezes my hand and walks me to the elevators.

A tall man dressed in a three-piece suit asks us what floor we're traveling to and presses the elevator buttons for us which strikes me as an odd job to have. But I guess if you're rich, and this place is undeniably for them, then you have someone whose job it is to do the most basic of tasks.

'Enjoy your evening.' He tips his hat as the elevator doors close.

Milo stands straight, and I lean into his arm, testing the waters on PDA. Milo doesn't make a move to wrap his arm around me like I had hoped he would, so I slowly pull away. He looks to me and smiles, and I mirror his expression.

'Have you been here before?' he asks as the elevator continues to climb.

I shake my head and let out a little laugh. 'I don't think a teacher's salary would even cover parking at a place like this.'

He smiles, but I notice he doesn't laugh. 'Well then, you're in for a treat tonight.'

The elevator comes to a stop on the top floor, and as the doors open, we're greeted by another man, dressed like the one who pushed the elevator buttons.

'Welcome to Matteo's.' He smiles and gives a small bow.

I'm not sure what to do, so I give a little curtsey. The gentleman smiles in reply while Milo does nothing. Instead, he guides us wordlessly over to the maître d's desk and gives him his name. Milo Barrington. The name sounds familiar. I'm a little embarrassed that I didn't even know the surname of the man who is taking me out. I'm also ignoring the fact that I slept with him on the first date without even knowing his surname. I think back to our meeting at the optometrist and his name tag definitely only said his first name. He never mentioned his surname. I feel like this is basic information I should know about someone I am currently dating. This fact makes me blush.

We take out seats, which are arguably the best in the whole place – beside floor to ceiling window seats that overlook the city as the sun sets. There's a small candle and three lush roses in a vase sitting on our small round table. The tablecloth feels heavy as I swing my legs under it, my chair held out by a waiter, not my date. I don't think anyone has ever held the chair open for me before. I decide instantly that I like it. The tables are spaced far enough apart to make you feel like you're in your own little bubble, but not so far away that the atmosphere is lost. There is an air of high class surrounding us, and I feel very out of place. On the other hand, Milo looks like he belongs, something I didn't notice before.

'Your surname sounds familiar,' I say as the waiter fills my glass with water.

'A lot of people say that, thank you,' he orders what I assume is a bottle of champagne as the name sounds French. I could be wrong. I guess I'll find out when it arrives. Milo adds, 'It sounds familiar because you probably see it every day in your classroom.'

I look at him confused, still unable to put two and two together. He undoes the button on his suit jacket and takes it off, swinging it over the back of his chair. The motion shouldn't be something that is attractive, but it is. I notice the way his checked shirt hugs those defined arms muscles that have no right belonging to someone who sits down in a dark room for most of the day.

'Stationery,' he finally says, but I've completely forgotten what the question was. My expression must tell him the same thing because he elaborates. 'Barrington stationery. Pens, pencils, whiteboard markers...'

'Oh my God! Yes. I use those in my classroom!' I finally make the connection.

'There you go. Most people know the name, but they don't know where from.'

'Huh. So, no joining the family empire then?'

He looks down at the place setting and moves his cutlery out a bit before looking back up at me with a very broad smile. 'Not really my thing.'

'You prefer staring into people's eyeballs all day,' I joke, and he lets out a chuckle.

'I benefit nicely from the family empire, as you put it.'

'The car?'

He nods. 'I don't make that kind of money in my job, but I am on the board of Barrington Stationary, so....'

So he's essentially being paid an allowance by his parents. I can't help but think how much my own parents would be dazzled by Milo, especially knowing he is an heir to a stationery empire. Is that right? Can you be an heir to a stationery company? I picture Milo in a crown made of four pens and giggle.

The waiter returns with a bottle of wine, not champagne, and a bread basket with a side of oil and vinegar for dipping. He pours a small glass of wine and hands it to Milo. He swishes the liquid in the voluptuous glass, takes in the aroma and then takes the smallest of sips. He nods his approval, and the waiter continues to pour us both a glass of wine. I guess it's just too bad if I don't like it.

I reach for the bread basket. 'The vinegar is the best part, and they never give you enough,' I say as I pull apart the rather stale feeling bread. In my enthusiasm for some carbs, my hand yanks at the bread, knocking into the wine glass. In what feels like slow motion, I watch as Milo tries to stop the inevitable from happening. We both reach for the glass trying to stop it from falling and spilling its contents, only I seem to make things worse and ensure the glass's demise. All over Milo's light grey suit pants. My hands immediately fly to my mouth, and I'm out of my chair, around to his side of the table in seconds.

'I. Am. So. Sorry.' I reach for the closest napkin and immediately begin rubbing it over the spill around his groin.

'Josie. Josie!' he whispers and grabs at my hand. 'I appreciate the help but what you're doing is really not helping.' His face is flushed, and I realise not only have I appeared to make the stain worse, but I've also managed to arouse him.

'Is everything alright, Sir? Ma'am?'

I jump and let out a little shriek as the waiter appears out of nowhere behind me. I look around the semi full restaurant and see many pairs of eyes are on us.

'I...I...I might just...sit. Back down. Here,' I say, scurrying over to my side of the table. As far as dates go, this one hasn't exactly gotten off to the best start.

'If you didn't like the wine, you could have just told me. No need to throw it at me,' Milo jokes, but it only makes my cheeks turn the shade of beetroot. 'We just need some help mopping up an accident.' He says to the waiter who promptly disappears to get what I can only assume will be cleaning supplies whilst I profusely apologise to my date for ruining his pants. Let's be honest, red wine ain't coming out of those pants.

'Josie, honestly, don't worry about it.'

'I'm not normally a clutz. Please let me get them dry cleaned for you.'

The pants themselves probably cost more than my fortnightly wage.

'I said don't worry about it,' he smiles. 'I think they're done for.'

'I–'

'Josephine?'

I pause. I must look like I've seen a ghost because Milo suddenly looks very worried.

'Josephine, honey, is that you?'

The unmistakable voice of my mother sends a chill down my spine. I plaster a fake smile on my face and turn to my left to see my mother approaching with my father.

'Mum. Dad,' I say shakily. This night couldn't possibly get any worse.

Chapter Twenty-Six

NICK

He's on time. The man could never make it out to one of my footy games as a kid but can damn well make sure he's on time to talk about his impending death. Sounds about right. I haven't had the chance to make dinner yet. I'm just not hungry. The TV is on, but truth be told, it's only been there for background noise as I've been staring out the front window: watching Josie leaving, waiting for her to come back, waiting for Ant to come home so I can bother him and miss what I'm about to sit through. I see my father's ute pull up and get to the door before he has a chance to knock. I let him in and offer him a drink.

'Nah, not for me mate,' he says and takes a seat on the couch.

I sit opposite him and pick a spot on the floor to gaze at. Who knew the pattern in my wooden floors boards was so interesting?

'When your mother told me–'

'Please don't bring her into this,' I interrupt, pain straining my voice. He doesn't have any right to talk about her. No chit chat. I guess we're just getting to the point.

'I need to get this off my chest, Nick. And you need to hear it,' He pauses and waits.

If he's waiting for me to give him the go ahead, he'll be waiting a long time. I don't need to hear his side of the story. I didn't come back into his life three years ago to rehash history. I came to get to know the man he is now and see if there was a way to move forward. I went through all the emotions as a kid; disappointment at him not being around for my games or my birthday, jealousy that he had started a new family and so easily cast me aside, and anger that he wasn't there when she died.

I remember the day I stopped wishing for him to return to us, the day I stopped trying so hard to get his love and attention. I was ten years old, and he hadn't shown up for yet another birthday. I promised myself then that I wouldn't ever need anything from him and, more importantly, that I would stop hero worshipping the guy. Love was a thing that I no long had for the man who was only ever part of my genetic makeup and nothing more.

When I decided I wanted to see him and get to know him after my mum died, it was on my terms. I *wanted* something from him which was to know him, and he was either going to give it to me or not. But I never *needed* to get to know him. There's a big difference. If he had turned around and said no, he didn't want to get to know me, then my next plan was to go backpacking through Europe. If that had happened, I would never have met Josie.

'Right then,' he sucks in a breath and continues, 'when your mother told me she was pregnant, I was in shock. We were only having fun, nothing serious.'

I sigh and sit back, picking at the leather on the arm of the chair. I've heard this before. They weren't serious, I was an accident, and he wasn't ready. Until he was – with someone else. I don't see the point in rehashing history.

'I wasn't ready to settle down, Nick. I wanted to get out there, explore the world. I didn't have a great father role model growing up,'

'The cycle continues.'

He narrows his gaze but doesn't scold me. 'I wasn't sure I even wanted to be a father. But your mum was hellbent on having you. She was a strong woman. Told me that I didn't have to be involved, that she could do it all on her own.'

'And she did. Is there a point to all this?' I snap.

'She sent me pictures of you when you were born, and to be honest, you looked like every other baby I'd ever seen.'

'How paternal of you,' I say dryly.

'It wasn't until you were about three years old, and I saw a picture of you playing on that yellow digger in a sandpit that I became interested in you. You know the one? It was one of your mum's favourites. She had it framed in the kitchen.'

My head snaps up. 'How do you know what she had framed in the kitchen?'

'I came round after seeing that picture. Nick, you looked just like me.'

And there it is. His only interest in me came when I started to look like him. What a narcissistic arsehole.

'I was there. We had afternoon tea. I wanted to meet you and your mother agreed, but you didn't want a bar of me. You couldn't have cared less. That's when I realised, that you and your mum had a good thing going on and that I would only be in the way. So, I left. I sent cards and gifts. And your mum sent me updates, and we left it up to you if you ever wanted to meet me.'

My jaw damn well nearly hits the floor. Of all the shi––

'Are you serious right now? Because that is not at all how I remember it going down.' My eyes narrow. Now I refuse to take them off him.

'You can remember it how you like, but that's the truth.'

I stare at him in stunned silence. He really believes the lies he just spun. He really believes that he was just a dad who came to his senses and wanted to be a part of his son's life, only to have a three-year-old dictate *no, sorry old man, you can't be my dad.* Bullshit. I have zero recollection of that day, and Mum never once told me about it. The way I remember it was that he wasn't interested. Yeah, sure, he sent cards and gifts at birthdays and Christmases, but any time I wanted to speak to him he was busy. Any time we planned to meet, he'd cancel at the last minute. I only ever knew him as a sort of twice a year twisted pen pal who sent cash in cards. I'm still deciding to challenge his version of events when he speaks.

'I didn't get it right, Nick. I should have pushed to see you, pushed to be in your life. It wasn't until I met Gina, and we had the boys that I realised what a monumental stuff up I had been. And by then you were a teenager and wanted nothing to do with anyone who wasn't your mate.'

'Are you blaming me?' I'm astonished. Of all the shitty things an absent parent can do, blaming the kid for their bad choices is just fucked.

'Did she tell you about our coffee dates? Your mum and I would meet up and talk about you. She'd show me your reports, pictures, things you made in wood shop.' He has the audacity to look proud. And no, I didn't know, but how could I ever verify this? The only other person there was Mum, and she's dead.

'I remember she was really worried when you had that girl-friend when you were about sixteen,' he chuckles. Chuckles! Like he has any right to share old time stories with me. 'She was worried you'd get her pregnant and that she'd be a young grandma.'

A pang of sadness hits my guts as I realise she'll never get the chance to be a grandma. And the man in front of me will never get to be a grandpa.

'She never told me.'

He sighs. 'I don't know why she didn't. She must have had her reasons. But I'm telling you this now, Nick, to show you that I did try. Over the years, I kept up with what you were doing. I helped your mum out a bit with money and stuff like that from time to time, but I just want you to know that I was always there.'

I don't know what to do with what he's telling me. Mum

can't validate his claims, and I don't know how this is supposed to make me feel because I feel nothing. No, not nothing. I feel exhausted. I'm exhausted from running through the gamut of emotions with this man. I literally have nothing left to feel.

'When you walked back into my life three years ago, I felt like someone was listening, like the universe was finally giving me a chance to right the wrongs. I gave you a job. I was able to see you every day. Get to know you. And that's when I knew. I knew I was going to leave the company to you. I just thought it would be well into the future and that I'd have more time to fix everything.'

What more can I say? This isn't about me, it's never been about me. This is about him and doing something to ease his conscience. His redemption story. He doesn't want to leave me the company because he thinks I'll do a good job or to keep his legacy alive. I'm sure if he wanted to do that, he could give it to one of his other sons. He wants to give it to me to show everyone what a great man he is, so someone can stand over his casket and tell a crowd of strangers what a great father he was. Make right in death what he was too cowardly to work hard at and make right in life. Fuck him.

'I don't want the company.' A low growl escapes my throat.

'Nick, this can set you up for life. The company is bringing in millions in profit each year and–'

'I don't want the company.'

It is his turn to looked shocked. 'I don't get it.' He shakes his head. 'Are you that stubborn that you won't accept this gift? I'm essentially gifting you millions of dollars here, Nick.'

I push myself out of the armchair and stand. 'I never wanted to be you.'

'You think that accepting this makes you like me? Being successful and wealthy and able to provide for your family...you think that's a bad thing?'

He stands. He's shorter than me but not by much. Despite the cancer that is ravishing his body, he still looks fit, if perhaps slimmer than usual. His dark eyes are as cloudy as ever. He's pissed off that I won't grant him the satisfaction of becoming a fatherly martyr in death.

I was serious when I came to him three years ago and told him I wanted nothing from him other than to get to know him. I wanted to see for myself who he was, and so I could call the shots on when *I* was done this time. I didn't expect to fall in love with Littleton Beach or the girl next door. And honestly, if those two things weren't a factor, I would have left long ago. I don't want to owe him anything.

If I take this company, I'll owe him for the rest of my life. Everything I ever buy or do with my life will have his fingerprints all over it. A reminder of how he bought my affection in the end. I'm not interested. I never needed his help growing up, and I don't need it now.

'I have no interest in running your company. Or any company. I just want to do my job and go home.' I walk towards the door to signal that this meeting is over.

He doesn't move. 'Think about it. That's all I ask.'

'I have.'

He moves to the door, ignoring that I have spoken. 'Let it sit with you. We'll meet at the end of next week, and you can give me your final decision.'

'My decision won't change.' I open the door for him.

'We'll see,' he says over his shoulder as he walks out of my house and into the night.

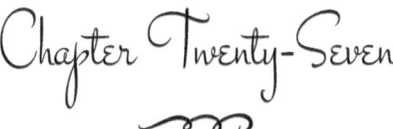

Chapter Twenty-Seven

JOSIE

Milo is a pure gentleman to my parents. I introduce them and he stands to shake both their hands, holding the napkin strategically over his crotch to cover the red wine spill.

'It's a pleasure to meet you, Mr and Mrs Russo.'

Mum is immediately dazzled by Milo's smile and charm, and implied wealth, no doubt. Matteo's is a well-known establishment for the upper class of society. Which begs the question, why are my parents here? They do well for themselves but not Matteo's kind of well.

'What are you doing here?' I try to sound jovial, but it comes out strained.

'Your father and I are dining with business associates.'

What she means is, Dad's wealthy golf buddies have invited them out for dinner.

'Milo, that's a lovely name,' Mum turns on the charm and faces my date. 'What is it that you do?' And she suddenly turns a little 1920s British. Her posture straightens too.

'I'm an optometrist.'

'A doctor, hey?' Dad interjects looking proud of himself. Or me. It's hard to tell.

'Ah, not quite,' Milo chuckles.

'Oh well, still, must be paying a pretty penny to end up at a place like Matteo's.'

'As lovely as this little reunion is,' I interject.

Mum completely ignores me. She has eyes only for Milo. 'And how is it that you know our Josephine?' she coos.

Her affectionate tone is performative and enough to make anyone who knows her gag. Milo seems to be buying it though. He looks at me as if asking if I want him to move them on. At least that's what I think he's trying to communicate. I give a small nod. To my horror, he begins to recount our meeting, not at all trying to move them on. I need to get better at reading people. Or reading him.

'I'm Josie's optometrist. She came in for an eye exam the other day and well...'

He leaves the end of his sentence hanging and a bubble of frustration dances in my chest. He leaves the rest to be interpreted by my mother who I can see planning our future wedding in her mind.

'Ah, yes, wonderful! Glad you're still having regular checks, Josephine. She was terrible about it as a teenager. Hated wearing her glasses, but I think they make her look more distinguished. Milo, has Josephine told you that she's a coordinator at the school where she works?' Mum lets out a knowing laugh, 'Which of course is a mere step away from being principal.'

I think she's miscalculated the steps there, but I don't get a chance to say as much as she continues to highlight my selling points as though I'm some property she's trying to offload.

'She also owns her own home.' Stretching the truth is a Lorella Russo speciality. I own it with Ant. But you know... details, details. 'Josephine also comes from a line of Italian landowners. Has she mentioned that?'

Milo graciously plays into my mother's hand by pretending to be impressed. Or maybe he is. I think we've established I'm terrible at reading people tonight.

'No, we haven't had a chance to discuss such things yet.'

'Oh well, plenty of time.' She pauses for a brief moment, and I seize my opportunity to move her along. 'As I was saying, you wouldn't want to keep dad's associates waiting.'

'Yes, of course. Come Lorella. Milo, good to meet you.' Dad gives Milo a firm handshake.

'Yes, lovely to meet you, Milo. I'm sure our paths will cross again soon. Josephine, I trust you'll be there Sunday?'

I give her a puzzled look. 'Where exactly?'

'Brunch. Don't tell me you forgot, sweetheart?'

I most definitely didn't forget because there has most definitely never been brunch on for this Sunday. I never forget a date with my mother. The mere thought of having to allocate my free time to her is anxiety-inducing let alone imagining the wrath that would rain down on me if I ever actually forgot. And so I do the most stupid thing I can do; I agree because I don't want to look any more foolish in front of Milo.

'Of course. Can you text me the information again, so I don't forget?'

Mum gives a curt smile and agrees before heading towards her table on the other side of the room.

'I am so sorry about that.' I all but crumple in on myself.

'Don't be.'

'I feel like all I have done on this date is apologise.'

'Hey, I started it by turning up late.'

We share a defeated laugh.

'This date is not going well, is it?' I concede.

Milo leans forward and takes my hand. 'I wouldn't say that. I'm out on a Friday night at one of the most popular restaurants in the whole country with the most beautiful woman I have ever laid eyes on. Who is apparently a wealthy landowner in Italy.' He wags his eyebrows in jest.

'Was there an optometrist joke in there?' I tease.

'You don't take compliments very well, do you?' The edges of his mouth curl upwards.

'I'm working on it. And don't take that land stuff seriously. My father's great, great grandparents owned a small farm which the family recently sold for barely anything. Mum likes to embellish the story a little. I think Dad ended up with a couple of thousand dollars in inheritance which barely covered the tiles in the ensuite bathroom they renovated at home.'

'Ah, I see.'

'Sorry to burst that bubble. Don't go around thinking we can merge our family empires and take over the world.'

Milo chuckles. 'Noted. Look, let's order and start the date over.' he waves the waiter over. 'We're ready to order.'

I scan the menu in front of me. I am most certainly not ready to order. I need to go back and forth over my decision at least five times, but Milo doesn't wait. He orders for us. 'We'll have the Chef's Selection for two. Thank you.'

'Very good choice, Sir.' The waiter bows.

I look to the waiter to see if he will confirm the order with me, to see if anyone will give me a say in what I'm about to ingest, but he doesn't. He keeps his gaze fixed on Milo before slinking away. It's not my place to speak up, not here in this very fancy and expensive restaurant that I'm being treated to, so I force a smile, trying not to let my panic show.

'W-what is on the Chef's Selection?'

'You'll love it. It's off menu. The chef basically has license to serve us whatever he wants. It's usually a couple of popular dishes and some that he is experimenting with. You know, before he decides to put it on the menu.'

Holy friggin' Gordan Ramsey nightmare, Batman! Experimental food dishes are not my thing. Not being given a choice about what I'm eating is also not my thing. What if it's some oesophagus stuffed monster dripped in sauce? Or under cooked meat? Or worse - something with mushrooms! Bile rises up in my throat, but I wash it away with a big gulp of wine.

'So,' Milo shows his hands, palms up. 'Start over?'

'Start over,' I confirm, my stomach still unsettled and worried about what will be served in front of us.

'How's the start of the school year going?' He lifts his glass to his lips and takes a sip.

'Busy. As always. You constantly feel like you're running on a treadmill, and someone keeps upping the incline and speed when you're not looking.'

He shakes his head in a supportive way. 'I don't know how you do it. I couldn't think of anything worse.'

I shrug. I hear this a lot. 'Young people are pretty amazing. Most of the time.'

'Well, I think it takes a pretty special kind of person to do what you do.' I smile and shift in my seat at yet another compliment. 'You must have the patience of a saint.'

'I mean, you realise pretty quickly that yelling and fussing gets you nowhere. They just want to be heard, to feel like someone is in their corner during a pretty confusing time. They're just trying to figure out who they are and who they want to be.'

'I couldn't do it.'

'It's not for everyone. Just like optometry.' I move the focus back to him.

'True. Funny the things we're drawn too.'

'What drew you to it?'

He looks over my shoulder as if the answer to the question is behind me. 'My dad gave me an ultimatum when I finished school. He told me I had to have another career lined up if I wasn't going to go into stationary. He said I had to do uni, so I just picked optometry.'

'You just picked it? Were you one of those annoying kids at school who were naturally academically gifted? Like, you didn't have to study for a single thing and still aced the tests.' The wry smile on his face confirms my suspicions. 'I hated kids like you.'

We share a laugh before he continues. 'The girl I had a big

crush on was picking it, so I thought I'd pick it to and maybe we'd end up at the same uni in the same classes.'

'And did you?'

He lets out a small laugh. 'I got in, and she didn't.'

I shake my head. 'I definitely would have hated you in high school.'

'Lucky we're not there now then.'

Milo leans into the armrest, casually folding the sleeves of his shirt up. I don't know why this one simple move has my heart all aflutter, but I file it away in my fantasy bank for later. Milo looks well put together. Everything he is wearing is coordinated. He's smooth, and if his anecdote is anything to go by, life for Milo has been easy with a capital E.

He's like a whole different Milo from the one who took me to the movies. That Milo was more causal, fun, down to earth. This Milo is a bit...aloof? Trying too hard? Which is the real Milo and how do I ask him which is the real him?

Our *first* first date was sweet; dinner at a quaint restaurant where they serve normal food, and I was allowed to pick my own dish, and then a movie. No fancy suits, cars or food. This Milo though...Is this who he is, or is he pulling out all the stops to impress me because he knows I'm seeing someone else?

I just don't know which Milo I would get if we got serious. More importantly, which one would I want? Movies Milo made me feel instantly at ease whereas Matteo's Milo is...well, let's just say I'm very aware of everything I say and do. And this dress feels like it has shrunk two sizes smaller since I put it on.

The waiter arrives with our first dish and I'm relieved to see it looks like a standard pasta entree. He informs us it is a traditional beef ragu with handmade rigatoni. Milo scoops a serving onto my plate before doing the same for his. The serve is small, and to be honest, I would have preferred to just have this as my meal and be done because upon first taste, all the flavours explode in my mouth. The pasta is silky smooth, the beef so tender it practically melts the second it lands on my tongue. I could happily eat this dish for the rest of my life. A satisfied groan escapes from somewhere deep in my throat. This seems to amuse Milo.

'Like it?'

'This is the best thing I have ever eaten. Just don't tell my Nonna.' My eyes dart to where my parents are sitting as though they may be listening in to our conversation and about to rat me out to Nonna. They don't of course because they look like they're having a howling good time with their own friends. As if she feels my eyes on her, Mum looks up at me and gives me a knowing look of approval. It makes me feel small.

Milo chuckles. 'Your secret is safe with me. Does your Nonna make her own pasta?'

'Pasta. Sauce. They have a veggie patch in their backyard. She's never liked my mum because my mum doesn't cook.'

'Ever?'

I shake my head. 'My dad does the cooking. Which of course is offensive to my Nonna. How dare her darling son cook for the family, you know.' I load my fork.

'Do you cook?'

'I can. I buy pasta and sauce from the supermarket though. I don't have time to make my own.'

'The shame!' he says dramatically.

I giggle. 'Nonna doesn't need to know because she won't come to anyone else's house to eat. She's always the hostess. Can you cook? Or are you one of those 'that's a woman's job' type of man?'

His cheeks flush ever so slightly. 'Not exactly.'

'Not exactly as in you can't cook or not exactly as in you believe a woman's place is in the kitchen?'

He wipes the corner of his mouth with the heavy napkin. 'I believe a woman's place is wherever she wants it to be,' my ovaries cheer, 'but I ah, I can't cook.'

'How do you get by?' He certainly doesn't look like a man who lives off pizzas and frozen meals.

'This is going to make me sound like a pompous arse...our home chef makes me meals and sends them to me once a week.'

'Home chef?' I almost choke on my rigatoni. I guess I know which Milo is the real Milo.

He runs a hand over his face, clearly uncomfortable. 'Victor has been our family chef ever since I can remember. He makes meals for my brother and I and sends them to us on a Sunday, ready for the week.'

My jaw drops. 'You're like, insanely wealthy.'

'Not me.'

'And entitled,' I tease.

His grin hides behind an embarrassed, knowing look. 'I can make food. I throw together salads just like I did for us the other night. And I can grill meat. It just saves time. And he's already getting paid so....'

I'm not sure how I feel about a grown man who is unable to fend for himself in a kitchen. But then again, I've never grown up with the kind of wealth he obviously has. My parent's house looks like we could be wealthy, and they certainly want others to think that. However, the truth is it's all for show. They know the right people and buy the right things to give the impression that they're wealthy. Take tonight, for example, there is no way my parents could afford to come to Matteo's and yet the only reason they're here is because they move in the right crowds. It's a perceived notion of wealth with my family.

I can't help but think about whether I would take advantage of a family chef if I could? Probably. Ant and I share the cooking and cleaning up duties, and more often than not, Nick joins us. So between the three of us, we've got a good thing going on. My mind flashes to images of the three of us in the kitchen and a strange feeling settles in my gut when I picture Nick's face. I wonder if he'll wait up for me? I take another large sip of wine to banish thoughts of Nick and try to refocus on what Milo is saying. I tuned out when he revealed that he doesn't cook.

'Victor did try and teach me how to make lasagne one summer when I was still in high school, but I just couldn't get it.'

'What's there to get? Sauce on the bottom of the tray so it doesn't stick, pasta sheet, ham, mozzarella, sauce, repeat. It's like the easiest dish.'

'But the béchamel sauce was—'

I gasp. 'No! No béchamel sauce. That's not the way it's done.'

'Maybe you can show me one day.' A smile settles on the side of his face, and it's endearing, but it doesn't send butterflies to my stomach. Interesting. Here is a gorgeous man, flirting with me over dinner, and I don't so much as feel a twinge of anything. Why is this so different to our first date when I felt like fireworks were going off through my entire body? Now, I can't even feel a spark. I decide that it must be because my parents are here ruining the vibe.

'The chef has put together this culinary delight for tonight,' says the waiter as he returns to place a dish with three, small, meat mousse squares in front of us. 'Suckling pig terrine with orange compote. This particular dish is one that shall appear on our spring menu.'

Milo's eyes widen with excitement as he rubs his hands together. It looks less than appetising to me. 'What exactly is pig sucking terrain?'

Milo chuckles, and the waiter restrains a smile. 'Suckling pig terrine,' he corrects, 'is a delicacy made from suckling pig, pork liver, kidney, herbs and finely chopped pistachio nuts which has been cooked in a steam oven and set. The orange and chilli compote contrasts nicely and refreshes the palette.'

I swallow hard. My parents are not the only thing ruining the vibe.

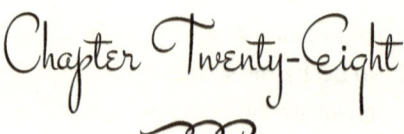

Chapter Twenty-Eight

JOSIE

Turns out the Chef's Selection is an eight-course meal of mostly inedible, unpronounceable products. By the time Milo delivers me home, I'm buzzed on wine and an angry, empty stomach. I'm a little wobbly on my feet as he walks me to my front door. I forgot to leave the light on, so I pull up the torch app on my phone and use that to help guide the key into the hole.

'Thank you for tonight,' I say. Hopefully it doesn't sound as slurred as I feel.

'Pleasure was all mine.' He leans in and plants his lips on mine.

I can't seem to make my mouth move, and so the kiss ends with me leaning so far backwards that I fall through the open door. I'm giggling as I sit on my butt in the darkened hallway of my unit. Milo crouches down and helps me to my feet.

'Are you, okay, Josie?'

I steady myself, holding onto his arm. 'I'm fine. Just a lil too much wine.'

He looks at me with his brows furrowed and his lips in a downward turn. He doesn't look impressed. 'Can I help you–'

'Nah,' I wave my hands dismissively, 'I'm fine. I'm going to take myself straight to bed.'

I look up at him and flash my most responsible smile at him, but I suspect I look more like a child on the verge of a nap.

'I'll call you in the morning.'

I give him a thumbs up and encourage him to leave by making a shooing motion with my hands. He hesitates before backing away and closing the door behind him. Unable to find the light switches anywhere – someone clearly moved them all – I stretch my hands out in front to help guide my way through the dark. I find the entry hall table and the wall. I trip over something on the floor – my own feet, perhaps – as I make my way quietly into the kitchen where the lights turn themselves on.

'Please, make more noise next time.' Ant stands shirtless in shorts at the end of the bench with an amused smile on his face.

'Oh!' I pull my hands up to my mouth before whispering, 'Did I wake you?'

'You could have woken the people two streets down. I thought someone had broken in.'

'I was super quiet though.'

'Uh huh.'

I take a seat at the bench which steadies the place from spinning and place my forehead against the cool marble. Ant busies himself behind the counter and places a glass of water and two painkillers next to my head. 'Drink this. Take those.'

I do as I'm told. 'Do we have anything to eat?'

Ant scrounges around in the fridge and pulls out a plastic takeaway container. 'Chinese?'

'When did we have Chinese?'

'*We* had it tonight.' There's a playfulness to his tone as he heats up the leftovers.

'We who?'

'Don't make a big deal––'

I gasp. 'I would never!'

'But I've being seeing a bit of Levi.' He shrugs like it's not a big deal when, in actual fact, it is. Ant hasn't had a serious relationship in years. Sure, he's bought people home, but never the same person twice and he never randomly hangs out with them. I remember that he was M.I.A earlier this evening, and it all clicks together.

'Is that where you were earlier tonight? How long has this been going on? Is he here now? Does Nick know? Am I the last to find out?'

'Slow it down, Eminem. Don't fire questions at me.'

A huge smile spreads across my face. 'I'm just happy for you, Ant.'

The microwave beeps. Ant fetches the leftovers and two forks. We eat out of the container together.

'Yes, that's where I was earlier. Not long. Yes, he's asleep in my bed although how he slept through the noise you made I'll never know——'

'You're a light sleeper.' I point my fork at him.

'Yes, Nick knows, and no you're not the last to find out.' He answers all my questions and then flashes me a sheepish smile. 'I know it shouldn't work, he's so much younger than me, than *us*...,'

'So young!' I agree.

'But we just work. I like him. Don't give me that look.'

'What look?'

'That one. The proud mum on the verge of tears look.'

I chuckle. 'I am currently not in control of my emotions on account of the copious amounts of red wine I drank to avoid eating baby pig liver and kidney.' The thought makes my stomach turn.

I'll never get the appeal of fancy restaurants. Yes, the pasta was amazing, but do I need to pay close to one hundred dollars for it? No. Not that I paid, mind you. Milo did. Still, I can survive on regular pasta, thanks.

'I would have done the same. Where on earth did you go? And what's with the car?'

'I know! Weird, right?'

'Nick texted me. He thought so. I believe he called him a try hard or words to that effect.' He says it so casually. The mere mention of Nick's name does something to my insides. I can't quite tell if they're turning or fluttering. It all feels the same at this point of the evening. I fill Ant in on the date, from knocking the wine all over Milo's crotch to my parents being there to the food.

'You don't seem all glowy like you were the last time you went out with him.'

I take stock of his comment. 'I feel drunk glowy.'

'Not drunk in love glowy.'

'Thanks, Beyonce,' I deadpan. 'It's just...he kissed me, and I fell through the door.' Ant's eyebrows shoot so far up they almost shoot off his head. 'Not in a good way. As in, like I was trying to back away. I didn't intentionally do it. It just happened.'

Ant gives me a knowing look. 'Interesting.'

I ignore his jibe and continue to ramble, unable to filter anything that comes through my mouth. 'And the car. I mean, what was that? He didn't bring it out on the first date. He did nothing to indicate that he was loaded on the first date, and he is loaded, Ant. Like, disgustingly wealthy. His parents own Barrington Stationery.'

Ant gasps. 'Marry him.'

'Ant!'

'I don't care. I love stationery. Imagine all the free stuff we could get! The pens! You know I love a coloured pen.'

We share a laugh and finish off the leftovers.

'He's probably showing off a bit. He knows he's in competition for your affections, so he's upped his game. I mean, he's upped it by one hundred and fifty percent–'

'Exactly. Tonight just felt...showy. You know? The Bentley, Matteo's...it just felt like he was showing off.'

'He didn't stay to help you inside, either,' Ant points out.

'He respected my boundaries,' I correct. 'I asked him not to.'

Ant shrugs. 'If I'm dropping someone home who is clearly drunk--'

'Tipsy,' I correct again, but he ignores me.

'*Drunk*, I'm at least helping them find the light to walk through the house and not wake up their roommate.'

'I told him it was fine to leave.'

'And he left you alone, drunk, in the dark. What? He couldn't at least flick on one light switch?'

'You know how straight men are, Ant. They don't always think of things.'

'Mmm hmm. I know what a gentleman does, straight or not.'

I wave my hands dismissively at him. 'It's no big deal.'

Ant gives me a look that tells me we are going to agree to disagree on this one. I don't see a problem with Milo respecting my wishes and leaving me when I told him to. I didn't want him to come in. I didn't want to give off the impression that anything more was going to happen tonight. He did look annoyed though, as if he were expecting something more to happen. I curse myself for sleeping with him on the first date. It sets a precedent, an expectation that I really didn't think too much about.

Maybe I'm the one making this weird between us. I bailed on the date at his house and tonight I got too tipsy to even give him a proper goodbye kiss. I need to get my shit together before our next date. If there is a next date. Wait, do I want a next date? The thought stuns me.

'I'm going back to bed.' Ant announces, pulling me from my thoughts. 'You gonna be okay?'

'Can you help unzip me?' I wave my hands to indicate the back of my dress.

In one smooth move, Ant unzips my dress and plants a kiss on my cheek. 'Sweet dreams, Josie.'

'Love you,' I reply with a smile.

I hop down off the stool, and the place starts to spin as soon as my feet hit the floor. I walk with purpose to my room, dropping my dress as soon as the door closes behind me. I don't bother with trying to take off my makeup or finding my pyjamas. I fall straight into bed and pray to the universe that the room stops spinning.

Milo doesn't call me the next day as promised. In fact he doesn't contact me until I'm sitting across from Franki at brunch, waiting for our mother and Daniella to arrive. I managed to fill Franki in on the details of the date in a joint call yesterday, so today she gives me a cautious look as I check my messages.

'It's him,' I state, almost in a whisper, as if Milo had sent spies to lunch.

'What does His Royal Douche want?' She sips her drink.

Franki is not impressed by Milo. She was not impressed when I told her he was late, and she certainly wasn't impressed when I told her about the display of wealth. She was absolutely dead against him when I told her about the awkward kiss and him leaving me alone in a dark house a tad tipsy. Elle agreed with me and didn't think it was that big of a deal until Franki went on a rant and rave, picking apart my date or 'red flags' as she called them, and managed to drag Elle onto her side. Although Elle text me later saying she was really on the fence. I guess maybe that's how I feel too. The first date was great. I could easily have seen us together, but then Ant got in my head about the second date, and then the official date trial date...well that was the worst of them. I reply to his check-in message with something as equally short and to the point.

JOSIE

I'm fine. Just waiting at brunch for my mum.

MILO

I've got a great idea for our next date. When can I see you again?

I show the message to Franki, and she simply rolls her eyes. 'Never?'

I nudge her with my elbow. 'I don't know what the rules are. Should I be waiting for Nick to take me out or should I get my dates with Milo done first?'

'Has Nick asked you out yet?'

I shake my head. I haven't seen him since I asked him to zip up my dress. I hope I didn't step over some bro code line. I'm not even sure where the line is anymore.

'Just ditch him now, Josie. Save everyone the trouble. He's not the one.'

'We don't know that. Come on, it's only been two bad dates.'

And they weren't even that bad. A home cooked meal and a dinner at the top restaurant in the country. I've been on worse dates. Franki doesn't get to answer me, and I don't get to answer Milo because Mum walks into the restaurant. The way she carries herself demands attention, and I see people looking at her, as if trying to place who she might be, if she might be someone of significance.

'Here we go.' Franki says under her breath.

I stifle a giggle. Our mother is wearing black pants and a white dress shirt, her hair is paired back, and her lips have been painted red. We stand to greet her with a kiss on the cheek and a small hug. I take in what Franki and I are wearing, and we look completely out of place.

Franki has let her natural curls fall down past her shoulders and isn't wearing a lick of makeup. Dressed in a flower print maxi, she looks like she belongs by a resort pool. And me? I threw my hair up into a sleek pony tail and found the cleanest shift dress from my floordrobe. I managed a scraping of mascara and a blotting of lip gloss but that's it. Mum looks at us, biting back her criticism of what we're wearing.

'Daniella must be running late,' Franki states, talking of our younger sister.

'She's not coming,' Mum says, and I try to fight the automatic frown that crosses my face. She notices. 'She has something on with Chad.'

Franki and I share a look. Being the baby of the family, Daniella is always getting away with things, like not coming to brunch. She never has to fear Mum's wrath because she kept herself at arm's length from the family. As soon as she turned eighteen, she moved out of home and only showed up when things suited her. I'm both envious and in awe of my little sister and the way in which she so easily navigates being a Russo daughter. Nobody presses Mum further.

We order and make small talk which is mainly Mum discussing some grand future plans she and Dad have for the house. They always have plans for the house, and mostly they stay plans. I think Mum enjoys the excitement of the possibility of change rather than actually following through on any of it.

Franki and I aren't really listening though because we know we've been summoned here for something. We're just waiting for Mum to drop the bomb. She keeps us in suspense as she further rambles on about a number of uninteresting and unimportant topics.

'Anyway, I hope everyone can make it to Luca's school play this year especially as he'll be the lead,' Mum says proudly.

Luca is the son of one of Mum's oldest friends and her Godson. She treats him like the golden son she never had.

'Of course, no one would miss it,' I answer on behalf of everyone.

'Josephine, will you be bringing your new boyfriend?'

Franki chokes on her food beside me, and Mum gives her a disapproving glare. 'Josephine has a new man in her life. One that took her to Matteo's on Friday night. Isn't that wonderful?'

Franki shrugs her shoulders next to me. 'If that's your thing.'

'Isn't Matteo's everyone's thing?' Mum looks baffled at Franki's indifference. 'What was it again, that your new boyfriend does for a living?'

'He's not my boyfriend. It was just a date.'

'But you will be seeing him again?' She poses it as a question, but it feels more like a demand. 'It's just so wonderful to finally have all my girl's settled to such accomplished men who can look after you all.'

'Way to set feminism back, Mum,' Franki retorts, and Mum narrows her eyes at my sister.

'Is it so wrong for a mother to want the very best for her daughters, Francesca?' I can see Franki ball her hands into a fist along the sides of her dress. I subtly shake my head in her direction. Her jaw sets tighter. 'I just want my girls to be married to men who are reliable and can provide the sort of lifestyle you all deserve.'

Her words make my stomach turn. I have never relied on any man for anything, and I don't intend to. Including any man who may be so lucky as to marry me. I am more than capable and willing to provide for myself. I don't say as much because there is no point in arguing with Lorella Russo.

'Francesca, darling, you and Josh are doing quite well. I imagine once you're blessed with children that Josh's job will be more than sufficient to support you all.' Franki stiffens besides me. 'Chad seems to be doing quite well with his gyms so Daniella can quit that God awful job of hers. And Josephine seems to have found someone who can take care of her too. I know how much the classroom stresses you out, darling, and how many hours you're working.'

'Excuse me,' Franki stands, 'I'm just going to the bar.'

'It's not even noon, Francesca.'

'And yet, I feel a drink is very much needed.'

Mum looks horrified. 'What has gotten into your sister lately? Josh told your father at dinner the other night that she has been very busy at work, and they're hardly spending time together.'

First I've heard of any of this although Josh also has a tendency to exaggerate the truth. 'I'll go check.'

I stand and walk towards my sister who has taken a seat at the bar. 'You good?'

A drink is placed in front of her and she's downs half of it in record time. 'Relax, it's virgin.' She says when she sees my jaw hit the floor. 'I can't do it, Jose. I can't stand to have that woman devalue us every single damn time we see her.'

'She just has very different values to us. She grew up in different–'

'In different times?' she gives me a warning look, 'Josie, don't make excuses for her. She grew up a snob. She's placed all these expectations on us since we were little. We always had to be the best at whatever we did. Get the best grades, win all the awards.' A hurt laugh escapes her. 'Do you remember she encouraged me to date Rhys Caulfield because he was the dux of my year every damn year?'

'Wasn't he gay?'

'Yep. We fake dated just to get her off my back.'

I let out a snort of laughter. I remember when Franki told me how in love she was with Rhys, and I was careful not to point out the obvious. Turns out she knew all along. We were never that close growing up. Mum always pitted us against each other in some weird competition to see which sister could outdo the other. She had us believing that we were each other's biggest rivals until we grew up, moved out of home and saw each other as our greatest allies. At least, that's what happened with me and Franki. United in our enlightenment that everything we were led to believe growing up was complete and utter bullshit. Although I've always felt like the odd sheep in the family, I've felt more of a connection to Franki over these past few weeks. Makes me think I might have started my own little rebellion. And I reckon we could draw Daniella to the dark side too. She's already distant with mum. There's hope yet for a full on Russo sister rebellion.

'Josie, don't settle for Milo just because of what she says.'

I jolt backwards. 'I wouldn't.'

She slams down the rest of her drink. 'Good.'

There's an edge to her tone, a sharpness to her glare that I haven't noticed before. I press her on it. 'You sure you're okay?'

She chews her bottom lip as if deciding whether or not to divulge the thoughts running through her head. It makes me nervous. Franki is usually careful with her words, always so considered and thoughtful. However I've enjoyed getting to know my sister in a different light lately, one who straight up says what's on her mind. It's how I remember her as a teenager. How she was before she settled down and grew up. 'Yeah, fine. Don't worry about me. Mum just gets under my skin.'

'You sure?' I don't buy it. I don't press further because I know my sister, and if she doesn't want to talk about something, she won't. End of story.

'Positive. Let's go back and get through this brunch so we can get on with our Sunday.'

She leaps off the stool and marches back to our table. I hang back and bring her empty glass to my nose and sniff. Just as I suspected, definitely not virgin.

Chapter Twenty-Nine

NICK

It's Sunday morning and while most people my age are either nursing a headache or tending to babies, I'm surrounded by the wisdom and wrinkly skin of a bunch of men in their seventies and older. And I choose to be here. Who would have thought it?

It's the third morning in a row that I've gone for an early morning beach swim, and the third morning in a row that I have ended up in the cafe listening to these men trade war stories and bestow their advice from a life well lived on me. Some of their wisdom is little nuggets of gold; other suggestions belong back in the nineteen thirties. One thing is for certain, though; they don't miss a beat and collectively have the working memory of an elephant. Case in point, George is currently harassing me about my date with Josie.

'Why haven't you asked her out yet? Are you chicken or something?' He then proceeds to cluck to prove his point.

I shake my head and stifle a laugh. 'I've had a few things on. Besides, she went out on a date with someone else on Friday. He drives a Bentley. How am I supposed to compete with that?'

In amongst thinking through my father's proposal, I've been overthinking things with Josie. I've now gotten to the point where, yeah, I am second guessing myself and psyching myself out. I didn't see what time they came in the other night because I fell asleep on the couch, but I know it wasn't before midnight. Ant texted to let me know that Mr Money Bags took her to Matteo's. I shouldn't have expected anything less from a man who drives around in the latest model Bentley, which retails at more than most people's home deposit. I know the significance of that is lost on Josie, though; she thought a Twin Cam was an actual model of car.

Besides, Josie doesn't fall easily for all that pomp and show. At least, she never used to. Who knows what Josie on a find-me-a-husband deadline will fall for. I keep going backwards and forwards about what our date should look like, and now I'm so confused, I don't know what to do.

'You don't need to compete with him,' George says, 'he's clearly just shown his hand. You know, over compensating for something.' Chuckles ring out around the table. 'It means he has a small dick,' George continues to make his point, just in case anyone missed it. It makes me laugh even harder.

'We get it George,' Clancy warns. 'Nick, just be yourself. It's been working for you for so far.'

'Clancy's right,' John pipes in, 'just be yourself.'

'But bring her flowers. Always bring her flowers. Not just when you're sorry,' Clancy nods his head.

'Have you thought about where you are going to take her?' John asks, sipping his latte.

'I was originally thinking the drive-in but then–'

George scoffs and Clancy shakes his head.

'What? Is that not a good idea?' I'm solidly confused. The drive in is something I thought these old timers would one hundred percent endorse.

'You can't talk at a movie, even the drive in,' Clancy says.

'I don't think Nicky boy has talking in mind.' George's eyes light up like a naughty school boy who made a rude joke in front of the teacher.

'Doing something together is much better. Sharing a laugh, son.' Clancy smiles. 'Anyone can sit in silence and watch a movie. You want to do something that will actually make the date fun. You young people and your apps and your phones and your internet. You've all forgotten how to be social, what a good time really looks likes.'

Is it weird that I think he kind of has a point?

'The bowls club!' Clancy exclaims.

'Oh Clancy,' George shakes his head.

'No, no, George, Clancy might be onto something. We're celebrating our seventy fifth year as a club next Sunday. We're running a barefoot bowls competition supported by local live music. The club rooms will be open for drinks and refreshments.'

I think I may have swallowed too much sea water because this actually doesn't sound like a bad idea.

'The last time we ran barefoot bowls we had lots of young people try it out,' Clancy says proudly.

'That's because they were offering five-dollar pots of beer.'

Sold! 'That sounds alright,' I chime in.

'You can't go wrong with a bowls date, mark my words.' Clancy wags his finger at me.

If I were a superstitious man, I would have taken it as a warning.

That's how Josie and I end up at the local lawn bowls club in our bare feet surrounded by people who are closer to John, George and Clancy's age than our own. The pints of beer were light beer, the refreshments were homemade slices being sold by little old ladies in flower aprons and the live music was three guys sitting down playing their instruments out of tune, all singing different songs. Josie and I spend the first ten minutes of our date shaking our heads in fits of giggles, whispering quietly to one another.

'So, is this what you do when you're not at our house on the weekends?' she teases, and I can't help but grin back at her. She looks amazing in some off the shoulder peasant dress. John, George and Clancy just happen to be a couple of lanes over from us, pretending they don't know me, all the while giving me a thumbs up whenever Josie turns her back.

'You know me,' I shrug in answer to her questions.

'I bet you've been charming the old ladies. Hope their husbands don't mind.'

'Gotta keep 'em on their toes.'

This earns me a belly laugh from Josie that resonates through my body. She doesn't have a damn clue at how beautiful she is.

'So basically, I just have to roll my ball as close to that other one as possible?'

'Jack.'

'Who?' Josie looks around confused.

'No, no, it's called a jack. The ball at the end.' I take confidence in my knowledge that I downloaded from three old dudes at coffee this morning.

'Okay then, I just have to get as close as I can to the jack.'

'And you can knock another player's bowl out of the way. Closest to it at the end wins.'

Determination clouds her eyes and a wicked smile spreads across her face. 'You ready to lose, Davies?' she taunts me using my surname. Game on.

I chuckle. 'Bring it on, Russo. Ladies first.'

Josie saunters up to the plate and bowls a pretty straight first ball. We both lean as the bowl curls towards the end and let out a series of 'oohs' and 'ahhs' as her first shot just misses the jack. I line up and take my first shot, bowling it with too much force so that it bypasses everything and ends up in the gutter at the back of the pitch.

'This is going to be fun,' Josie says, placing her hand on my forearm. The touch is only feather light, but it's enough to send an electric current all the way to my groin.

'Care to make it interesting.' I cock an eyebrow at her.

She laughs. 'I think it already is but sure. What are you thinking?'

I look to the end of the pitch and then back at her. 'Alright, we're playing best of three,' she nods in agreement, 'the winner of each game can decide the prize.'

'Stated ahead of each game.'

'Fair.'

'What about the overall winner? What do they get?' Eager delight dances in her eyes.

I remind myself that this is a first date to show Josie that I'm serious about committing to a relationship and that making the prize my dick wrapped in a bow is probably not the way to show her how seriously I am taking this...competition. That's what this is, right, I'm competing against the Eye Doctor for her. I reign in my thoughts and keep them PG.

'A week off from cooking.'

I think I'm a genius. Whilst it's not exactly the prize I'd really like to be claiming, it does guarantee me a whole week of extra time with Josie that the other guy won't get. *Genius.*

'Does that mean you'll cook for Ant too?'

'You're so confident that you're winning, Josie,' I drawl.

'Oh I am. After that display,' she points to where my ball ended up in the gutter, 'I'm very confident.'

'How do you know I'm not lulling you into a false sense of security?'

She thinks it over for a moment. 'True. Still doesn't answer my question.'

'Okay then, yes. If I lose, I will cook for you and Ant.'

'And clean.'

'What?!'

'I'm just upping the stakes,' she says innocently, 'the loser not only has to cook but also clean up the dishes once we're done.'

'Fine.' The more time I can spend with her, the better.

'And, it has to be a cooked meal. No takeaway. No frozen dinners. Proper, home cooked meals.' She sticks her hand out.

I pretend to think it over when in fact I was sold from the second I brought it up. I'm no Master Chef, but I do alright in the kitchen. Hell, I might even throw this thing so I can show her just what a fucking domestic God I am. That can only work in my favour, right? I'm compiling a menu in my head when I take her hand in mine and shake it.

'You got yourself a deal, Russo. By the way, I like my steak medium rare.'

She laughs. 'You should know, we do meat free Mondays and tofu Tuesdays.'

I grimace. 'How can you be a picky eater and eat tofu?'

'It's all in the herbs.'

'You'd need a bucket load of 'em.'

She gives me a wry smile. 'Stop stalling, Nick, let's do this. What are you playing for in this first round?'

I rub my hands together. 'If I win, you let me buy you a drink.'

'They only have light beer.' She pokes her tongue out in disgust.

'I didn't say from here.' The corners of my mouth lift into a slow smirk.

Josie looks up at me from beneath her long lashes and my heart damn near beats out of my chest. 'Touché.'

'And you? What do you get *if* you win?' I place emphasis on the 'if' part.

'You mean, besides the glory of beating Nick Davies at a sport?' A mischievous grin spreads across her face. 'I want my car washed.'

'That's a big prize.'

'Hey,' she holds up her hands in defence, 'there were no rules about what the prizes could be. Not my fault you're thinking small.'

I chuckle and rub my hand over my beard. I'm more than

happy to play this game with her. 'Deal, Russo. You still drink vodka raspberries, yeah?'

'I guess you'll never know.' She picks up her next ball and bowls it straight down the line.

The ball lands next to her last one and they look like they're forming a wall around the jack. This is going to be tougher than I thought. She turns back to me and winks before letting me take my turn. This time my ball stays on the pitch but falls too short to be in contention.

'Just warming up,' I say as I head back to my spot behind the mat. I roll my shoulder as if I'm limbering up. 'Have you played before?'

Josie shakes her head. 'Beginners luck,' she says as she bowls another that falls in line with the rest, and I have a sneaky suspicion I'm being played.

Game one is done. We're sitting on the bench for a quick break while I look through the weather app to find the perfect day to give Josie's car a wash. We settle on the end of the week, so she has enough time to ensure the car is caked in dirt and grime. Again, the silver lining to all this is that I get to spend more time with Josie. Even if it entails her telling me I missed a spot and ordering me to keep scrubbing.

'If only I could put essay marking up as a prize,' she jokes as we sit down sipping our drinks in between rounds.

'Even I draw a line at that.'

'What,' she says playfully, 'you don't want to read twenty-five essays on how *Animal Farm* is an allegory of the Russian Revolution?'

I shake my head. 'I'd rather scoop my eyeballs out with a spoon.'

We share a laugh, and I'm reminded of how easy everything is with Josie. We've got history and friendship on our side, or on my side, depending on how you look at the situation. I had no reason to be concerned about how the date would go. We could do anything and manage to find the fun in it.

'Okay, Russo. You've won yourself a car wash. What's next on your wish list?'

'Ohhh.' She folds her arms over her chest, making the line of her dress dip into her cleavage. I sneak a look at her full chest. She notices and subtly squeezes them tighter. A smile tugs at the corner of my mouth while my jeans tug tighter over my package. 'My car is getting washed, and I won't have to cook and clean for a week,' she steals a glance at me, and I jokingly shake my head. 'I guess this time...hmmm, oh! I know! You can make my lunches for a week.'

'These are all very tame.' I give her a look.

'This is a first date, Nicholas. What kind of girl do you think I am?' She mocks offence.

'You and I both know what kind of girl you are,' I lean in closer so my lips linger near the crook of her neck and her breath hitches, 'or what kind of girl I can make you be.' She swallows hard and colour paints her cheeks. 'I'm playing for a kiss.' My voice is low and gravelly, not because I'm trying to turn her on but because I've already turned us both on and my mouth has gone so dry it's like the damn Sahara desert.

We stay in that position until she asks who's going first this round.

'I think you better. I might need a minute before I stand.'

She sucks in a short breath and slowly stands, making her way to the mat. The first bowl she throws down is completely offline and too fast down the pitch. I can't help but wonder if she wants that kiss as much as I do.

'You distracted me,' she says by way of explanation.

A knowing smirk spreads across my face. I stay silent and take my turn. My bowl lands so close to the jack, it's almost touching. We take the next few turns in relative silence, stealing knowing looks over the rims of our drinks. I make absolutely no secret of the fact that I am checking out her arse during every shot she takes. She knows because after a while, she begins to jut her sweet rear out a little further. It sends me wild. It's my final turn, and to be honest, it's looking pretty even. I need to knock one or two of her balls out of the way so that I have the upper hand and win this round. I'm desperate for that kiss. As I walk to the mat, Josie calls out to me. 'Watch out!'

I spin around in time to see a magpie flying right for my face. I try to duck and throw the bowl at it at the same time. The swooping magpie misses me by mere centimetres, but I can't say the same for the bowl. It lands with bone cracking accuracy on my foot, and I let out an almighty roar.

'Oh my God! Nick, are you okay?' Josie runs towards me, hands covering her mouth in shock, and I suspect covering a laugh as well.

'Yep. All good.'

'It doesn't look good.'

'I'm fine.'

Chapter Thirty

NICK

Turns out that I am very much not fine. I drew the crowd at the bowls club and the consensus was that my ballooning black foot was something that needed urgent medical attention. Which is how my date ended up driving me in my car to the hospital, and why we are now waiting in a packed emergency waiting room with other sick and injured people.

The guy to my left looks like he took a hammer to the head and the women sitting on the chair in front of us couldn't possibly have any more vomit left in her system. Not to mention the guy who is as high as a kite and yelling at the triage nurse. *Yeah, great date, Nick.*

'How's the pain?' Josie asks, concern lacing her voice.

The one good thing, and maybe the only good thing to come out of all of this, is the fact that the hospital is short staffed, so Josie has taken up the position as my personal nurse which means her hands have been all over me. Okay, all over my foot, but I'll take it.

'They've given me Panadol, Josie. I may as well have been throwing back M&Ms for all the good bloody Panadol is doing.'

'I guess they can't give you the good stuff until you're admitted.'

I look around the waiting room. 'I don't need a bed. Just x-ray my foot and chuck me in a chair. Surely it can't be that difficult.' I try to keep my temper in check. I'm not the most patient of people so being kept waiting for something that seems so simple to me really makes my blood boil. It's not a good combination when added to the excruciating pain in my right foot.

'Do you think it's broken?' Josie asks in all seriousness.

I hope not. That will put me off site for weeks, and I don't have that kind of leave up my sleeve. 'Nah,' I lie, 'probably just bruised.'

'It's definitely bruised alright.' Josie looks down at my foot, 'You actually have really nice toenails.'

Her offhand comment makes me chuckle. This chick. 'That's random.'

'Hmm, most men have like ingrown crusty nails. Yours are good.'

'I like to take care of myself. Everywhere.'

'Hmm, I never noticed before.'

'You have a sudden foot fetish or something?' That earns me a playful punch in the arm. 'Speaking of fetishes....'

'We weren't,' she interjects.

'What happened in that second game? If I were a betting man, I reckon you tanked a few of those bowls.'

'How is that in any way, related to fetishes?' she laughs.

I shrug. 'I couldn't think of a smooth segue.'

'So you went with fetishes.'

'I hurt, Josie,' I play up the victim role.

She rolls her eyes. 'Whatever.'

'You haven't answered my question.'

'Sounded more like a statement,' she taunts, and I can see she is buying time, deciding whether or not to tell me the truth. She doesn't need to; it's written all over her stained cheeks and in her smile.

'Would you care to support or challenge that statement then, Ms Russo?'

'I can neither confirm nor deny the allegations being thrown my way by Mr Davies.'

I let out a hearty chuckle which draws the eyes of those around us, but I don't care. Let them look at my chump arse with the hottest woman in the whole ER. Not a sentence I thought I'd be uttering, but here we are. 'Admit it, you want that kiss as much as I do.'

She shrugs. 'I guess we'll never know because the game was still in play. It was looking pretty even until that bird swooped in.' She fights a giggle.

'That bird was probably sent by your boyfriend to derail our date.'

An older lady looks disapprovingly at me. I can't be bothered to explain the weird situation that I find myself in, so I let her think whatever the hell she wants.

Josie is now laughing so much that she is crying and gasping for air. 'It...swooped...bang...foot.' She wipes tears from her eyes.

'Keep laughing,' I say dryly, and she leans into me for support, her body vibrating with laughter. I don't mind in the slightest.

'Sorry,' she gathers herself and lets out a deep breath, 'woo! That was funny.'

'I think I was going to win that one,' I say confidently because I definitely was. 'Besides, I'm hurt, so that should automatically make me the winner by default.'

'I'm not giving you the win,' she argues before a nurse finally calls my name.

Josie stands and waves at the nurse to tell her that we're here before she pushes me in the hospital wheelchair through the doors and onto the emergency ward.

. . .

I'm not exactly sure what the rules are dating wise, so as she helps me through my front door, I can't help but feel like I've found another loophole to spend more time with her. Granted, it's a big, black throbbing loophole that is going to make my life difficult over the next week but a loophole nonetheless.

She places her arm around my middle while I loop an arm around her shoulders, and we both pretend that she is carrying my weight through the front door and onto the couch. My body reacts to her familiar touch and heat radiates from just below my ribs where her hand is resting. I carefully sit and she immediately uses some nearby cushions to make a tower for my foot to rest on.

'There. Is that comfortable?' She looks at my foot, assessing her handiwork.

'About as comfortable as I can be.'

'I'll go and grab the crutches from the car.'

'I'm not using those things.'

She places her hands on her hips. 'The doctor said–'

'The doctor doesn't live here. Look around, Josie. I can literally walk through my unit leaning on the furniture. It's not like I'm living in an expansive mansion. I'll manage just fine.'

She throws her hands up in defeat. 'Fine. Be a baby. I'll leave them by the front door for when you go out. Did you call your dad?'

I shake my head. 'I'll be right by tomorrow.'

She stares at me like I'm from out of space. 'The doctor said you needed to rest it.'

'He said I'd be able to go to work.'

She rubs her hand over her temples. 'He said that you *might* be able to start walking on it by the end of the week.'

'Midweek. And if I can walk on it, I can work.'

Josie looks exacerbated. 'What have you got against rest and recover?'

Everything. I don't do well sitting around the house feeling sorry for myself. I don't do still. If I do still then the noise in my brain gets louder. If the noise in my brain gets louder, then the panic attacks happen. I am not sitting around doing nothing for the next week. It's not broken, just bruised. It'll smart to walk on but hey, I can handle it. It's better than the alternative. Of course, I don't mention any of this to Josie, not in as many words. 'I don't like being still.'

'I know you get bored easily, Nick,' it feels like a loaded statement, 'but I think you should listen to the doctor, otherwise you'll risk doing further damage.'

'How?' I'm just being difficult now because I can. And because I don't like being told to sit still and be a good boy.

'I don't know! I'm not a doctor.'

'Exactly.'

'I'm just relaying what the doctor said.' She flops down on the couch next to me and rolls her head to the side. She looks at me with her dark eyes as if weighing something up. I hope it's the same thing I'm weighing up because not being able to reach out and kiss her, or hold her like I normally would, is torture. What I wouldn't give to be inside her head right now.

'This isn't exactly how I pictured our first real date going,' I say softly, my eyes bouncing between hers and her full lips. 'It's had the same desired outcome though.'

'What's that exactly?' Her eyes focus on mine.

'You back here with me.'

Her smile is soft. 'You went to extreme measures to make that happen.'

'I'd do anything, to make that happen. Josie, you belong here. With me.'

'I think that might just be your meds talking.'

'Or maybe they're just giving me the courage to say what I've always felt.'

Her eyes dart so quickly to my lips that I think I imagined it. 'Tell me again when you're not hopped up on pain medication.' She stands to leave, but I catch her hand, and she stills in place. 'I better go and make sure Ant put those flowers you bought me in a vase. Can I help you with anything before I leave?'

Her offer is sincere. It always is. I shake my head in response. 'I'm good. Thanks.'

She lets go of my hand and walks to the door. I can hear her pause, so I peer over the top of the couch. 'I think you won that second game, Nick.'

A grin spreads across my face. 'Does that mean I can claim my prize?'

'Only after I've claimed mine. Fair's fair.' The corners of her mouth lift into a small smile.

I have the distinct feeling that nothing about this whole situation is fair.

Chapter Thirty-One

JOSIE

After both first dates, I'm no closer to knowing who I have stronger feelings for. Milo and I had such great chemistry the very first time we went out, chemistry unlike I've ever had with anyone. It felt electric, but since then there's barely been a spark. Surely if it was there before, we can find it again?

As for Nick, I just can't move past the nagging feeling in my gut telling me something isn't quite right. I question the timing of his intentions and whether or not we're better off as friends. Franki and I catch up with Elle at her house on Wednesday. Once Harlow and Jaggar are asleep, we eat our weight in charcuterie board and talk through my dilemma.

'Do you think you're looking for excuses to not fall for Nick?' Franki says, popping another cracker with soft, creamy camembert on it into her mouth.

'No.' I say because, honestly, the thought never crossed my mind. I have enough reasons not to fall for Nick. I don't need to look for excuses.

'Your sister may have a point,' Elle concedes.

'Whose side are you on? One minute you're Team Nick and the next you're Team Milo. You tell me to give Milo the benefit of the doubt, and then you tell me Nick and I are perfect for each other.'

Elle runs a hand through her hair. 'I know! My mind is all over the place.'

'Everything okay?' I probe. It wasn't so much what she said but how she said it. Despite being best friends, Elle can be a really private person which means that I only know when things are bad after they've come good again.

'I'm fine. Just sleep deprived and trying to keep up with your drama.' She throws a single, discarded nut in my direction which I catch in my mouth. We cheer loudly only to have Elle's husband Rich come in and shush us. We all pause as if frozen in time, waiting to hear if our cheers have woken the kids. After a silent moment or two, we resume our discussion.

'I think,' Franki says, curling her feet under her, 'that you're trying to make something happen with Milo, so you don't have to face your feelings for Nick.'

I roll my eyes. 'That makes no sense. If I'm looking to settle down with someone, why would I ignore my feelings for Nick?'

'Because you're in a rush to do all of this by your next birthday and you're not thinking clearly,' Elle adds as if it's obvious.

'And because you have more to lose with Nick. You guys have been close enough to dating for the past two years, and if you start to label it and voice your feelings now, you'll have more to lose if anything goes wrong. A bigger heartbreak, if you will. And a destroyed friendship.'

'Not that anything will go wrong,' Elle rushes to add.

'Pick a side, Elle!' Franki and I say in unison which makes the three of us giggle.

I'm not afraid of my feelings for Nick. They're there. I know I have them and I know that right now he thinks he has them for me too, but I just can't shake the feeling that his are fleeting.

When I first met Nick, he told me that he never stuck at anything longer than four years; not jobs, not friendships and not relationships. Next year, we will be coming up on Nick's fourth year in Littleton Beach. That means his fourth year in his unit, working for his dad and in our friendship group. I can't afford to give my all to someone who is only going to pack up and leave in less than twelve months.

'And perhaps your hesitation around Milo is because you know where you should be.'

'But it makes no sense, Elle,' I moan and fall backwards into the couch. 'How can Milo and I have such great chemistry one moment and then have it fizzle out after having sex. Shouldn't it get better?'

'It should,' Franki states, matter of factly, 'and it does. With the right person.'

'You and Nick have been hooking up for two years, and it hasn't affected your chemistry one little bit.' Elle wags her finger at me like I'm a naughty child.

'Does it bother you that you're always right?' I groan.

'Just stating facts,' she shrugs with a knowing smile.

'Okay, so what, I just forget about Milo?'

'No.'

'Yes.'

Elle and Franki speak at the same time.

'No,' Elle says, placing emphasis on the vowel, 'give him one more date. See if that chemistry is still there. I mean, maybe he's nervous too. You did tell the guy he is essentially competing for your love. If the chemistry is not there this time, then you'll have your answer.'

I groan. 'This would be so much easier if Zac Efron just suddenly appeared to sweep me off my feet.'

When I drive into the shared driveway of our block of units, I see Nick and Ant arriving home. Ant is baring the weight of both of them as they hobble up the driveway with Nick's arm slung around Ant's neck. I pull into our driveway and meet them at Nick's front door.

'What are you two doing?' It comes out like a scold.

'He wanted to go for a walk.' Ant shrugs. 'Guess he's not quite ready.'

I follow the boys inside and help Ant take Nick to the bedroom.

'What is it with you boys and not listening to medical advice?'

'The doctor said I should be fine to do some light walking on it now,' Nick pleads.

'The doctor said that in the belief that you were going to rest it and stay off it for a couple of days. I haven't seen you do that yet.'

Nick pulls himself to a sitting position on the bed, and I help arrange the pillows behind him, so he is comfortable.

'I'll grab you a drink and some more pain meds. Josie can help you get undressed.' Ant winks mischievously before slipping out the door.

Nick looks as if he's holding back a laugh whilst stretching out his arms to welcome me to do as Ant suggested. I take in his grey sweat pants and t-shirt. 'You're fine in what you're in.'

'I normally sleep naked, you know that,' he chides.

'Well, tonight will be an exception.'

He chuckles. 'Jose, you know I wouldn't expect that of you. I'm just mucking around.'

I do. I know that Nick would never expect anything from me that I wasn't comfortable doing. Despite his stubbornness, flirtatious nature and dirty mind, Nick is, overall, a good guy.

Ant enters the room with a glass of water and a packet of pain killers. 'I'm just making you some toast. Shouldn't have those on an empty stomach.' And just as quickly as he entered, he leaves the room again.

'He's gonna make such a good husband to someone one day.' Nick comments.

I take a seat on the bed next to Nick. His hand instinctively falls to the small of my back. I let his thumb circle for a brief moment before shifting.

'Sorry,' I say quietly.

'I won't bite, Jose. Unless you want me to.'

The joke brings a smile to my face and eases some of the tension. His room is as familiar as my own, and my body tingles with anticipation. Confusion engulfs me. I shouldn't be having this strong physical reaction to this space, *his* space, and yet I am. His blue eyes draw me in, and I drink him up.

What does it really say about me that I find his vulnerability attractive right now? I'd like to think it's the affect powder-grey sweats and a backwards cap have on me, but there's something more that hangs in the air around us. It's getting more difficult to deny.

'Ant looks like he's got a handle on this, I might just head home.' I point to the door but don't move.

I find myself wanting him to ask me to stay. Silently, I beg him in my head. Need me. Want me. Tell me you want me to stay. He opens his mouth as if to say something but thinks better of it and offers me a straight, strained smile.

'Goodnight then, Josie.'

Disappointment clogs my chest. 'Goodnight, Nick.'

I slowly exit his room, hoping he'll call me back, but he doesn't. The last sound I hear is Ant asking if the plates in the dishwasher are clean before I close the front door behind me and walk home.

Chapter Thirty-Two

NICK

I should have asked her to stay. We both knew I wanted her to stay, so why couldn't I say the damn words? Our date didn't go perfectly, but it ended on a pretty good note. She all but promised me a kiss. At least, I thought that was a good note. She's been checking in on me all week but tonight she seemed different. There was an awkward aura around her. I hate that term, but I have no other way to describe it. I need help. I need an inside woman to give me the lowdown. Ant's given little away, and I have a feeling that what Josie discusses with Ant is different to what she discusses with Elle. I pull up the message thread that I have with Elle and begin to type.

NICK

Need your help. I need the inside scoop.

ELLE

I was wondering how long it would take
before you came begging for my help.

NICK

Consider me on my hands and knees with my tail between my legs.

ELLE

As cute as that is, sorry Nick. Girl Code. You get it.

NICK

You wouldn't be breaking girl code. You'd be helping your best friend of many years, who you love dearly, live happily ever after.

ELLE

Let me guess...happily ever after with you, right?

NICK

Right.

ELLE

How do you know I'm not #TeamMilo

NICK

Ummm, have you met me? I'm irresistible.

ELLE

And soooo modest.

NICK

I just need to know where Josie's heads at? She's so hard to read atm

ELLE

She's confused. What else can I say?

NICK

More than that! Am I at least winning?

ELLE

It's not a game, Nick.

NICK

I didn't mean it like that. Sorry! Elle, I'm just...

I run a hand over my beard. I didn't mean to make it sound like a game. I know it's not a game. I sigh wondering how much I should tell Elle. There's every chance she'll screen shot this and send it to Josie. You know, Girl Code and all. Wouldn't be so bad if she did though. Might make it easier to tell Josie how I feel.

NICK

I don't want to lose her, Elle. I can't lose her.

ELLE

Then tell her that! She's worried that if she picks you she's buying a one-way ticket to heartbreak town.

NICK

She said that?

My heart sinks. Breaking her heart is the last thing I would ever want to do. I don't know what more I need to do to prove to everyone that they've painted the wrong picture of me.

ELLE

Not in so many words. That's more Franki's conclusion, and I happen to agree.

NICK

Her sister? Her family hate me!

ELLE

I can assure you that's not true. Franki is very much #TeamNick. Besides, have you met you? You're irresistible.

NICK

Very ducking funny, Elle. HELP ME!

ELLE

duck emoji *crying laughing face emoji*

NICK

bloody auto correct.

ELLE

Just tell her how you feel. Lay it all on the line. Don't leave her guessing. You know how she gets in her own head sometimes.

NICK

That simple, huh?

ELLE

That simple xo

Chapter Thirty-Three

JOSIE

I arrive at date number two with Milo with an open mind. If I'm serious about settling down and starting a family with the right man, then I need to make sure my judgement isn't clouded.

Seeing Nick helpless and somewhat vulnerable, well as vulnerable as he'll allow me to see him, very much clouded everything. The whole time I've known Nick, he's had this macho male bravado about him. I've been trying to tear it down; however, I haven't gotten very far. Until now. Our talk on the beach and now having him actually accept help with his foot, however minimal it is, feels like I've finally broken through that barrier, and it's...alluring. I wonder if it's been the missing piece to seeing him as something more. But I have to push all that out the way right now because I need to focus on Milo, give him that benefit of the doubt that Elle was talking about. Or at least, that's where I think she currently stands.

Currently, *I'm* standing on the dock at Littleton Beach Marina looking at a small yacht with a very handsome Milo smiling down upon me. Dressed in khaki shorts and a polo top with Ray-Bans shielding his eyes, and his dark hair looking perfectly windswept, Milo looks every inch the poster boy for sailing. Sign me up!

'Have you ever sailed before?' He smiles at me and helps me aboard.

'I don't think I've ever been on a boat before.'

'How can you live by the water and never been on a boat before?'

'Well, you know, sharks, giant octopus – that's enough to make me stay on dry land.'

He chuckles and shakes his head. 'Well, I promise we won't see any of those today.'

'You can't promise that! The ocean is their home. And I forgot about whales. I've seen videos on the internet of whales causing all sorts of damage to boats, even ones bigger than this one.'

'You need to stop Googling things like that.'

I settle on a cushioned spot at the front (the bow? Or the stern?) of the yacht. 'I don't Google these things, Milo. It's the algorithm. What sort of things do you get on your For You pages?'

'Nothing. I don't really have social media.'

My jaw almost hits the ocean floor. 'How? How is that possible?

He smiles. 'I just don't have the time. Or interest. I'd rather be doing something like this.' He gestures around, and I'm aware we're suddenly moving.

'How are we moving?' I try to grip onto something, but the cushions fall through my fingers.

'It's okay. Whilst I'm more than capable of sailing this yacht by myself, I've charted it for today, so you and I can enjoy our time together.'

A little part of me relaxes as I realise this means that he won't be shouting at me to tie knots and let sails down. We have a captain and crew for that which is a good thing because I clearly have no idea what I'm doing. I don't even know the bow from the stern!

Milo opens a small picnic basket unpacking an array of delicious looking treats alongside a bottle of champagne and two glasses. We toast to 'new adventures' and the bubbles help me relax further.

I think I quite like yachting. Is that what it's called? The water is calm, the breeze is warm, and the sun is glorious. I get what Rose meant when she told Jack she was flying on the Titanic. There's something about the wind in your face and rhythmic dip of the yacht that makes you feel like you're gliding through the air.

'I can see why you love this so much.' I recline back into Milo, cuddle up to his side. He cups his arm around me. 'Do you prefer sailing it yourself or being chauffeured like today?'

He smiles down at me. 'Right now, this is pretty much perfect.'

He leans in and plants a gentle kiss on my lips. I part them slightly as an invitation for him to kiss me deeper which he takes. Our mouths move to the rhythm of the dipping of the yacht, slow and deep, hypnotic. Without breaking the connection, I feel Milo twist his body away slightly to place his glass down, before taking mine from my hand and doing the same. He then reaches his free hand to slowly caress my thighs, edging bit by bit under my skirt.

We stay like that, kissing for what feels like an eternity. I can feel his excitement pressed against my thigh. I run my fingers through his hair and down his back as he shivers under my touch. He withdraws from my lips, and I find they're not the only part of me aching for more.

'Why did you stop?' I pout, running my fingers through the ends of his hair. He lets out a satisfied groan, and I make note to do that again just so I can hear him make that noise.

'Because if I don't stop now, I won't be able to.'

He shifts off me and onto his side, adjusting himself in the process. I sit up, reach over to grab my glass and take a sip of champagne that has gone warm. This is a different Milo to Restaurant Milo. This is more like the First Time We Met Milo. Maybe it's the fresh air, but he seems different. More likeable. Restaurant Milo was too...arrogant. Will the real Milo Barrington please stand up?

'What do you think of your first sailing experience so far?' A smile dances on his lips.

'Can't complain,' I smile back. 'I bet all the girls say that though,' I tease.

'I wouldn't know.'

'Oh bull.'

'What?' he proclaims innocence.

'Don't try and tell me I'm the first girl you've bought sailing.' I roll my eyes behind my glasses.

'You're right, you're not. But normally I try to impress them by sailing it myself. Turns out women don't really like to be made to work on a date. Or so they say.'

'So they do complain.'

'They don't stick around long enough to complain. Usually, it's the dealbreaker date.'

'And yet here I am, on your deal breaker date.' I say carefully. Maybe he's testing me as much as I'm testing him.

'The difference is we're being chauffeured, as you put it.' I wish I could see his eyes right now to gauge the sincerity in his voice. 'I'm pulling out the big guns, Josie. I want to impress you.'

Butterflies make waves in my stomach. 'You think you need all of this to impress me?'

'I don't know. Maybe.'

I shuffle closer to him. 'I don't need the big guns to be impressed. I'm not that kind of woman.'

'I know. That's what's slightly terrifying about you.'

'Me? *I'm* terrifying?' I can't help but laugh in disbelief. 'I'm about as terrifying as a butterfly.'

'Hey, some people have legitimate phobias of butterflies.' He makes a point, then smiles to let me know he was only joking.

'You're terrifying because I can't quite read you. Like that first dinner we had,' I nod to show I remember, 'that was...wow! That was great! Amazing, even.' I can't tell if he blushes at the memory, or if it's a reaction to the sun. 'Then you came over for dinner and things were weird.'

'Weird,' I confirm.

'Then at Matteo's...I don't know. Things just felt off. I just keep wondering how we went from...whoa!' He makes a hand gesture like an explosion. 'To, whoa!' Another gesture that very clearly signals stop.

There's an awkward sort of comfort in knowing that he also noticed the weird trajectory this courtship has taken.

'I started thinking maybe I had done something wrong or maybe it was the other guy you're sort of seeing.'

A pang of guilt contracts my chest as he says the words. I stop myself from asking if it bothers him because I have every right to date who I want. We've made no commitment to each other and I resent the fact that as a woman, I'm expected to be loyal to even the slightest interest in me.

He continues, 'So I thought if I showed you at Matteo's, you know, that I'm wealthy, it might make a difference. Might make things go back to the way they were on the first night.'

'So you think I'm materialistic?' I try not to let the offence influence my calm tone, but on the inside, I'm fuming at the insinuation.

'No, no,' he drags his hands over his face in regret, 'not in the slightest. It was a dumb move, and I felt awkward the whole night. I'm not *that* guy. And then at the end of the night, I was mad at myself for putting on such a stupid show. Then you didn't even want me to help you inside. I thought I'd blown it.'

'So, charting a yacht isn't a big display?'

'It probably is. But I guess this is more me, out on the water. This is what I like to do with my spare time, sailing, skiing, swimming. The guys are only here because I wanted to spend time with you.'

I believe him. I think I'm also flattered that someone has gone to so much effort to try to impress me.

'I can even teach you to sail one day, if you'd like,' he adds sheepishly.

I lean in and kiss him. 'Thank you.'

'For what?'

'Being honest. For trying so hard. I know this has been...I mean, I've been confused too. I've thought the same as you, like why was it so amazing the first time and then it's been...maybe it was the sex? Maybe we rushed it...'

'I thought that part was pretty incredible.'

I make a noise to acknowledge what he said. Incredible? Not so much. I may have led the boys to think that the morning after, but they were being rude, and I was in the mood to be petty. Besides, I couldn't very well let Nick believe anything different. He and I have had incredible sex before; the night we spent together in the middle of nowhere in his broken-down ute waiting for a tow truck is the bench mark that all other experiences are measured against. What Milo and I did was good, fun. But incredible? I can't commit to that. I try to banish memories of Nick and that night from my thoughts. They're not conducive to keeping an open mind with Milo. They refuse to leave.

Milo obviously reads my muffled sounds as if I agree with him about our night together being incredible because he rushes to kiss me with his tongue, hungrily poking around my mouth. I lean back and break away from the kiss.

'We can always do a do over of that night,' he suggests.

I wriggle out from him, sitting up straighter. 'I can't, Milo. Not while I'm...'

'Still seeing the other guy,' he finishes the sentence for me.

'I'm sorry.'

He waves his hand dismissively. 'I get it. It's fine. In a weird way, it's a relief to know you're not *with* both of us.'

I try not to let offence be the first emotion I feel, and I try to think about how I would feel if the shoe was on the other foot.

What if he is seeing someone else? He said it was only me, but what if he's changed his mind? Should I ask him? That would be hypocritical.

I keep thinking about myself and the choice I have to make at the end of the three dates. It never really occurred to me that he might be seeing someone else too. That I might be competing for him now. My heart palpitates at the thought. Something takes over, a moment of jealously? A moment of pity? Whatever it is, I find myself launching back into his arms and kissing him like the world is about to end. I don't know if the kiss is reassurance for him that I'm still interested, or if I'm staking a claim against someone I'm not sure even exists, but it is enough to make me forget everything else for the rest of the afternoon.

Chapter Thirty-Four

NICK

I didn't want to make a big deal about my foot, but apparently I live next door to two overly dramatic people who have relentlessly pestered me about following up with a second medical opinion. As a result, Ant and I pull up to my place, with me sporting a shiny new moon-boot to wear for the next six to eight weeks thanks to a hairline fracture in my foot. Remind me to never again go barefoot anywhere near a ball or bowl of any kind.

'What in the...,' Josie exclaims as she sees me arrive home.

She looks like she's just arrived home too, although her date is nowhere to be seen and for that I'm grateful. And smug.

'What happened to your foot now?'

'This old thing,' I shake my foot with the boot and try not to wince in pain. Dumb idea. Noted.

'Hairline fracture in his foot,' Ant answers for me.

Josie follows us inside. 'I feel so bad.'

'Why?'

'Well it was my date that caused it.'

'So, are you saying you're calling this whole ridiculous thing off then?'

She gives me that teacher look of hers, and I know the answer immediately. Need to do more than break my stupid foot to get her to dump a Cup of Milo. Roger that.

'And then I laughed at you. Nick, I'm so sorry.' Her apology is sincere.

We each take up a seat at the table.

'You should ring your dad to let him know. You probably won't be able to go to work. Won't it violate some insurance thing or another?' Ant reminds me.

'I'll deal with it later. How was your date?' It kills me to even think about her date let alone to come straight out and ask her about it. I think I might be part sadist.

'I can't tell you.'

She's acting like a giddy teenager with something to hide. That isn't good. 'Why not? You know word will get back to me anyway so why not cut out the middle man.'

Her gazes shoots to Ant who doesn't even try and deny it. 'I've already told you that I'm firmly on Team Nick.'

'Should we get t-shirts made up?' I say to annoy Josie more than anything. Although t-shirts saying Team Nick do sound like a fabulous idea.

'Fine! We had a great time. We went sailing.'

'As in on a boat?'

'As in on a yacht. We ate chocolate covered strawberries and drank champagne. It was really lovely. Is that enough detail for you?'

Too much.

'Sounds like something *The Bachelor* cooked up,' Ant jokes, and we mentally high five each other.

'Well, no one ended up in the hospital, so I'd say it was rather dull and uneventful,' I tease.

She tries to hide a grin that refuses to be locked away around me.

'You hate the ocean,' Ant adds.

'I didn't mind it today,' she adds coyly.

I hate to admit it, but she seems to be glowing. Fucking glowing. And I don't mean because she got sunburnt. I mean the glow of a satisfied woman. I should know. I've seen that same look on her many, *many* times before at my own doing. My stomach churns in knots and there's a quiet, jealous rage burning in my chest. I don't want to ask. I have no right to ask, but my brain and my mouth are under different management teams.

'Did you two–'

'Did you have to sail it yourself?' Ant talks over me, sensing I was about to say something stupid. I shoot a quick thanks in his direction.

Josie shakes her head. 'He had it charted.'

Of course he did. Old Money Bags pulling out the lavish dates while all I manage to organise is lawn bowls with the oldies and a trip to the ER.

A knock on the door helps to stop me from blurting out something else stupid. Ant answers it and the blood drains from my face when Tori walks in with two shopping bags full of groceries, wearing little more than a crop top and booty shorts.

'I was just on my way home from the gym,' Tori beams, and Josie clears her throat. I get it. Tori looks like she's stepped out from an activewear shoot rather than the gym, but I give her the benefit of the doubt, 'and thought I'd pop in. Ant was telling me this morning that you had broken your foot, so I picked up some things up for you in case you couldn't get to the shops.' Tori smiles innocently.

I shoot Ant a warning look which he expertly deflects. I hadn't even had it x-rayed yet, and he was running his mouth. Proves his ambush of taking me to the hospital was pre-meditated. The nerve.

'That's thoughtful of you, Tori. Isn't that thoughtful of Tori, Nick?' Ant encourages.

I catch a glimpse of Josie looking between everyone standing in my small kitchen dining area.

'I'm sorry, I don't believe we've met.' And just like that, my nightmares come alive as Josie walks towards Tori, hand outstretched. 'I'm Josie, Nick's...neighbour.'

Neighbour? That's how she wants to introduce herself? Her date with Milo must have gone better than I thought. Although how does one describe our current situation? We're neighbours who have been sleeping together for the past two years and are now dating?

'Tori. Nick and I are seeing each other.' Tori smiles as she takes Josie's hand for a pretty flimsy handshake.

My stomach drops. Ant stifles a laugh whilst Josie looks like one of those cartoon characters whose eyes have bulged out of her head. Tori, on the other hand, looks like the cat that got the cream. I notice that her smile doesn't radiate the way Josie's does.

'Hello? Anyone home?' A voice comes through my front door.

'You have got to be kidding me,' I mumble and scrape my hands over my face.

My dad pokes his head around the corner and takes in the people before him. 'Ah, sorry. This a bad time?'

'Is there any other time?' I groan.

'I'm Greg, Nick's dad.' He gives an awkward wave around the room, his eyes lingering on Tori and Josie trying to figure out what is going on. 'Ant rang and told me you've got a bit of trouble with your foot.'

I shoot daggers at Ant who looks like he's rather enjoying my current situation, not at all remorseful for causing it.

'It's fine. I can walk on it.'

'Doesn't look good, mate.'

'I'm sorry, you're *seeing* each other?' Josie turns to me for an explanation.

'Not really–'

'What was the other night then, Nick?' Tori slams down the shopping bags with more force than necessary.

'Oh, I remember you from the other night. When I came to see Nick.' Dad wags his finger at Tori, and I want to die. Right here. Right now. 'I didn't mean to interrupt anything.'

Kill me.

Josie's eyes practically bug out of her head.

'It's not what any of you think.'

'Oh, you don't know the things I'm thinking right now, Nick.' Josie's voice is thick with anger.

'I bought some things to make a pasta. I thought I could cook for you, Nick,' Tori offers. 'Would you like to stay?' She turns to my dad and he accepts.

Josie shakes her head and now has her gaze locked on Ant. They appear to be having some sort of telepathic conversation, no doubt her plotting my demise. It's all too much, and I snap.

'Stop! Dad, you're not staying for dinner because Tori you're not cooking me any. Thank you, but I can cook my own. I have a small fracture in my foot, I'm not completely incapacitated. You,' I point at Josie who looks stunned, 'you don't get to be mad at me. Tori and I are not seeing each other, but even if we were, you have no right to judge because you're seeing me *and* Milo.'

Tori whimpers behind me, and Dad scratches his head. I leave no time for explanations as I continue my rant around the room. 'Tori, I'm sorry but it's just not like that for us. I shouldn't have led you back here that night knowing it was never going to be a thing.'

Her face heats up and now she is shooting daggers at me. I wait for her to say something, but she doesn't, so I continue. 'And you,' I round on Ant, 'you've got the biggest fucking mouth of anyone I know. Stop talking about me to people!'

The room falls silent. Tori is the first to leave. Dad is the first one to speak. 'I can see this is a bad time. I'll swing by tomorrow, and we can talk about that thing that I asked you about.' He leaves.

Josie and I pick a different spot on the floor to fix our gaze while Ant stands with his arms folded across his chest. I'm in his direct line of sight. 'You know, man, if you just opened up to people once in a while....'

'I didn't need you to tell my dad on me,' I say. It's light-hearted and eases the tension.

'Yes you did, you clown. You hadn't even told him that you hurt your foot. He's not only your dad, but your boss as well. He needed to know.'

'You're like the snitchy little brother I never wanted.'

Ant scoffs. 'More like the big brother who'll kick your arse to keep you in line.'

I huff out a chuckle. 'Tori?'

'I swear,' Ant dramatically holds his hands up in defence, 'I saw her at the gym this morning, and she asked where you were. I said you had mostly likely broken your foot and that I was taking you to get x-rays today. That's it. It was a five second conversation.'

'I'm so confused,' Josie mutters.

'Tori works at the gym. She's his gym stalker,' Ant explains.

'So...you're not seeing her?'

A smile hitches the corner of my mouth. Josie is jealous. As bright as day, Josie is one hundred percent jealous. It gives me hope. Jealousy is a sign that she cares. 'I told you, I'm only interested in you.'

'She's delusional. I *never* thought she'd come here with groceries. I mean, A plus for effort. Girl tried to shoot her shot,' Ant muses.

'I think we need to find a new gym.'

'I think I need to go and lie down.' Josie walks towards the door.

'Hey, Josie,' I call out to her and she pauses and turns towards me. And because I'm a jerk, I tease her, 'You like me.' She scoffs, but I continue, 'You can't deny it. You wanted to rip Tori's hair out when you thought we were together.'

'You looked like fire was about to come out of your mouth at any moment,' Ant joins in.

'You like me, Josie. Admit it,' I call after her as she turns and walks out the door, flipping us both the bird.

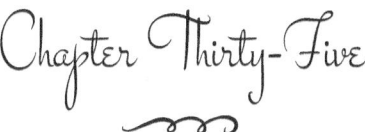

Chapter Thirty-Five

JOSIE

I feel like I am suffering emotional whiplash. The last half an hour has been...something. Arriving home from my date with Milo, I was on a high. The date was amazing but seeing Nick immediately afterwards made me feel like a huge wave of guilt was crashing down around me.

To see him in his boot created a sense of urgency to be with him. And then when Tori said they were dating...well, I've never felt so much blind rage. Then the wave of guilt hit me again because who the hell do I think I am?

As Nick so rightfully pointed out, I'm seeing two men at once. I don't get to be jealous and yet today the thought of either man dating someone else has seen me wear a shade of jealous that feels ugly. I can't figure out what it means. Does it mean I care for both of them? Or does it mean I'm just a selfish brat? Not long after I leave Nick's place, Ant arrives home and flops down on the couch beside me.

'How bad is his foot?' I know Nick won't ever divulge the true extent of his injury or just how sore he actually is. He is the walking stereotypical Australian male with the 'she'll be right' kind of attitude.

'For once he's not downplaying it,' Ant responds. 'It is just a hairline fracture. The boot will help. Doc says he can walk with the boot on and everything.'

'I hope his dad can find something for him to do because he'll be a nightmare if he has to sit around the house all day.'

'I'm sure they'll figure something out. I'm heading out for dinner. Not sure when I'll be home.'

I waggle my eyebrows at him. 'Or if?'

'Shut up.'

'You're blushing! Ant, I don't think I've ever seen you blush before.'

'Are you done?'

I shake my head. 'Not in the slightest.'

'Well, tough luck because I'm hopping in the shower and then I'm out. See you at work tomorrow, yeah?'

'Don't stay out too late on a school night, Mr Mavrakas. Wait, why don't you have any Sunday night prep like me?'

'Because I'm more organised than you.'

'Bull!'

Ant chuckles. 'You're right. I'll just wing it tomorrow.'

We laugh, and he disappears into the bathroom. I mindlessly flick through the television channels thinking about dinner and ignoring the piles of lesson plans and marking that are calling my name.

Not long after Ant leaves, I peel myself from the couch and rummage through the cupboards and the fridge. All of which are fully stocked, but none of which take my fancy right now, so I take out my phone and send a text message to Nick without even thinking about it.

JOSIE

Takeaway?

NICK

Thank YOU! Cbf cooking.

JOSIE

Maybe you should have asked Tori to stay then *winky face emoji*

NICK

Couldn't trust she wouldn't put a love potion in my food.

JOSIE

I think you need to be more worried about poison after today.

NICK

Did anyone check my tyres on the way out??

His message makes me giggle out loud. The image of petite Tori worked up into such a rage that she slashes Nick's tyres is funnier than I would have thought.

JOSIE

Ant has abandoned me for a hot date, and nothing here looks like tacos or burritos.

NICK

I'M IN!

NICK

Wait - does this count as date number two?

JOSIE

This is a neighbourly act of kindness.

NICK

This sounds like bending the rules. Which I'm all for btw. If you like me best, Josie, just say so.

JOSIE

> How about I go and get the food and drop it to you. No eating together. No broken rules.

NICK

> I'm not even sure YOU know what the rules are anymore. I sure as hell don't.

JOSIE

> Do you want tacos or not?

NICK

> Extra sour cream this time.

NICK

> Please.

As I wait for our order at the local Mexican place, I read over our last text conversation.

I'm not even sure YOU know what the rules are anymore.

I'm not sure I do either. Until now, I never realised just how intertwined my life was with Nick's. From casually popping over to offering to buy us both takeaway, I've never had to question my actions before. It just feels normal.

And yet, now I'm questioning everything. Should I only see Nick when we have our dates? That's all I'm giving Milo. But it's different. Nick lives right next door. I can't avoid him. But then why did I offer tacos anyway? I could have just ordered takeout for myself, completely ignoring the fact that I also could have cooked for myself. I didn't need to involve Nick in any food related decisions. And yet, I involve him in everything. Is it just habit or something else?

I don't have more time to contemplate as my order is called and I walk briskly back to the units. What I really love about our little unit block is that it is within walking distance of almost everything important in town; supermarkets, post office, bottle-o, the beach, everything. By the time I make it back to Nick's place, the food is still hot. I don't bother knocking. Instead I make my way straight through the door to his unit as if it were my own.

'Food's here,' I call out and see his head pop over the couch. 'Plates?'

'Nah, just bring it straight here. I'm starving.'

'I got you extra cheese because I remembered that last time you said they didn't put enough on. And I got you the loaded veggie burrito because I have been trying to get you to try it forever. Now that you're somewhat incapacitated, this was the perfect opportunity.'

'I can still walk over and put it in the bin, you know.'

I hand him the food along with a serviette. 'But you won't, because not only do you hate to see food go to waste, but you also hate to waste other people's money. And since I paid for everything....'

'Whatever. I'll eat the damn burrito.'

'Trust me, you won't regret it,' I sing to him, smug about my win.

I turn to leave, and his face softens. 'You're really not staying?'

'Nope. Rules are rules.'

'What rules?' He sighs. 'You know, Josie––'

He's cut off by the ringing of his phone beside him. He answers and immediately all of the colour drains from his face. My heart drops to my stomach. I clench the takeaway bag in my fist, waiting for him to finish the call. He gives nothing away, only talking to the other person on the end of the line in one-word answers. Mainly 'yep.' He hangs up and lets the phone drop to the couch. It takes moment before he speaks. 'It's my dad,' he says, his expression blank, 'he's in the hospital. He's had a heart attack.'

The air thickens around us, making it difficult to breath. 'Is he...?'

Nick shakes his head. 'He's breathing. I don't really...I need to go.'

I place the food on the nearby table. 'I'll drive you. With your foot....'

'I can drive myself, Josie.'

'You look like you're in shock, Nick. I'm not letting you drive like that.'

We leave the food at his place and scramble out the door. Nick's breathing is shallow and quick as we buckle into my car. He tries to cover his laboured breathing by letting out a fake cough. His eyes are wide with fright, reminding me of the night he showed up on my doorstep at midnight. The night we went to the beach. Nick is teetering on the edge of a panic attack, just like he was on that night.

My heart races, and I try to still everything within me so that I can be here for him in this moment. 'Nick, I need you to breathe,' I say calmly.

'I need you to drive, Josie. Now's not the time.'

I place my hand on his thigh. 'I'll get you there, but I just need to get you there without me needing to call the doctor upon arrival because you've blacked out or something.'

He turns to me, his eyes cloudy, pained. He takes in a deep breath, inhaling through his nose and then gives one long exhale through his mouth. I join him. We do it twice more, our eyes fixed on one another. I lift my hand from his leg and cup the side of his face, running my thumb in a circle over his cheek. We let all of the unspoken words fall between us in silence.

A cry for help.

A reassurance that I'm here.

A promise to stay for as long as it takes.

Or maybe just a promise to stay.

There's a quiet acknowledgement between the two of us before I put the car in drive and make my way to the hospital.

Chapter Thirty-Six

NICK

I hate hospitals. The smell of disinfectant burns my nose and the brown stains on the creamy coloured walls turns my stomach. The second I step foot inside the doors, I'm taken straight back to four and a half years ago when Mum was taking her last breath. It wasn't at this hospital, it was one in the city, but they're all the same. They all feel like death's waiting room.

Josie is looking at the directory, trying to find our way to the ward that my step mum named. Lucky she's here because I didn't take in a damn thing Gina said. What I do know is Josie rang Gina back on the way here to get all the details my brain couldn't hold. He's been placed in a ward and not in I.C.U. which gives me some hope.

Inside the world's slowest elevator, Josie reaches for my hand, and I instinctively pull away. I don't need to look at her to know that hurt is written across her face. I'm not thinking about her now. I can't. I'm in self-preservation mode. I can feel myself shutting down. It's my default response to any sort of crisis, a way to control what feels overwhelming. As I stare at the numbers, willing them to light up faster, I feel a tingle in my fingers before my hands starts to shake. I roll both palms into a fist. Next is the wave of nausea. I know this pattern all too well although now I am able to recognise what it means – panic. Last year, I had my first panic attack since the funeral, in front of my dad. Back then, I didn't stop to recognise the subtle symptoms creeping up on me, so it got out of hand real quick. It wasn't until I was doubled over with chest pain and unable to breathe that I let Dad call an ambulance.

I had been so good at keeping it in check until then and hadn't had an attack in front of anyone. My dad was the last person I wanted to see me in that state. No, scrap that. Josie is the last person I want to see me in that state. I don't want her to see me as weak. I don't want her to have a tainted view of who I am. I wanted to keep last year's attack a secret, but Dad went and called Ant who has been sworn to secrecy not to tell Josie about my anxiety. It was Ant's idea to go to the gym together. He believed it would help and, to my surprise, it has. Keeping active helps my mind settle and when my mind settles, my anxiety settles too.

Right now, in this metal box, I have nowhere to run, and my anxiety is pushing through all the cracks. Josie runs her hand over my back and instead of wanting to sink into it, it makes me stiffen. Sensing the shift under her touch, Josie stubbornly presses harder into my back, the soothing circles now stiff and determined.

The elevator doors open, and I bolt out looking around for signs of my dad. We make our way up the corridors to the sounds of machines beeping, a chaotic rhythm of life and death. We turn the corner and find a small waiting room where my stepmother and half-brothers sit, looking anywhere but at each other. My half-brothers, Cal and Cam, barely in their teens are the first to look up at me. Both are sporting red eyes and aggressive pouts. They're angry. They think this is unfair. I know because their expression is my own mirrored back at me. Gina shoots out of her chair and wraps me in a hug as though we embrace like this all the time.

'Oh, Nick. I'm so glad you made it.' Gina pulls away, wiping away tears that fall steadily. 'He's in with the doctors now. He's awake and breathing on his own—'

'What happened?' My tone is gruff and impatient.

Gina shakes her head. 'One minute he was standing there talking, laughing, the next he was pale and clammy, clutching at his chest and saying he couldn't breathe.'

I look up to the ceiling and draw in a deep breath. It seems too sudden. My brain can't seem to make sense of the man I just saw and what Gina is describing. She suddenly sees Josie beside me and wipes furiously at her cheeks.

'I'm sorry,' she says by way of encouraging an introduction.

Josie steps in for my lack of etiquette and tells Gina that we're friends and neighbours. I almost laugh at the absurd nature of what's going on right now.

'Excuse me, Mrs Rockman? Your husband would like you to come in now,' a nurse dressed in blue scrubs interrupts. Hearing his surname, different to mine, reminds me that I'm intruding on this family.

Gina nods. 'Nick, will you come with me?'

She looks up at me with grey eyes full of panic and dread. I don't know this woman, not like I should. After all, we're family right? I have no obligation to support her, and yet I find myself going numb. I agree more because I want to see my dad not because I want to be a good stepson and support her. That makes me some sort of arsehole.

'Can we come?' one of the boys ask. I don't know which one because, again, I've done everything I can to distance myself from them.

'No, sweetheart. I need the two of you to wait out here a little while longer while I see what state Dad is in.'

When Gina calls him Dad, I feel like I'm suffocating. Why should I get to go in and see the man who has only been in my life for three years? Here are two young boys who he was there for when they were sick, had fevers; who he taught to ride a bike and play catch; I bet he even went to their Saturday sports games. Hell, maybe he even coached their team. What right do I have to be going in there to see a man I know better as a boss than I do as a father?

'I need, need a minute.' I stumble to the closest exit which so happens to be a small balcony patio off the back of the waiting room. There are benches and bins overflowing with cigarettes. Josie follows me out.

'Hey,' she soothes.

I reach for the railing to hold me upright and suck in as much oxygen as I can. She goes back to rubbing my back, but I shake her off. 'I need a minute,' I bark.

'Hey, I know this is scary.' Her voice is soft, concerned.

I let out a humourless laugh. 'Why am I here?'

'What?'

'Those boys in there. He's their dad. He's not mine.'

'Nick–'

'Why should I even care? He never cared about me until I found him. And now he's dying, and he wants me to take over his company, a company that belongs to his sons.'

'You *are* his son.'

'I'm just some by-product of a night out. A mistake.'

'Is that how you really feel, Nick?' Something in Josie's tone makes me swing around to look at her. I wish I hadn't. She stares back at me with those big dark eyes of hers.

'Why didn't he come for me, Jose? I was a kid. Why wasn't I enough for him?'

The words spill out of my mouth before I have time to catch them. And then I see the look of pity on Josie's face and I hate myself for saying anything out loud. I rub at my chest where a dull ache has presented itself. *Fuck.* Not now.

'Nick,' Josie's hands land on either side of my hunched shoulders. She's trying to get me to hold her gaze. 'Nick, look at me. You need to breathe. Here....' She begins to show me how to take deep breaths like I'm a child. And like any sullen child, I shake her off.

'I know how to breath, Josie.'

'I'm only trying to help.'

Shit. I know she is. She's the one person I want beside me right now, to fold into, to help make it all stop. But she's also the one person I want to avoid right now. I can't let her see me like this. I press the palms of my hands into my eyes.

'Nick, it's okay. You're allowed to feel like this.'

'I know, I just...,' I suck in a deep breath, 'I can't stop feeling like this. All the time. Sneaks up on me.'

'Anxiety?' she asks, her voice dripping with concern. I nod and she continues, 'Nick, please let me help.'

I can't stand it. I can't stand her seeing me like this. I can't stand to hear the pity in her voice. I stand tall, cracking my knuckles. 'It doesn't matter. Forget it, Josie.'

I turn towards the door and completely ignore her calling my name.

I enter the room behind Gina who practically falls into the bed with my father. He runs his hands through her hair and kisses the top of her head. He mumbles something to her that soothes her, and as if remembering there are other people in the room, namely me, a nurse and a doctor, she stands up, straightens out her jumper.

'Mrs Rockman,' the doctor says to Gina and looks to me. 'I'm Doctor Jodie Smith.'

'This is Greg's son, Nick.' Gina introduces me which I'm thankful for because my mouth is dry.

'He's doing well. Preliminary tests show there has been no damage to the heart, which is a good thing.'

'What caused this? Is it the cancer?' Gina inquires.

Doctor Jodie shakes her head. 'We don't believe so. There is a family history of heart disease so it's not completely surprising,'

Maybe not to you, I think. I make a mental note that there is a history of heart issues in my DNA that I didn't know about ten seconds ago but need to mention the next time I'm at the doctors.

'Although, the body is under a lot of stress fighting the cancer and from the medications he's taking. Also, stress can be a contributing factor. Greg tells me there has been an increase in stress surrounding his business.'

Although no one looks at me, I feel as though all eyes are upon me. Thanks, doc. I did this. I wouldn't give him the 'right' answer about the business which increased his stress levels which landed him here. Son of the year.

'So now what?' Gina asks.

'We will keep him in for observations––'

'And then what? He just comes home? Life is back to normal?' Gina has a bit of pitbull in her. I certainly wouldn't want to be on her wrong side.

But maybe that is what is supposed to happen when someone you love ends up here. You fight for them. I wouldn't know. I was only ever in a position to give up any chance I had at fighting for my mum. I had to watch as all the choice was taken away from me. I had to watch her draw her final breaths knowing there was nothing more I could do.

'I spoke with Greg about reducing the amount of stress in his life,' Doctor Jodie says, her words bringing me back to the present.

'She wants me to give up work,' Dad says in a gravelly tone, eyes locked with mine.

I shift on the spot, and my hands find their way into the pockets of my jeans.

'I think it would be in Greg's best interest if the business could be handed over sooner rather than later.'

'Just need someone to hand it to.' Dad coughs, and everyone in the room stills until he recovers.

'I will leave you to it. I'll be in again in a couple of hours. Jess,' she points to the nurse, 'will be here should you require anything.

She has my direct number.' The doctor gives a curt nod and swiftly exits the room.

Nurse Jess turns back towards the machine watching his vitals on the screen, trying to give us as much privacy as possible in this moment. The things she must hear as a nurse.

'So, how's about it son. You ready to talk now?'

I'm not. I don't want to run a company, I don't want to be tied to something so definite. I don't want to have my whole life planned out in front of me at thirty-one. I don't want to take something that isn't rightfully mine. He built that company to give to his other sons, not me. Had my mum not died, had I not come to find him, he wouldn't have left me so much as a bread crumb upon his death. I haven't needed anything from him in life and I certainly don't need anything from him in death.

I don't say any of that though. Instead I see the frail man with thinning grey hair hooked up to machines, and all I can say is, 'I'm ready to talk.'

Chapter Thirty-Seven

JOSIE

I give Nick a wide berth for the next few days. I tried checking in on him the day after his father was admitted to the hospital, but he wasn't home, and he wasn't answering my text. He is, however, talking to Ant and I can't help but feel a little jealous and hurt. What have I done to earn the cold shoulder?

This is what Nick does. He shuts down and shuts people out until he processes and deal with whatever is going on, and then he'll re-enter your life as though nothing has happened. He's totally incapable of letting anyone see him vulnerable. By day three I've had enough and corner Ant on our shared oval yard duty at lunch time. 'Day three and Nick is still avoiding me.'

We stand at the opening of the oval and watch the various small groups of boys playing different ball sports, and the small group of girls who seem to stand there watching them.

'He'll come around. He always does.' Ant shrugs carelessly.

'Easy for you to say. He's not avoiding you. Don't think I didn't hear the two of you go out for a walk at midnight last night.'

'What do you want me to say, Josie?'

'I want you to tell me what I can do to help!'

'Give him space—'

'It goes against my natural instincts to give my friends space when they're obviously hurting.'

'So, is this about what you need, or what Nick needs?'

Ouch. Ant has never been one to shy away from bluntly telling it like it is. His comment stops me in my tracks. I do have a need to help my friends, but my need is only out of care for Nick.

'Nick's a big boy. He knows how to cope.'

'Yeah? Well his coping mechanism of avoidance and pushing people away is unhealthy.'

'Or maybe he just needs one person to confide in, not twenty.'

'What's that supposed to mean?'

'You cope with things by dissecting them with everyone close to you. You like to hear everyone's opinion on the matter before you make any kind of decision. Which I don't really understand because it only ends up confusing you further until you get stressed and go with your original decision.'

I am not prepared to be called out right now. 'And you don't talk anything through with anyone.' It's a cheap shot, but it's like water off a duck's back to Ant.

'Precisely. I'm confident in my own decision-making skills while you're stuck in people-pleasing mode. Nick, he doesn't need all the extra noise. He internalises it, deals with it and then it's done.'

'So he's not confiding in you? What are the walks about then? And at midnight!'

'He talks, I listen. He doesn't want advice, he just wants to hear his thoughts out loud. Look, Josie, sometimes you have to know the difference between when someone just wants you to listen and when someone wants your advice. You and Elle go straight to advice. Always. It's like a default.'

Chewing my bottom lip, I think over what he says trying not

to get defensive. I can listen. I'm a great listener, but when I try to think of time I've only ever listened, or if I've ever asked someone if they want me to listen or give them advice, I cannot think of a single example.

I'm a rescuer. That's me. That's what I did at the hospital. Nick was pacing like a caged animal, and I couldn't help but jump in and force my help onto him, forcing him into a corner where he pushed me away. I feel awful. I want to call him and apologise and then curse myself immediately. *Some people just need space, Josie.*

Ant and I stand in silence as we let the weight of his words hang between us. Two groups of students join together, and my teacher instincts kick in to focus on them.

'Is that Connor James?' Ant says, hyper focused on the same group of students.

'Wouldn't surprise me. That kid makes it his business to be in everyone else's.'

'Hmm, sounds familiar.'

I nudge him with my elbow. 'Don't you dare compare me to that Lynx Africa-soaked bonehead.'

'That bonehead looks like he's mouthing off...'

Ant and I walk briskly towards the group of students. 'At this point, I should have Connor's mum on speed dial.'

Staying back after work to conduct a suspension meeting always drains me. Despite the fact that Connor James's mum wanted the school to throw everything we had at him and was in full support of a suspension, it still takes up a lot of energy that I no longer possess after three p.m. I finally leave school, a good two hours after the final bell for the day, only to be called by Elle on my way home. I ignore the first call, preferring to just listen to whatever playlist is on when she calls again.

'Hey, sorry I just missed your call. My Bluetooth was playing up,' I lie as I connect the call through my car.

'Mine's been doing that lately too. Drives me nuts. Hey, listen, I won't keep you long. I need a huge favour. I'm stressing out.'

'What's wrong?'

She groans. 'Rich has these tickets to a Fleetwood Mac tribute band in the city for Friday night. Our babysitter just cancelled, and my parents are away, and, well, you know I can't trust Rich's parents.'

I let out a small laugh at the statement. Not trusting Rich's parents is an understatement. Elle doesn't trust anyone with her kids. I've babysat on a few rare occasions and that's only because I was her last resort. And the job came with a two-page directory of emergency contacts, doctors names and numbers and a detailed list of what medications the kids can take, how much and when to administer it.

Elle trusts her parents to look after her kids, but only if her mum is there. Poor Rich's parents will never live down the one time they babysat the kids, and Jaggar ended up in the hospital getting a couple of stitches in his head after tripping over a bit of concrete.

I know how much Elle and Rich both love Fleetwood Mac. It's their music. They've claimed the group as a couple so either she's about to ask me to babysit or offer up the tickets. To be honest, the tickets would be amazing and perhaps something that Nick and I could go to, to help brighten him up.

'Can you please babysit?' The daydream bubble bursts. 'I wouldn't ask if we weren't desperate. Rich and I really need this night out together.'

'Everything okay?'

'Yeah, yeah,' she says flippantly, 'just typical parents-of-young-kids-stuff. All our time is spent on the kids or talking about the kids. We're just a little disconnected at the moment. Nothing dire, but it'll be good to go out.'

How could I possibly say no to a friend in need. After my

conversation with Ant early, the irony is not lost on me. But this is totally different. 'I'm more than happy to babysit.'

'You sure? Harlow is teething, so she's a bit grumpy at the moment.'

'Are you trying to talk me out of it?' I joke.

'No, just want to make sure you're fully aware of the terms and conditions.'

I laugh. 'Elle, it will be fine. I've babysat them before. Besides, what kind of Fairy Godmother would I be if I said no to babysitting my God-children?'

'It doesn't interfere with your *dating life*?' She says the words with mock drama.

'I think that's on hold for a bit. Nick's dad is in the hospital.'

Elle gasps. 'Is he okay?'

'He had a minor heart attack.'

'How is a heart attack minor? That's awful.'

'I know.'

I feel heavy. Heavy in my body. Heavy in my mind. Heavy in my heart. I want to just push a giant pause button on life right now.

'Let me guess. He's gone silent on you?'

I nod before forgetting that we're talking on the phone and respond, 'Yep.'

'Look, give him the space he needs. Doesn't stop you from seeing Milo again. Just don't let it be Friday.'

I chuckle, and as I turn into my street, I'm surprised to see Nick walking in the direction of the units. 'I gotta go, Elle. Text me the details, and I'll see you Friday night.'

'You're a life saver. Thank you.'

We say goodbye, and I pull the car over a few metres in front of Nick and climb out. Dressed down in a backwards cap, hooded jumper and shorts, he doesn't look surprised to see me pull up in front of him. He walks towards me and my parked car. 'Got car trouble?' he smirks and comes to lean on my car next to me.

'Got neighbour trouble.'

He scratches his beard. 'Need me to go rough him up a bit?'

I turn my body towards his whilst still leaning against the car. Keeping in mind what Ant said earlier today, I try not to let the overwhelming sense to push overtake me. 'Just need him to know that he can talk to me. He doesn't need to push me away.'

'You want to write it down, and I'll pass him a note?'

'I'll friggin' hire a plane and write it in the sky if you think it will help.'

This earns me a chuckle and it's nice to see Nick smiling again.

'I don't know, Jose. Maybe you were right all along.'

'How do you figure?'

'Talking. Letting people get close to you. Commitment.'

'Is this where you run away?'

'Usually.' He kicks the dirt beneath his shoes. 'No attachments...'

'No hurt feelings.' I finish the sentence for him, and he nods. My heart breaks a little hearing the defeat in his tone. I restrain myself from adding further to the conversation, remembering what Ant said about listening - *sometimes you have to know the difference between when someone just wants you to listen and when someone wants your advice.*

To my surprise, the space gives Nick time to think about what he wants to say next. 'You're the same.'

My head juts back in surprise. 'I'm the same?'

He nods. 'Why do you think we work so well together? And why do you think you're avoiding making something real of it?'

'Because I'm scared of this. I'm scared that when things get tough, you'll shut me out.'

He shakes his head. '"Nah, that's not it.'

'Oh no?' I say sarcastically.

'You're just as afraid of commitment as I am. You avoid labelling what we have because it looks too much like a relation-ship and that scares you.'

'Says you.'

'Exactly. I see it in myself, Josie. Falling for you is the scariest thing in the world. The further you fall, the more you have to lose. I've been there. I've lost the one person in this world who was there for me through everything, who raised me...I can't go through that again.'

'So, what are you saying?' My heart catches in my throat as I watch a cloud descend across his face. I can see Nick disassociate in front of me.

'Give Milo a chance. Go all in, Jose. You deserve everything, and he can give you that. You deserve to be happy.'

I hear the words, but I don't really believe they're coming out of his mouth. How can he go from saying he's falling for me to telling me to be with someone else? I don't buy it. Anger swirls in my belly. 'And you don't deserve to be happy? What kind of world do --'

'I want to *stop* being in love with you Josie because all that is going to happen is that I'm going to lose you.'

My whole world stops spinning and everything else melts away between us until it feels like Nick and I are the only two people left on the earth. I falter, 'You-you love me?'

An exhausted sigh escapes his mouth. 'You're surprised?'

I am. Love is big. Love is...

'Anyway, it doesn't matter. Anyone close to me just ends up sick or dead, and I don't want that for you.'

I shake my head trying to make sense of what is happening between us. 'That makes zero sense. Don't they say it's better to have loved and--'

'Don't quote that bullshit at me.' He takes his cap off to run his hand through his hair and places the cap back on. 'Whoever said that has never lost anyone they love. Look, I'm fine. Honestly, Jose, this whole thing with my dad has just reminded me of why I don't get attached to people or places.'

'So that's it?'

'My dad wants to leave the company to me. I told him I'd keep it in a trust for Cal and Cam until they're old enough to take over, but I don't want it. Doc says the cancer is aggressive. He's not going to be around much longer. I figure, when he's gone, I'll sell the unit, get someone to run the company, keep it strong for Cal and Cam. I'll be no more than a name on a piece of paper. Was thinking I might head north for a bit.'

My jaw practically hits the ground when he speaks such soulless words. It's like the Nick I've known is nowhere in sight, instead a bot is using his flesh as a disguise to blend in with the human race.

'Seems you've got it all figured out then.' I bite back the tears that threaten to escape. 'Where do the rest of us fit into your plans?'

He shrugs. 'We can stay friends. Keep in touch.'

Keep in touch. Seriously? I push off the car and stalk to the driver's side, aggressively pulling the door open.

Keep in touch.

Get stuffed, Nick.

Chapter Thirty-Eight

JOSIE

I'm not proud of how I behave when I'm angry and upset. Despite the long day this was turning out to be and the emotional rollercoaster I appear to have bought an unlimited ticket to, I decide to call Milo and ask him out for our third date.

Technically, Ant and Elle were going to organise the third and final date, but I've given up playing their stupid game. This is *my* life, *my* thirtieth birthday is edging near, and I am not any closer to finding a husband and baby daddy.

Screw Nick. I can do commitment. I want commitment. That's what this whole thing has been about! I am ready to commit to someone and begin a life with them. That's all I want. So that's what I'm doing, going all in as Nick put it. Milo agrees to meet me at the local bar for a drink. It's not the most creative date but I need to spend time with him without all the flashy distractions.

'Come here often?' The deep baritone of his voice sends a shiver through my soul.

I spin around on my stool at the bar and am greeted with a

smile that could light up the night sky. Immediately my body relaxes as he cups my face and brings our lips together.

'Is that your best pick-up line?' I smile as we part.

'I actually don't have a pick-up line.' He chuckles as he takes a seat beside me. The bartender comes over and he orders a scotch on the rocks. I'm still nursing the fruitiest cocktail I could find on the menu and decline the offer for another drink. 'I literally have no game.'

'Your face is the game.'

This earns me a heartier chuckle and another kiss. 'What brings you out on a school night, Ms Russo?'

'Just wanted to see you,' I coo.

'I'm glad you called. I've been thinking about you.' He keeps his voice low, just between us as though we're two people meeting up for a secret rendezvous. The idea gets me excited.

'I hope they haven't all been nice thoughts.' I wink, and he lets out a low groan.

'I don't even know what to say to that. See, no game.'

My turn to giggle. I lick my lips. I'm being way too obvious, and I cringe inwardly. I shake it off and ask how his day has been. We trade stories. I leave out the Nick parts to spare my own feelings and not bring the mood down. I find the more I talk to Milo, the more relaxed I feel. He offers me support when I tell him about Connor and the suspension, and I feel I take can refuge in his words. Something about Milo screams stability, beyond just his physical presence. I'm reminded of just how commanding his presences is as he sits awkwardly folded in the bar stool that looks like it was made for a toddler.

'Can I ask you something serious?' I say, my second cocktail granting me liquid courage.

'You can ask me anything, Josie.'

'Real talk.'

'Real talk.' He smiles back at me, flashing his delicious dimples, and I almost lose all my senses. How unfair.

'Future. What does it look like for you?'

'As in, what do I want?'

'Yeah! What do you want from the next sixty years of your life?'

He contemplates the question not because he's scrambling for the answer but he's thoughtful in how he wants to deliver his response. What I've learnt about Milo is that he likes his answers to be considered even if they're not always finished.

'Without sounding like I'm being fed some lines from a reality TV producer,' I giggle again before he continues, 'I want what everyone wants – happiness. My mum says she still gets butterflies when my dad takes her out. They're so in love with each other even after thirty odd years of marriage. They have each other's back no matter what. I want that. I want someone to be my true partner, someone to have my back, and I'll have theirs. Someone I can come home to every night and forget all the stresses of the day.'

I can practically see the love hearts floating above my own head like a Looney Tune character. A real-life Prince Charming saying exactly what my heart wants. 'And kids?'

'A bunch of them.' He beams. 'What about you?'

'Can I just say ditto to everything you just said? You literally just describe my perfect life.'

He smiles looking down at his drink. A blush rises to his cheeks. He covers it by taking a long swig of the aged scotch in front of him. 'Glad we're on the same page.'

'Me too.'

Chapter Thirty-Nine

JOSIE

I surprise Elle by showing up half an hour early for my babysitting duties which is a good thing because she is still running around in a ratty old t-shirt trying to get Harlow in a nappy. Harlow thinks it's hilarious to make her mother chase her and is currently hiding under the kitchen table letting out that glorious toddler chuckle sound. Tell me a happier sound in the world. You can't. I enter the dining room offering to get the nappy on Harlow so that Elle can go and get dressed for her date with her husband.

'Good luck,' Elle huffs, flinging the clean nappy at me.

I coax Harlow out with a sing-song voice and much to Elle's horror, Harlow crawls out from under the table immediately and happily lays down and allows me to cover her bare bum with the nappy. Elle stands there, hands on her hips, mouth hanging open.

'I have been chasing her for ten minutes trying to get that thing on her.'

I'm quietly proud of myself. Parenting must be in my genes. I can totally see this being my life in the next two years. Being around Harlow just makes my desire to settle down even stronger.

'Can't have been trying very hard,' I mock, knowing full well just how difficult Harlow can be.

Elle rolls her eyes and lets out a little chuckle. 'We'll see if you're still singing the same tune by the end of the night, my friend.'

'Go and finish getting ready, or you won't need me because you'll have missed the whole thing. I've got this. What do I need to do?'

'I've got some left-over spaghetti in the fridge. If you heat that up, you can give them their dinner. That way they'll be distracted when we slip out.'

'Sure. I mean, it'll be fine either way. How hard can it be?'

Turns out, if you utter those words then you are setting yourself up for failure. Approximately five minutes after Elle and Rich leave, I find out just how hard it can be. Harlow has had enough spaghetti which meant instead of just pushing her plate aside, she grabs fistfuls of it and throws it in the direction of her brother and the crisp white walls behind him. Which prompts Jaggar to cry because spaghetti sauce get in his eyes. I throw them both in the bath and a fight over a Paw Patrol pup is the catalyst for an all-in water fight that displaces water to every conceivable crease and corner of the bathroom. Jaggar decides it is funny to do a nudie run through the house whilst I try to dry Harlow, who takes off after her brother the second I put the towel down.

I take back what I said about a chuckling toddler being the best sound in the world. It's not. It's a demonic call to arms for more mischief to occur. Her laughter mocks me. I try to make a game of the running around, saying the last one in the lounge room is a rotten egg. However I'm it. I'm the rotten egg standing alone in the lounge room with two sets of pyjamas and a clean nappy because apparently kids of this generation are smart and do not care about being rotten eggs.

It's then that I remember kids are usually transfixed by screens and after battling with five different TV remotes, I finally land on the kid's channel which is playing a high-pitched cartoon. This brings the nude little devils into the lounge room, and, as predicted, they're frozen to the spot, eyes glued to the TV.

This gives me enough time to dress both of them. I usher them towards the couch so I can clean up in the dining room and the bathroom. I do a quick wipe up of the mess these little tornados have made and flop down, exhausted, next to them on the couch.

'I thought we were going to take it easy on Aunty Josie tonight, huh?' I say, ruffling Jaggar's wet mop of hair.

I haven't been game to run a comb through Harlow's precious curls and decide that Elle can deal with that in the morning. *Sorry, bestie.* Harlow scoots over to me and without taking her eyes off the TV, makes her way into my lap and snuggles in for a hug. All is forgiven. She places her thumb in her mouth and begins to suck. I know Elle wants to discourage the thumb sucking, but I find it too adorable to stop and make a pledge to help pay for her braces later in life. My phone buzzes, and it's Elle checking in.

ELLE

How are my babies?

JOSIE

Fine. Jaggar invited some friends around to play poker. They've started at ten bucks a hand. He says you usually say fifteen, but I told him he needs to build up to it.

ELLE

Ha. Ha. Very funny.

JOSIE

They're FINE. Stop worrying and enjoy your night out with your husband.

ELLE

He is looking rather like a snack tonight.

> **JOSIE**
> Did you just use young people slang? Next you'll be making out behind the school hall.

> **ELLE**
> Just make sure my babies are in bed soon.
> Just trying to make it easy on you.

> **JOSIE**
> They're fine. Fed and bathed. We're just watching some talking pig who has a rather questionable looking face and then they're off to bed.

> **ELLE**
> Enjoy Aunty J x

> **JOSIE**
> Enjoy you two xo

I don't recall when my teeth came in but I certainly don't remember them being this painful. After Harlow drank her bottle, all she has done is scream, which has in turn has woken Jaggar up, who decides that the most helpful thing he can do is cry too because he's overtired.

I feel like joining in the chorus and crying too. How does Elle do this? I go into Harlow's room and pick her up in her armless sleeping bag. Her little red face is scrunched up in pain. Her hair is wet, plastered to her forehead, and she's tugging at her right ear. Jaggar sits on the floor in her room and cries, clutching at his favourite teddy.

I put Harlow down on her change table, unzipping her and freeing her from the oven-like sleeping bag.

I coax Jaggar to follow me out to the kitchen where I make up another bottle for Harlow. While it's warming in the microwave, I bend down to wrap my free arm around Jaggar.

'It's okay, sweetheart. You're okay.'

'Mummy,' he cries.

'Oh honey, Mummy will be home soon.' I check the clock. It's not even nine o'clock. The band has probably only just started. 'Aunty Josie is here. I'm here.'

He snuggles into my shoulder, rubbing his nose against my jumper leaving a trail of snot from one end to the other. I guess I deserve that. The microwave rings, and I reach up for Harlow's bottle, testing it on the inside of my wrist like Elle taught me to do when Jaggar was a baby. Perfect. She grabs at it, furiously sucking on the teat. It seems to settle her for a moment. I take Jaggar's hand and walk them both into the lounge room where I struggle to find anything on TV for kids.

'Do you have a DVD or anything?' I ask Jaggar.

He looks up at me confused. I guess not. Are DVDs already obsolete? I scan the Cartoon Network only to find cartoons that are for older kids, still Jaggar seems distracted, so I let him watch it. How on earth am I going to get these two to bed? I pick up my phone and dial Franki. As the older, married sister, I assume she should know what to do.

'I have no fucking idea what to do with kids!' she says in a panic down the phone to me.

'I thought you'd know what to do!'

'Yes, Josie, because I have so many children of my own,' she deadpans down the line.

'Fine. But you're older. You helped Mum with Daniella and me. Surely you picked up a trick or two.'

'I couldn't have cared less about you and Daniella as babies. Seriously, I made sure I was in a different room to you until you were about four and fun to hang out with.'

'You're a great help.'

'Look honestly, kids aren't my thing.'

'No kidding. Does Josh know he's practically going to be raising your children alone until they're *fun to hang out with*?'

She's silent on the phone, and I panic, thinking I have offended her. 'Franki?'

'I'm here. Look, I don't say this lightly, but why don't you call Mum. She raised us.'

'I'm not entirely sure we didn't come out already toilet trained and self-sufficient.'

'You have a point. But at this stage, what are your other options?'

I think it over knowing full well she's right. I don't want to call Elle because it will ruin her night. She'll come home early, and I'll never be allowed to babysit again. Ant is impossible to get a hold of these days. I wouldn't put it past Daniella to have changed her phone number and not told anyone. I can't call Milo because I don't want him to think that I can't handle this mothering thing, and Nick is avoiding me. Or I'm avoiding him. Whatever, we're not talking to each other and the thought hurts my heart.

I thank Franki for nothing and dial my mother's number, swallowing all my pride in the process. 'Hey, Mum,' I sing down the line.

'What trouble are you in now?' She sounds bored.

'What makes you think...'

'Very rarely do you call me when you aren't in trouble or needing money.'

I let the punch land in my gut before responding. 'Actually, I need some advice, some parenting advice.'

I hear her breath hitch, and I realise what it must sound like to her. 'Sorry, not like that. I'm babysitting Elle's kids.' I can feel her disappointment over the phone. 'Harlow is really unsettled. I think she's teething. She's tugging at her ear. And Jaggar can't sleep because his sister is making too much noise.'

'Have you given her anything for the pain?'

'Yes, but it hasn't helped.'

'She seems quiet now...'

'That's because I've given her a bottle.'

'Does she have a dummy? The sucking motion often helps when teething.'

I get up from the couch, holding the phone between my ear

and my shoulder, whilst carrying Harlow in my arms. I open all the cupboards until I find a small Tupperware container hiding behind the biscuit tin housing two dummies.

'Got them.'

'Run it under some cool water and let her suck on it once she's finished the bottle. The chill can help with the pain.'

'How do I get them both down though? Harlow seems to be okay if I'm holding her, but that means I can't put Jaggar to bed.'

'Okay, here's what you're going to do. Download a baby sleep soundtrack on your phone. Something calming, much like the music at your favourite spa. Then put Jaggar to sleep with the music and a lamp on. Then you're going to cuddle that baby to sleep and when she is in a deep sleep, you will put her down in her bed, be careful not to make a sound, and then slip out.'

'How will I know when she's in a deep sleep?'

'You'll know. She'll become like a dead weight in your arms. And her breathing will change.'

I sigh. 'How did you do it, Mum?'

'I never had to do it alone. Your father was always there, and I knew I could count on him to stick it out, no matter how long you girls took to get to sleep.'

I breathe out a small laugh. I was the one who was notorious for being the most difficult to get to sleep at night.

'Mum?'

'Yes, Josephine.'

I can't believe I am about to ask my mother for relationship advice. I must be catching Harlow's fever or something.

'How did you know Dad was the one? Could you always count on him?'

'Oh honey, your father is the man he is today because of me,' she chuckles down the line, and I don't doubt it for a second. 'Your father is an incredibly stubborn man, which, like I said, meant I knew I could count on him because he wasn't going to let anything beat him. Not even little, brown-eyed girls who had him wrapped around their little pinkie fingers.'

Harlow finishes her bottle, and I see her eyes begin to well with tears. I flip her to my shoulder for a burp and then cradle her in my arms, placing the dummy in her mouth. She takes it immediately and closes her eyes.

I think about having to do this, be wholly responsible for another life outside of my own. Maybe I am jumping into this settle down, have babies thing too quickly? Despite my biological clock ticking and society telling me I should be ready, am I actually ready?

'Josephine?'

'Yes?'

'Who did you want to call tonight?'

'Pardon?'

'Your father was always the first person I wanted to call whenever I needed help. Or if something good happened. He still is. You asked me how I knew your father was the one. That's it. Does this mean you're thinking about that young gentleman we met at Matteo's a few weeks ago?'

'I...I...'

'Josephine, you called me out of necessity. I have the experience you need. If it weren't for that, when you were in the thick of it, who was it that you wanted to call for help? Who was it that you wanted by your side tonight, even if they too had no clue what to do?'

Only one face flashed in front of my eyes as she spoke, and I let out a gasp.

'Does that settle it then?' she asks, a little tired of the conversation.

It does. Holding Harlow in my arms and watching a tired Jaggar rub his eyes, I know exactly who I want by my side to share these moments with, and I can't wait to tell him.

Chapter Forty

NICK

I can't bring myself to care about much. It's not a depressed feeling, just a numbness that kind of washes over me. I've been here before, after Mum died, so this feeling is nothing new. I never thought I'd feel anything again until I met Josie, and to an extent, Ant and Elle. While they reminded me of what it was like to have real friends who had your back, Josie reminded me of something more.

I'm not sad that I cut ties with her earlier this week. I'm not anything. It's for the best anyway, for everyone. I can't bring myself to fall in love with Josie, have a family and be constantly looking over my shoulder wondering when it will all be taken away from me. I should have known better than to even entertain the thought. I may have let things get a little too comfortable here in Littleton Beach but seeing Dad in hospital was a wakeup call that nothing is permanent and serves as a reminder that getting close to anyone only ever lands in heartbreak. I take a sip of the soft drink in my hand just as Josie's name flashes across my phone screen. I decline the call. She doesn't leave a voice message.

It's the first time she's reached out since I told her that we can be friends. I felt sick when I said those words and even now, my stomach churns at the thought. That day, I shattered my own heart into millions of pieces that I have no intention of ever gluing back together.

I've tried not to replay the conversation with Josie over and over in my head this week. The moment her doe eyes flash into my mind, I mentally push them away again. I'm getting better at it. If I keep telling myself that it doesn't sting to see the hurt in her eyes, then I might just start to believe it.

I wouldn't say the week flew by, but it certainly went by in a blur of bad television and non-alcoholic beer, which tastes as bad as it sounds. My hands have had a constant shake to them all week and this itch, oh man, this itch just won't quit. No matter how many times I scratch at the back of my neck, it doesn't seem to resonate deep enough to stop the damn itch. I've steered clear of alcohol which I know from experience is a one-way ticket to breakdown when I'm like this.

Only now I don't have anyone to help fish me out. Dad's sick, Josie's gone, I've blocked Elle's number, and Ant has finally taken a hint and is putting his energy into the one dude who wants it, Levi. The sound of silence in the unit is deafening. I'm about to get up and push some weights to stave off an intense wave of anxiety kickstarting in my gut when there's a knock at the door. I answer without looking through the window, and I must say, I'm not surprised to find who's behind it. I was expecting her to come.

'Hi. Can we talk?'

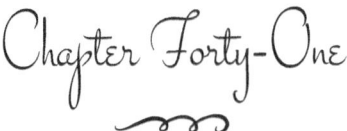

Chapter Forty-One

JOSIE

I shouldn't feel nervous, but I am. My mouth is dry, and my heart is beating rapidly as he opens the door. My brain rapid fires word vomit, and I can't remember the speech I practised on the way here. It all but melts away when I see him standing in the doorway.

'Hi. Can we talk?'

'Of course,' Milo swings the door open, 'I wasn't expecting you today. This is a nice surprise.'

He leans in to kiss me and I move to present my cheek. 'Sorry, I should have called first.'

'Please, you're welcome here any time, Josie.'

I follow Milo through the entry way, taking in the neat order of his home. Everything has its place and I bet if I slid my finger over the side table in the hallway, I would not find a speck of dust.

I can't remember the last time Ant or I picked up a duster and wiped our entry table down. I make a mental note to do that as soon as I get home. I take in the rest of Milo's house because that's what it is, a house not a home. There's nothing warm and inviting about it, a little bit like the perfect man in front of me.

I wonder if it's a smokescreen for an empty life. It dawns on me that outside of work, Milo's life is lonely. On our dates, he never once talked about the friends he has or memories with his family. The only glimpse I got into his private world was when he spoke of the staff that cooked his weekly meals or sailed his yacht. Where would a relationship fit into all of this? Where would kids? The life I dream of is the same as I have now, full of friends and family and memories made together. I see a husband and children as adding a richness to the full life that I already have.

'I'm not spoiling any Saturday plans am I?'

'Not at all,' Milo holds the kitchen stool out for me, 'can I get you something to eat or drink?'

I focus on the monochrome aesthetic he has going on. Apart from the Marvel memorabilia, there's little character to the place, little of Milo in the place. At least, I think there is little of Milo. Unless this is him.

'Josie?' Milo's voice pulls me from my thoughts.

'Huh?'

'I asked if I could get you something to eat or drink?' His tone is a little clipped.

I shake my head, tugging the ends of my sleeves over my hands. 'I never noticed how tidy your place is.'

He chuckles proudly. 'I like order.'

Order and chaos don't generally mix well together. I can't help but think about what this place would look like with kids in it. Would they have designer toys? Would they even be allowed to have toys? Kids are messy.

I clear my throat. 'I was at Elle's last night.' It suddenly occurs to me that he has no idea who Elle is. The thought stops me in my track momentarily. How could the guy I'm dating not know one of the most important people in my life? I guess he's not the only one who has kept parts of himself hidden during our dates. I clear my throat again and continue, 'Elle is my best friend. Anyway, I was babysitting last night and there were toys everywhere.'

What I want to say is that it felt homely, lived in, the exact opposite to his place. I want to ask how he imagines kids living here under his preference for order. I wait for him to ask a question or try and join in this conversation I seem to be at the helm of, but it is very clear that I am talking to myself.

'My place is like that too,' I add trying to keep the conversation alive, 'I call it organised chaos.' I let out a performative laugh and cringe inside. Am I turning into my mother? S.O.S

'It's very different here,' I say awkwardly. *Catch my drift? Say something. Say anything. For the love of ice cream on a hot day, SAY. SOMETHING.*

He shrugs. 'It's just me here, so it's not that difficult to pick up after myself.'

'What about when you have kids?'

'I assume my wife will be at home with them, so she can keep on top of things. If it's too much, then I'll hire a cleaner.'

I still.

My wife will be at home.

As in, my wife will be a stay-at-home-mum. End of discussion.

I clear my throat again with little care that it is making me look like I have some sort of respiratory illness and need a throat lozenge.

'You expect your wife to stay home?'

'Why not?' He lets out a humourless laugh as though the answer is obvious, and he can't believe I'm even questioning it. 'She won't need to work. Money is not a concern she'll have, so she can stay at home and be with our children, raising them.'

I can practically see my mother clapping her hands together with glee. Another man to take care of her daughter. But I don't want to be taken care of. I want a partnership. I want to be equal in a relationship, and I want to work. Yes, my job is stressful at times, but I love it. I don't want to give away my career and my passion just because I have children. And I certainly don't want to be stuck inside here all day, every day, making sure that order is kept. Cleaning all day? No thank you. It confirms that my gut instinct last night was right.

'Milo, I umm...,' although he must know what is coming, he doesn't make it any easier on me, he just waits for me to speak. I silently curse him in my head. 'The thing is Milo...I just...,' I take a deep breath. 'Milo, I'm in love with someone else.'

The admission catches us both off guard. Love is big. Love is... Nick. I love Nick. Coming to the realisation and saying it out loud is freeing. Milo's expression doesn't change, and I wonder if he's actually heard me.

'I'm sorry. You're a great guy–'

'Just not your guy.'

Oh, so now he interrupts.

'Was it the stay-at-home wife thing?' he asks, confused.

I bite my lip. That comment was the nail in the coffin but we were already dead. 'A little...I love my job, Milo. And I love to work and create and see progress in my students. And I love to learn and challenge myself.'

'I think you'll find that will change when you have kids of your own.'

I jerk my head back. 'It's a big part of who I am, Milo.'

We sit in the silence, unsure of how to move past this moment. A break up as an adult doesn't seem as clear cut as it was when you're a teenager. Simply saying, 'You're dumped,' doesn't cut it. I don't want this to be awkward and the people pleaser in me doesn't want Milo to feel bad but it's clear that our values are misaligned.

'We had a great time. I had a great time. And you're a great guy.'

A small, defeated smile spreads across his face. 'Great.'

We share an awkward laugh. I should leave it there. I should go home and tell Nick how I feel but there's some sort of sadist in me that keeps wanting to draw this out. 'I mean it, Milo. You really are a great guy, it's just...'

Nick. It's always been Nick. I haven't been with anyone else or wanted to be with anyone else because I was content with the way things were with Nick. We had each other and I realise that's all I've ever needed.

Sitting here in Milo's perfect house, with his perfect pin-up looks and his perfect dates, I realise this life is just not me. If I chose Milo, I'm choosing the version of myself that my mother has tried to force me to be. I would never be able break free of that perfect mould no matter how hard I tried. I'd always feel like I dimmed myself to be someone I'm not. Nick would never ask that of me.

'It's love. I'm sorry I can't give you any more than that.'

Milo rubs a hand over the back of his neck. 'You're going to be a tough one to get over, Josie.'

'Are you mad?' I roll my eyes at myself for asking such a stupid question.

A dimple appears as he tries to ease my own feelings by slapping on a smile. 'A little. I guess I'm trying to figure out where it went wrong.'

'It wasn't so much that it was wrong...'

'It just wasn't right?'

I nod in agreement. Not my Mr Right.

'Josie, did I ever stand a chance?'

I think back over our dates, and the excitement I felt before each one. I think back to the sparks that flew the very first time we went out and how I felt after sailing. It felt good to feel something new. It was exciting, but in between all of that, I came home, and Nick was there. Nick was always there, even on our dates, Nick was there in the forefront of my mind. No matter how many times I tried to push thoughts of him away, I couldn't do it.

'I don't think I stood a chance against my own heart,' I confess.

He holds out his arms as an invitation to crawl into his embrace. I stride over and wrap my arms around his waist.

'Any tips on how to make the next girl stay?' he asks with a small sigh.

'Just be yourself Milo. You don't need anything else.'

'Sounds simple enough,' he concedes.

'And definitely re-think your whole stance on the stay-at-home wife thing. It should be a choice, not an expectation.'

His arms tighten around me. 'Thanks, Josie.'

'Does this mean you won't be my optometrist anymore?'

He lets out a hearty chuckle. 'I'll always be your optometrist, Josie.'

I can't help feeling that maybe everything will turn out just right, for both of us.

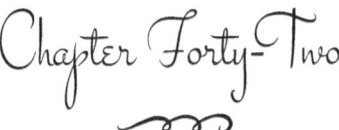

Chapter Forty-Two

NICK

'Can we talk?' Gina asks again after I blank out and don't respond to her original request.

'Yes, sorry. Come in.'

'Are you listening to Adele?'

I shift awkwardly. 'A friend leant it to me.'

I'm certainly not about to admit that the woman has the voice of an icon and her songs can make a grown man break out into karaoke in his living room.

I open the door wider and make a welcoming gesture. We move to the kitchen table where I shut off the music and take a seat. I offer to make her a tea, but she declines. She looks as though she has aged ten years in the last week. The wrinkles around her eyes are more pronounced than they were before. Or maybe they were always there, and I just never noticed because I don't know this woman.

I haven't taken the time to get to know her in the last three years I've been in Littleton Beach which means I feel nothing for her on a personal level when the silent tears sporadically roll down her face. I'm not heartless. I feel for the woman like I would for anyone whose husband or wife was sick, but I don't feel anything for her beyond that of a mutual respect for a stranger.

'I won't stay long, Nick, I just want to talk about the business.'

I hold up my hand. 'Look, Gina, I already told–'

'I know what you told him. You two may have talked privately at the hospital but don't for one minute think my husband doesn't share every goddamn word ever said to him with me.'

I sit back, a bit affronted by Gina's attitude.

'I'm sorry,' she sucks in a deep breath and then slowly exhales, 'I need you to hear me out.'

She stares me down with steely determination. It's more of an order than a plea, and I nod curtly nod for her to continue. I can tell she is going to make me listen one way or another.

'Greg knows he hasn't been the best father to you.'

I scoff, and she sends me a warning glance that makes me feel like I'm twelve again. I take note not to make another sound.

'Nothing can change any of that. When he said he wanted to leave the company to you and not to Cal or Cam, I'll admit I was a little taken aback.'

Her and me both. I can only imagine how Cal and Cam feel too. Ripped off. Probably pissed off too. They don't need to be because I'm not taking it.

'But the more I listened, the more I understood,' Gina continued.

'He's trying to atone for his abandonment.'

'He's trying to make it up to you. Cal and Cam will be just fine. They'll always have a part of him that you won't, the memories. And do you know how much that kills him?'

'He could have come to find me at any time.'

'And he tried. But your mother and him decided it was for the best if he didn't. They both thought you had adjusted well to life with your mum, and that if he came back into the picture, it would only complicate things, and you'd resent him for having another family.'

'Look–'

'Do you resent him, Nick? Be honest. No bullshit.'

I look at her as she implores me to look within myself, a place I'd rather not travel to. A small nod escapes, and she lets out a disappointed sigh. I, however, feel a little bit lighter. It's as if admitting to feeling resentment towards him allows someone else to help carry the burden of all that extra emotional baggage. Who would have thought?

'He wants you to have the business to have a piece of himself, to make up for everything he never did for you when you were younger. He's not a perfect man, Nick. Nobody is. He's made some big, big mistakes in his life, but you shouldn't let your resentment stop you from accepting this gift that will set you and a family up for life.'

I laugh humourlessly . A family? That's no longer on the cards for me. I made sure of that by pushing Josie away.

'You're stubborn, just like he is.'

'No, that's not it.' I shake my head.

'Then what is it?'

'I don't want to be tied down to something that I have zero interest in running. I only took the job to get to know him. I like what I do enough to stick at it bit, but I don't love it. I'm not him.'

'No one is asking you to be, Nick. Do you know how many people your age would kill for an opportunity like this?'

'That doesn't mean I have to take it if it isn't right for me. I'm sorry, Gina. My mind is made up.'

She shakes her head. 'I'm sorry I've been unable to convince you to take the business.'

She's right. I am stubborn, but I also know my own mind and heart and neither of those two things are in it. When I told him at the hospital that I wouldn't be accepting his offer, I felt as though a huge weight had been lifted off my chest and even more has been lifted after sitting down with Gina.

I realised something at the hospital that no one else seems to understand yet. I don't need a piece of him to remember him by. The business and him wanting to leave me something is about his legacy not about my future. I could never run that business without people constantly comparing me to him. *Greg would have done it differently. Greg would have done it better.* The company would be one more way to keep tabs on me from beyond the grave, and I don't want to be trapped.

I'll remember him in death as he was in life, in truth to my experience with him not the history he wants to rewrite. My time in Littleton Beach is coming to an end and with that, so are any ties I have to him and his family. There's a sense of freedom in that.

I walk Gina to the door. She places her hand on the door knob before turning around to say one last thing to me. 'I wish we had the chance to get to know you better, Nick. I really do. I'm truly sorry things have worked out this way.'

I nod. I don't need to say any further goodbyes, I'm all out of those. I open the door to see Josie standing on my doorstep mirroring my own shocked expression.

'Sorry, is this a bad time?'

'No, I was just leaving.' Gina gives us both a strained smile and departs.

I really don't have the mental energy for anything else today, so I don't move to invite Josie in. And it hurts every inch of my soul. Standing there in jeans and a worn old jumper, her hair in a ponytail and her glasses slipping off her nose, she looks more beautiful than ever before. Maybe it's the determined look in her eyes, or maybe it's that I know she's the only woman to have ever held my heart, but something tugs at my guts and brings down my defences. 'I don't have the ener–'

'Tough luck, Davies. You're going to listen to what I have to say. Now you can move aside, or I can push you aside.'

The corners of my mouth lift and a chuckle bubbles in my chest. This woman. I don't test her because I can see just how fired up she is. I have no doubt that right now, she could knock me over. But then again, she could always knock me over with just a look. Whatever she's come to say, I'm going to hear it whether I like it or not.

Chapter Forty-Three

JOSIE

Why is it easier to stand in front of a room full of teenagers and speak to them than it is to stand in the living room of one man and talk? Nick sits on the couch looking up at me expectantly, his blue eyes radiating hurt. There is an invisible barrier between us growing thicker by the second. I need to find my verbal sledge hammer and break it down.

'You're an arsehole.'

He laughs. 'Good start, Josie.'

'I mean it. You are a complete arsehole for telling me that you love me and then pushing me away because you got scared of your feelings. Well, guess what? I'm not having it.'

Maybe aggressive isn't the way to go judging by the stunned look on his face, but I have no control over anything my voice is doing. Not tone, not volume and certainly not the sounds it is making to form words. It is all completely, unpredictable rapid-fire word vomit. I'm just as much an audience member as Nick at this point.

'I spoke to my mother last night.' We both scrunch up our

faces. 'I know, but wait, she actually had some good advice and was all motherly.'

Nick gives me a bizarre look, the one that says he's trying to solve a complex puzzle.

'Trust me, I was just as shocked as you. We may have even had a bonding moment.'

'I don't want to detract from whatever point you're trying to get to, but why were you talking to your mum last night?'

'Harlow was teething, and she wouldn't stop crying. Turns out she also has an ear infection which Elle found out this morning after taking her to the doctor, which would have been handy to know, but still, I managed to get her and Jaggar to sleep by myself despite battling spaghetti wars, teething and the now obvious ear infection. I was like freaking Superwoman!'

'Ah, Jose?'

'Right, the point, sorry. I was babysitting, and I was having trouble getting Harlow and Jaggar to settle, so I called her for advice. She asked me who it was that I really wanted to call, like, who did I want by my side in that hectic faux parenting moment?'

'And? Who did you want?'

'You. I wanted you, Nick. I always want you. When I'm lonely and want someone to eat takeaway with, I want you. When I've had a rough day at school, you're the one I want to come home to. And I know this is going to sound all kinds of messed up, but when I had a really great date with Milo, I wanted to come home and tell you all about it.'

'You're right. That's messed up.'

I stride over to the couch and sit as close as humanly possible to him. 'I know! Even more messed up is that I spent most of my dates with Milo *thinking* about you. Don't you see, Nick? Our lives are so intertwined that one doesn't exist without the other. And I realise now that it has been like that for a long time.'

'Josie...'

'Nick, please. I'm not saying all this perfectly like I had planned. Please just-just let me finish.' He nods, and I continue,

'Nick, I realise now that it has always been you, and that I was projecting my own fears of commitment onto you. I thought that if they were your problem then it would hurt less if things didn't work out. But I realised that I'm not scared of commitment. I'm scared of you.'

'Um,' he scratches his cheek, 'you're scared of me?'

'Yes, because I love you. I'm all in, Nick. And I don't believe all that stuff you said by my car the other day. I just don't. Nick, you told me that I deserve to be happy and so do you. You deserve to be happy. You really do.'

I reach for his hand, taking it in mine and holding on for dear life. His expression is hard to read, and I don't know whether I am convincing him or sinking the ship further. 'I'm not giving up on us, Nick.'

I force myself to maintain eye contact with him, searching for something, some indication that my sledgehammer has made some kind of dent or crack in his veneer, but there are no signs. He runs his free hand through his hair and then over his beard, running his fingers through it a couple of times.

'I'm pretty sure I'm supposed to do all the begging, you know.'

We share a desperate laugh. The light behind his eyes comes back, and they shine.

'I'm fighting for you. I realised that no one has ever fought for you before. Your dad didn't fight to stay. Your mum never fought for you to see him. Well, I'm fighting for you. Stay. For me. Fight for me.'

In one swift movement, Nick's free hand cups my face and pulls me in, his lips on mine pressing firmly, passionately. I match the urgency in the kiss until we part. There is no need for urgency, not anymore, and with that shared thought, we kiss again, this time long and slow. I let go of his hand and throw my arms around his neck. Sliding effortlessly into his lap, my legs relax, straddling him.

'Fight for us, Nick,' I whisper as we break apart, his hands tangled in my now loose ponytail.

'Don't hurt me,' he whispers, his voice cracking under the weight of giving in to feelings that are overwhelming. 'I couldn't stand to lose you.'

'I'm not going anywhere.'

He ducks his head and captures my mouth once more, massaging his tongue against mine, slowly, deliberately. Warmth encompasses my body as I melt into his.

'I'm a mess, Josie,' he whispers leaning his forehead against mine.

'I like messy.'

'And I can be stubborn.'

'And thoughtful, and funny and supportive,' I counter.

'You forgot horny.'

I throw my head back with laughter, tears of happiness welling in my eyes. His joke helps to ease some of the tension around us. I've said the big words. I've told him I love him, and they've been left hanging.

'I'm sorry it took me so long to realise that my Mr Right was right next door this whole time.'

'I told you that you liked me.' A familiar, playful smirk dances across his face.

'I said I love you. Not like. Already not listening to me.' I run my fingers through his thick head of hair.

'Oh no, I heard you. I just wanted to hear you say it again.' He winks and I'm a goner. Hook, line and sinker, Nick Davies has my whole heart.

'Jose, I'm sorry I pushed you away. Multiple times. I didn't want you to see me as anything...less.'

'I'd never think that, Nick. Never.'

'I promise I'll work on it. I, ah, I might need a little help, a few reminders every now and then.'

'I can do that.'

He draws me in with his gaze and if I ever have to describe what it looks like when someone looks lovingly at you, it will be this moment. I've never been seen the way Nick sees me right now.

'What I wouldn't give to be inside your head right now.' I smile, and he reflects one back at me.

'I'm just wondering how I ever got to be so lucky as to be the guy that gets your heart. Josie, you are my world.' His hands slide down my waist to caress my thighs. 'I love you. I think I always have. I'm sorry it took me a long time to let you know that, but I promise from now on, you'll never have to question what you mean to me. Or what's going through my head. I'm all in too, Jose.'

I draw him closer, taking in everything of the man who snuck up on me and stole my heart. My very own Mr Right Next Door.

Epilogue

JOSIE

Singing in the Rain was, as the kids would say, epic. Even Nick thought so. With his musical cherry well and truly popped, he most definitely has a taste for it now.

'I hear *Moulin Rouge* is coming back to town. Maybe we should get some tickets,' Nick suggests and the three of us walk back to our city apartment.

Cashing in my birthday present has been nothing short of amazing. The apartment Nick organised has the most romantic views of the Melbourne city skyline with our room looking directly over the Yarra river. Nick drops his arm around me, pulling me in close to keep warm from the early autumn chill. Ant and I share a knowing look. We recognise a musical nerd when we see one.

'What?' Nick says defensively, 'You two have already seen it, haven't you? Surely there's something we can see that neither of you have seen?'

'Oh, we've seen a lot. You should ask your girlfriend here

about the immersive theatre experience she dragged me to where we had to wear capes and sex masks,' Ant chuckles.

I roll my eyes. 'They weren't sex masks.'

'It was weird.'

'It was art.'

'Sounds kinky,' Nick adds before kissing my temple.

The apartment is only a short distance from the theatre, and we make it back in no time, even after we stop off for an obligatory ice-cream cone.

'Ooh! They have fairy floss flavour.' I give Nick a knowing look.

'We'll take two scoops in a cup. One bubble gum and one fairy floss for her and I'll try bubble gum and liquorish,' he orders.

I already know his will be a flavour disaster, but we will not be defeated in our search to find a flavour of ice cream that compliments bubble gum. I have a feeling that I'm onto a winner though. Ant picks up two cups, both with banana and choc chip ice-cream and when we make it inside the apartment, we see Levi sitting on the couch.

'I told you not to wait up.' Ant scurries over and plants a kiss on his boyfriend's lips, showing zero disappointment that Levi did in fact wait up for us. He hands Levi the ice-cream he bought.

The two of them have become inseparable over the past few months. Turns out Levi was who Ant was sneaking off to see when he said he was going to the gym. After Nick broke his foot, and after Tori showed up at his place unannounced, the boys decided to find a new gym, with Ant taking on the responsibility of scouting out new options. Turns out the only thing he was scouting was Levi's bed!

Nick wasn't too bothered to be honest. Since his foot has healed, he's taken up ocean swimming and meets up with a group of elderly men each morning for a swim. Most mornings he'll then go over to his dad's place and have a coffee with him. He still trying to palm the business onto Nick in his frail state, and Nick is still reluctant to take the offer. I have, however, managed to convince him to stay in Littleton Beach, which let's be honest, took very little convincing. Nick and I still live apart although most nights I stay at his house to give Ant and Levi some space to enjoy their new relationship. Turns out Levi isn't as young as we all thought, and Ant might just be as smitten with his new boyfriend as his new boyfriend is with him.

We join Ant and Levi in the lounge room. Nick chooses to sit in the recliner and pulls me onto his lap.

'So, how was it?' Levi asks while finding just the right position in Ant's arms.

'Amazing, of course,' I answer.

'I think we've converted Nick into a musical theatre geek like the rest of us,' Ant teases.

'Opened my eyes to a whole new world.'

'Oh babe, you ain't seen nothing yet.' I lean in and find his lips beneath his bushy beard.

My phone buzzes in my purse, and I bring it out to see a message from Elle.

ELLE

I told Rich! He's excited of course. I can't believe we're having another baby!!!

JOSIE

I'm SO happy for you guys. Does this mean I can tell the others now?

ELLE

Yeah sure, we'll just pretend you kept it a secret.

I let out a laugh. She knows me too well. Of course I told Nick the moment Elle told me. He then let it slip to Ant who of course told Levi. I may have also accidentally on purpose told Franki too. She, Elle and I have become much closer over the past couple of months. I'm still determined to bring Daniella into this girl group. She's a work in progress.

'Who is it?' Nick nods his head towards the phone.

'Elle. She finally told Rich so now you can all officially know.'

'Tell her congrats.'

'From all of us,' Ant smiles.

> **JOSIE**
>
> Everyone is happy for you!

ELLE

Thank you! Love you xxx Oh and Josie, that's the last time I let you babysit!

> **JOSIE**
>
> Hey! I didn't get you pregnant.

ELLE

No, you're right. We can blame a really bad Fleetwood Mac tribute band and too many wines for that! Enjoy the rest of your stay in the city. Love to all xxx

> **JOSIE**
>
> Night xxx

I place my phone down and snuggle closer into Nick.

'That's great news about Elle. Guess you two will be next.' Levi wags his eyebrows at Nick and me.

'A bunch of little Nick's running around sounds good to me.' Nick pats the sides of my thighs.

'Sounds chaotic to me!' Ant chimes in.

'I think we're going to enjoy being a couple for a little bit first and then...'

'Whatever happens, happens,' Nick finishes my sentence.

'So we're not freaking out about the whole fertility dropping in a few months' time when you turn thirty?' Ant teases.

'We're not freaking out about anything anymore,' I say confidently because truly, I'm not.

Life is good. If you had told me three months ago on my birthday that this is where I would end up, a small part of me would have believed you. I think deep down my heart has always known what my head took a while to catch up on.

'Someone's popular tonight,' Nick nods in the direction of my ringing phone, 'who is it?'

'Franki,' I say, confused.

'Hello?' I answer, unsure if she meant to call me or did so accidentally.

'Hey, where are you?' She sounds startled.

'I'm in the city. Why? Where are you?' I rise from Nick's lap and pace in the very small lounge room of our city apartment.

'I'm at your place.'

'Franki, it's after midnight. What are you doing at my place?'

I can hear her thinking over what to say. 'Sorry, I didn't mean to worry you. It's nothing. Don't worry about it.'

'Franki! What's going on?'

She pauses for a brief moment but long enough for every horrible scenario to run through my head. My heart stops. 'I think my marriage is over,' she says down the phone.

I gasp, and everyone in the room moves to the edge of their seats ready to jump if I ask them to. 'What do you mean, you think your marriage is over?'

Ant's eyes bug out of his head. Levi's hands whip straight up to cover the gaping hole his mouth is making, and Nick jumps up to stand beside me, placing a hand on my hip ready to catch me if I fall. I won't, but the sentiment is nice.

'I want to divorce my husband.'

Acknowledgments

Did you know that this is the most difficult part of the book to write? It's really difficult to encapsulate the writing, editing and publishing process in a few words whilst also expressing my deepest gratitude for those who have helped me along the way.

To the bloggers, bookstagrammers, Tiktokers, librarians and readers in general, thank you for your ongoing support. Without you shouting about how much you enjoy reading my stories, I don't think I'd have a courage to continue on.

To Farrells Bookshop, thank you for supporting local authors and helping us realise our dreams of seeing our books on the shelf of a bookshop.

To my writing friends, thank you for sharing the highs and lows of this whole process with me and cheering me on. The writer community is a special place and I'm happy to be among my people.

To my family and friends who continue to support my books, it means the world to me that you show up each time with such enthusiasm.

To my beta readers, your feedback was invaluable and I appreciate you. Emma, what would I do without your eagle eye? Thank you.

Thanks to my editor, Laura Boon.

To Mel, my incredible cover artist and designer, I'm so honoured to be working with you on this series.

To Mum, I couldn't do any of this without you. I am so

grateful that you introduced me to the wonderful world of books from a young age. I love you.

My biggest thanks is reserved for my children, thank you for giving me time and space to disappear into my imaginary worlds and play with my imaginary friends. I hope I make you proud. I love you.

Finally, to my husband, I'm inspired to write love stories because I'm loved so deeply by you. Thank you for supporting me and all my crazy ideas. I love you.

Also by Katie Montinaro

The Girl In The Sunflower Dress

A Holly Jolly Christmas

Coming Soon:

Mr Right Here

Mr Right On Time

*

Please consider leaving a review on your favourite sites so that other readers will find my books.

About the Author

Katie Montinaro is a Melbourne based romance author. When she's not writing, you'll find her hanging out with her kids, watching movies or designing something for her husband to build - again! Katie loves to hear from her readers so make sure you stop by her Instagram page and join in the fun. You can also sign up for her newsletter at her website:

www.katiemontinaro.com

www.ingramcontent.com/pod-product-compliance
Lightning Source LLC
Chambersburg PA
CBHW030614120726
47904CB00006B/1889